NEW LIFE

Visit us at www.boldstrokesbooks.com

By the Author

Live and Love Again

Best Laid Plans

New Life

NEW LIFE

by
Jan Gayle

2017

NEW LIFE
© 2017 BY JAN GAYLE. ALL RIGHTS RESERVED.

ISBN 13: 978-1-62639-878-8

THIS TRADE PAPERBACK ORIGINAL IS PUBLISHED BY
BOLD STROKES BOOKS, INC.
P.O. BOX 249
VALLEY FALLS, NY 12185

FIRST EDITION: MAY 2017

THIS IS A WORK OF FICTION. NAMES, CHARACTERS, PLACES, AND INCIDENTS ARE THE PRODUCT OF THE AUTHOR'S IMAGINATION OR ARE USED FICTITIOUSLY. ANY RESEMBLANCE TO ACTUAL PERSONS, LIVING OR DEAD, BUSINESS ESTABLISHMENTS, EVENTS, OR LOCALES IS ENTIRELY COINCIDENTAL.

THIS BOOK, OR PARTS THEREOF, MAY NOT BE REPRODUCED IN ANY FORM WITHOUT PERMISSION.

CREDITS
EDITOR: SHELLEY THRASHER
PRODUCTION DESIGN: SUSAN RAMUNDO
COVER DESIGN BY JEANINE HENNING

Acknowledgments

Jules Gourley, thank you for all the professional midwifery knowledge; Shelley Thrasher, thank you for your amazing edits. You make my stories the best that they can be. And Bold Strokes Books, thank you for taking a chance on me. The professionalism of this publishing house cannot be matched.

Dedication

Dedicated to my dad, for teaching me the love of woodworking.

Prologue

It was only two p.m. when I finished the ceramic tiles in the kitchen we were remodeling, and on the drive home, the perfect idea came to me. I rushed the twelve miles from the job site, bouncing in my truck along the gravel road to our house. As soon as I got there, I plugged in my laptop computer to charge the batteries, then ran out to the storage shed and pulled out our air mattress. I unfolded it in the back of the truck, after I had unloaded all my tools from work. After just a few minutes connected to the compressor, the queen-sized mattress was filled with air. It fit snugly in the back of my full-sized pickup.

Then I rummaged through the spare-room closet and dug out two old comforters that we mostly used for camping. I laid them out on the air mattress with four fluffy pillows. After that I searched through our DVDs until I found the perfect movie. With the battery fully charged, I tossed my laptop on top of the comforters and rolled down the truck-bed cover so my great work would be hidden from view. It was nearly four p.m. when I finished, and Karrie would be home in about an hour. I still had plenty of time to pull off my plan.

In September, the evenings could get pretty cool in the high desert, and we'd actually been having a bit of a cold spell lately. It was the best time to have a movie out on the mesa, where the city lights didn't obscure the night stars. I would score loads of romance points for this. Karrie loved our desert movie dates.

I ran into the house, showered, and quickly dried my hair. Then I put on a pair of basketball shorts, a comfy tee shirt, and a pair of flip-flops. I made a quick call to our favorite restaurant before I wrote a note for Karrie.

Babe, please change into something comfy and be ready to go when I return. I love you, beautiful. T.

I drove over to the liquor store and picked up a bottle of Riesling and some Dixie cups. Across the street, I pulled into The Fat Squirrel for our food. I'd ordered me a big beef cheeseburger, but I got Karrie her normal veggie burger. She'd taught me to like sweet-potato fries, so I asked for one order for us to share.

"Where's Karrie?" April, our normal Friday-night waitress, asked when I walked into the little family-owned pub.

"Special date night tonight—movies in the desert. I'm picking up a to-go order."

"Oh, good for you. She'll love it." April smiled. "Let me see if Tommy has it ready."

Within seconds she returned with a large bag. "I think he gave you a few extra fries."

"Great. Tell him thanks."

"What else do you need?"

"Uh. Napkins, lots."

I paid and was back on the road in minutes. When I pulled up, Karrie's Highlander was right where it was supposed to be in our drive. I was so excited and pleased with myself, I ran into the house.

"K, you ready?"

She met me in the kitchen. "Yes, but what am I ready for?"

"Hi, hon." I kissed her and pulled her out the door.

"Don't I even get a hint?"

"Nope. Just do as you're told," I said as we climbed into the truck.

"Mmm. Well, I might not know where we're going, but I know what we're eating. I smell Tommy's burgers." She twisted around to look in the backseat. "Oh, Trig, are we having a movie night?" She asked as we headed west into the desert. The sun was already falling fast.

"I knew you'd figure it out."

It only took about fifteen minutes before we were on a dirt road in the dark desert west of town. "How's this?" I pulled off what was left of the dirt path I'd been following and parked between two squat little juniper trees.

"This looks great. Thanks, honey. What a perfect ending to a busy week."

"I know, right? Grab the food. I'll roll down the top." I jumped out to get the Toyota open-sky cinema ready.

There was already beginning to be a chill in the air, and with just shorts and tee shirts on, we burrowed into the blankets and began to devour our sandwiches.

"Oh, my God, Trig. I'm so stuffed. How many orders of fries are in here?"

I laughed. "I just ordered one for us to share, but Tommy was feeling generous, I guess." I grabbed two more fries. "I'm stuffed too, but I can't stop eating these. You still up for a movie?"

"I'd rather just sit here and cuddle with you and…well…see what else happens."

"I like the way you think." I tossed all the trash into the backseat, and we burrowed into our comforters.

"Trig, if I forget to tell you later, thank you." She kissed me, then snuggled into the crook of my arm.

"You're welcome, babe."

We lay there looking up at the stars so long I almost fell asleep. Karrie was right. It had been a long week. We were both exhausted. Except for today, I'd worked ten-hour days so we could finish the job. Karrie was just starting a new semester, and she was putting in a lot of late hours as well. Just as I was about to doze off with Karrie safely next to me, she spoke softly.

"Are you asleep?"

"No. I'm awake."

"I've been thinking." Karrie pulled herself around me and laid her head across my stomach.

"Oh, you have? What have you been thinking?" I was so relaxed I had no idea what was coming.

"I think I'm ready to get pregnant now."

"What?" I was wide-awake.

"I'm ready to have a baby now. It seems like everything's right, and I'm ready. Aren't you?"

"Um…well…I. Things are great just the way they are. Aren't they?"

"Yes, they are, and I think that means it's a perfect time to start our family. We can't wait forever." She laughed a little and then looked up at me.

"I didn't know you still wanted kids." I couldn't even remember the last time she'd said anything about it, and I wasn't about to bring it up.

"Of course I do. You know that." She twisted around and sat up next to me cross-legged in the middle of the air mattress. "I've always dreamed of having a family with a full house. I want them to all be close, and I want us to go on family trips and adventures together. You can take us all camping, and I can take everyone to art museums. I feel like I missed something not having any siblings, and my parents always worked too hard."

"A house full?" I tried not to look too surprised. I knew she wanted children, but in my mind that never added up to a houseful, and I was always sure she'd get over it.

"I'll settle for two. We can both have one." Karrie winked at me.

"Ahh. I don't want to have a kid."

"You don't want to have one, or you don't want to be pregnant?"

"Ahh…I…don't want to be pregnant." I didn't want children at all, but telling her that seemed like the exact wrong thing to say.

"Okay. I'll have both. I just think we should get started. We should at least look for a donor and a midwife."

I paused a little too long and saw her frown. "You really sure you're ready now?"

"Trig, are you okay with this? I thought you understood how much I wanted a family. Do you not want one?"

"Yeah, of course. No…I mean…you just took me by surprise. I want you to be happy."

"Well, then I'll start doing some research." She lay back across my lap.

"Okay. Yeah." I pulled her next to me. I had no idea how I was going to deal with this situation, but I was sure I had months to try to work it all out. Maybe I could even convince her that we were the perfect family without any additions.

Chapter One

I opened my eyes to the soft morning glow filling our bedroom. It's always been my favorite way to wake up—no harsh buzzing from the alarm clock shocking me from sleep like a bucket of ice water. Karrie's warm body was tucked tight against me. She was pulled up so close I could feel her nascent round belly against the small of my back. I liked it to be cold in the house at night, mostly because if I turned the air conditioner to a lower temperature, she'd snuggle up next to me. Sometimes our king-sized bed felt like we had a vast wasteland between us, but right now, even with her self-described pregnancy hormones heating her body, she nestled close, and I was loving it.

I lay perfectly still. She always seemed to sense when I woke up, and she'd wake up too. I wanted to let her sleep and to just enjoy her warm body next to mine. It felt like home. As I lay there, I couldn't stop thinking about the tiny creature growing inside her. I couldn't believe we were going to have a baby, and I had no idea how I would pull off being a mother.

It scared the crap out of me. I'd never had any desire to have kids. Even after I told her I wanted her to be happy—and if having a baby would make her happy, then she should have one—even then, I didn't really want them. I meant it about her happiness. Since the day we met, that had always been the most important thing in the world to me, but I just couldn't imagine me with a kid.

When she told me she was pregnant—well, actually showed me—and I saw her excitement, I felt a love for her I didn't know was possible. During the insemination, I'd secretly hoped she wouldn't get pregnant, but when she walked out to my workshop with that little pregnancy test stick in her hand smiling with tears streaming down her face, her joy was contagious. My heart seemed to actually grow larger. The overwhelming feeling of love was almost physically painful because I just couldn't express it to her. Neither of us could speak; we just stood there in the middle of my dusty workshop and cried, holding each other tight. For that one moment, I was crying tears of happiness. Ever since then, I'd been worried about how I was going to be what she and this baby needed.

Despite my anxiety, I could never quite get close enough to her after she told me. I held her hand everywhere we went. I touched her arm or put my hand on her lower back, so I was always in contact with her. She truly was glowing. It seems all that hype about a pregnant woman is true.

I was terrified not only of the maternal part, but also the financial responsibility for another person nagged at me constantly. I had to keep reminding myself that at thirty-six I was actually quite successful at running my own business, and we'd be okay. I had five people working for me, and in nearly twelve years, I'd never been more than a week or two without work. A lot of times things were really slow though, and then money was tight. I was a small building contractor, with a team of three women and two men working for me. We would do practically anything, but we were best at interior remodels.

Turning gold-and-green 1960s and 70s bathrooms and kitchens into something that belonged in the twenty-first century was our real specialty. RJ and Jason could work miracles with plumbing and electricity. Justine and Danielle, my two best friends from college, were the most creative interior decorators in the state. They could transform a brick shit house into the Taj Mahal, if that's what was required. That left Janet and me to do most of the carpentry work. Between the two of us, we could overcome pretty much any challenge, but everyone helped out.

Last year, when things were slow, we bought and remodeled an old house—popularly referred to as flipping, but we called it damned hard work. We finished in half the estimated time and made way more money than we ever imagined we would. It was a huge risk though, one I was sure I'd have trouble taking on again knowing that someone else would be depending on me now.

Karrie was a brilliant associate professor at the state university, and there was no chance she'd ever lose her job. Sought after by many other colleges and universities, Karrie could easily get a position at any of the top art schools in the country—much more prestigious institutions than our state university—but we loved the desert Southwest. Karrie had the opportunity to travel all over the country doing seminars and working with other great artists, and she seemed happy with that.

It took both of our salaries to live comfortably though. We'd just purchased our brand-new adobe home, and I had big dreams of building a stand-alone workshop for me and a studio for Karrie. I wanted to design furniture full-time one day, and I wanted to set Karrie up so she could paint whenever she wanted.

I'd always felt responsible for taking care of her. As a feminist, I thought that sounded stupid, but I was probably a bit old-fashioned. Karrie would say I was just old. She was three years younger than me, and she never let me forget it.

"Why are you pretending to be asleep," she whispered in my ear, and I felt her warm breath on me.

"How do you always know when I'm awake?" I stayed still as she kissed my neck—her soft, moist lips felt like velvet.

"I never sleep. I just wait for you to wake up and make love to me." She pulled me toward her, and I rolled over. "If it's any consolation, I didn't hear you come in last night. I was exhausted. I can't wait for this supposed second-trimester energy to kick in."

"I'm glad I didn't wake you. I was sure I did. You were pretty restless when I climbed in the bed." I leaned into her kisses.

The monthly meeting of the Sandia Volunteer Search and Rescue Council had run late last night, so Karrie was already in bed when I got home. I've been a member since I moved out West after I graduated from college. I loved the outdoors and had been hiking, biking, skiing, camping, and horseback riding my whole life. Pretty much if it's done outdoors, I do it. I've even done a little rock climbing. My dad took me horseback riding when I was barely old enough to hold my head up. He sat me in front of him in his big western saddle, and I would sleep there as long as he would ride. I'd much rather be out in the elements enjoying nature than trapped inside a perfectly controlled environment.

Being a part of the SAR Council had started out as a good deed with benefits, including the opportunity to camp in the woods and perfect my outdoor skills, but over the years, I got so invested I'd become a permanent member of the advisory board. The first year I volunteered, I assisted in finding two teenagers lost on an off-piste skiing adventure. The scared kids were both in bad shape from exposure and dehydration by the time we got to them. The look on their faces when we finally found them sold me forever. RJ, one of my employees, and I have been running the survival training program for the last five years.

Karrie pushed my hair away from my face. "Nope. I didn't even know you were home until I woke up a little bit ago, but I'm glad you are." She wrapped her leg around mine. "How'd the meeting go?"

"It was good. We have three new volunteers, and we really needed them. We've lost several experienced folks this past year. It sucks with winter just around the corner." I pulled her leg up higher on my thigh. "I was going to talk to you about the best weekend for a training session. RJ has a few options open, and I wanted to make sure they didn't conflict with anything you may have planned for us." Karrie moved her hand under my shirt and caressed my breasts. "Mmm…that feels good." I closed my eyes and sighed heavily as she stimulated every sensitive nerve around my nipple. "Maybe we can talk later."

"Yeah. Let's discuss it later. There's something else I'd like to do right now." Karrie pulled me into a deep, passionate kiss, and I felt her tongue exploring my mouth. I tasted the minty tingle of toothpaste.

I pushed her away gently, trying to look mad. "How do you do it? You can get up and brush your teeth, and I don't know it, but let me just open one eye and you're wide-awake."

She laughed at me and pulled me back to her. I wanted to go clean my teeth as well, but at this point it wasn't going to happen. I felt a rush of pleasure between my legs, and all I wanted to do was make love to my beautiful wife. This scared me too, but I couldn't seem to stop myself. I let my hands travel all over her smooth, sexy body. We'd made love since she told me she was pregnant, but this was the first time since I could actually see the little round bump on her abdomen. I raised myself up over her and met her lips, and she pulled me tight against her. Her tongue tangled with mine, and a wave of passion ran through me. My heart rate increased as I reached for the bottom of the oversized tee shirt she slept in and tugged at it. She took in a deep breath and responded by raising herself up enough so that I could pull it over her head. I couldn't help but stare; my stomach did a little flip.

"They're bigger." Her normally full, round breasts were just noticeably larger and absolutely gorgeous.

"You like?" She smiled and cupped both breasts in her hands, putting them on display for me.

I lowered my mouth to her nipple and ran my tongue across it, gently pulling at it until the sensitive skin turned rock hard. The unmistakable flood of desire swelled within me, and I wanted her so badly. Karrie moaned, and I was encouraged to move to her other breast, lightly caressing them both with my hands, teasing her with a soft touch as I tasted my way across the smooth curves. She tugged at my shirt, and I knew what she wanted. I rose and pulled it off, exposing my own bare breasts. She reached up to touch me and inhaled deeply. I could see the desire and passion in her eyes.

We loved to be naked when we made love—to experience the stimulation of flesh on flesh. It was one of the things we didn't want to miss out on—no matter how impatient we might have been for each other. I lowered my upper body across hers, careful not to put any pressure on her stomach. I was scared of hurting her. With my breasts pressed against hers, I ached to be inside her. Feeling Karrie's body beneath me sent a tingle through my lower body.

I pulled her into a long kiss. Karrie opened her mouth and met my tongue. Her soft lips seemed to devour me, and she gasped as I explored her mouth with my tongue. Karrie squeezed me tight to her and caressed my bare back and shoulders. Her skin on mine felt electric. We couldn't get close enough. She pulled away briefly and gulped in deep breaths. I traced the side of her body to her thigh. She reacted to my every move.

When I reached her panties, I hesitated until I heard her throaty groan. I moved my hand under the band and between her legs. Her thighs instinctively slid apart and rose to meet my hand. Her closely shaved mound felt like silk, and I could tell she was already wet. My body reacted, and I felt my own juices flood through me. I struggled with her panties, and with her help they got lost in the blankets at the end of the bed.

"Please touch me." Karrie trembled as she pushed my hand hard against her swollen clit.

I pulled my hand away and started moving down her body, licking and tasting her as I went.

Karrie entangled her fingers in my hair and pulled lightly to stop me before I could reach her crotch. "No, honey, please. I just want you inside me. Now!" She exhaled heavily.

"Are you sure it's okay?" I covered her with my hand and ran my fingers through her slick folds but couldn't bring myself to put my fingers inside her. Her body jerked at the sensation.

She pulled my face to hers and kissed me hard, sucking my tongue into her mouth. She raised her pelvis to my hand. I slowly moved one finger inside her wet vagina and exhaled audibly—she felt so warm and soft inside. Karrie rose harder against me. She pulled her mouth away, and breathing deeply, she moved her hips against me. "More, please."

I slid a second finger inside her, still moving slowly and way too cautiously for Karrie's desire. She rocked hard into my hand and held me to her when I tried to pull away. "Trig, please... please," she begged me. I moved with her and quickened my pace. I lowered my head, moving my tongue across Karrie's erect nipples. I heard her making soft sounds and covered her breast, sucking a nipple into my mouth. I filled my mouth with her sensitive flesh, feeling closer and closer. I knew what to do to make her come, but my fear of hurting her caused me to ease up even when I knew she wanted me to go deeper.

"Trigena, please...fuck me. I need you." She practically cried out, so close to coming, but my hesitation kept her from the edge she was seeking. "Trust me," she whispered through heavy breaths in my ear, and I thrust deep inside her and moved with her. We found a perfect rhythm, and she whined a sound of pure pleasure and called out, "Don't stop, please."

I would never stop now, not when I could feel her pure desire. Karrie's breathing increased. She slowed her rhythm and spoke words I couldn't understand, but I knew the meaning. I felt her shiver and then explode. Her thighs tightened hard around my hand, and her muscles contracted around my fingers. I stopped moving to let her take in the pleasure. She wrapped her arms around my neck and pulled me tight against her.

"I love you," she said as she caught her breath.

"Mmm. I love you too, babe." The musky scent of her perfume lingered on her neck, and I inhaled. Before I could pull out of her, she tightened her thighs around my hand again and stilled me.

"Oh my God, you feel amazing inside me. Just stay there a minute." That was an easy request to fulfill. It felt fantastic for me too. Making love to Karrie was always exciting, but somehow her being pregnant made it even more pleasurable. She relaxed her legs, and I moved to her side and lay next to her. After only a few seconds she rose and kissed me, thrusting her tongue into my mouth. That overwhelming rush filled my gut and thighs again as she moved down my body, already pushing my panties down.

"It's okay, babe. I'm completely satisfied," I lied, and caressed her shoulder to urge her back to the pillow next to me.

"I'm not." She slid her tongue across my belly and looked up at me. "Trig, you're going to have to get over this pregnancy anxiety. I have nearly six months to go, and I can already tell I'm going to need a lot more of this. I want you more than ever." Her tongue moved down to my closely trimmed bush. "I won't break. It's good for the baby."

"Hmm. Maybe I'll have to keep you pregnant."

"And barefoot," she said and smiled.

I felt her tongue brush across my clit and called out. Karrie breathed deeply and her mouth settled over my clit, sucking it hard, rubbing her tongue against it. I squeezed the sheets and rocked my hips, so wet and hot from her orgasm I was close to my own just from her touch. I wanted it to last, but I felt my body rising to a climax—responding to Karrie's instinctive touch. She stopped sucking and thrust a finger deep inside me. I was so close, the flick of her tongue across my oversensitive clit sent me to the edge. I pushed into her and she rocked with me.

The orgasm came hard. It was so intense, the release of all my anxiety and fear came with it. I couldn't hold back a scream of pure pleasure and squeezed my weak legs tight around her. Karrie rose slowly from the grip of my thighs. I just lay still on the bed and took in short, quick breaths. Karrie's hands moved slowly now, softly caressing me. I just relaxed and enjoyed her sweet touch.

❖

When Karrie got up to shower, I finally found strength in my legs and headed for the kitchen. I knew she'd be hungry. She'd been starving since morning sickness ended and was having cravings of the wildest kind. But she was sticking to her healthy diet, just lots more fresh-ground peanut butter and green, leafy vegetables. And honey—honey on things that no normal person would put it. Her favorite was a combination of honey and peanut butter. Thankfully, I hadn't seen her put any directly on the leafy green veggies, yet. Karrie was always an extremely healthy eater, to the point of being really annoying to my Midwestern meat-and-potatoes palate. Although I sometimes snuck away to satisfy some of my own need for deep-fat fried food, mostly she'd converted me.

I pulled out the whole-grain pancake mix. This was one of the items I still had to pretend to like, but I knew peanut butter on pancakes would make the baby happy. I had a small stack ready by the time Karrie came into the kitchen with her hair still wet and wrapped in a towel.

"Being pregnant is working out pretty well for me." She picked up one of the cakes and started eating it with her hands.

"K, we have silverware." I turned and pulled a fork out of the drawer for her.

"Hmm." She sat at the island across from the griddle I was working at and smothered the remaining pancake with real maple syrup. "Thank you, hon."

I moved over beside her and kissed her sweet, sticky lips. "No peanut butter?"

She shrugged, indicating she had no control. "What do you have planned for today?" she asked without looking up from her task.

"Ahhh, I was going to work in the shop awhile. I need to finish the kitchen cabinets for the Fergusons so we can install them next week. We need the money from that job, before I can buy the wood for the crib." I looked over at her. "What is it that you wanted me to be doing today?" I flipped the pancakes cooking on the griddle.

"Well, we need to go to the grocery store. We're out of everything." She had finished the first two pancakes and appeared to be coveting the ones cooking on the griddle. "Here, you take those, and I'll put some more on," Karrie said and started to get up.

"No, here." I stacked the cakes on the spatula and slid them onto her syrupy plate. "You need them more than I do." I poured two more pancakes on the hot surface. "If we're out of honey and peanut butter, then the governor might need to declare a state of emergency."

"You're funny. Thank you for the pancakes." She smiled that perfect, gorgeous white smile, and I would've made pancakes and walked around a crowded grocery store all day long for her.

"You should have an egg too, right? The midwife said you should get protein every meal."

"Trig, the midwife has a name. It's Jules. And you're right, but I'm good for now. Pancakes fill me up quickly, but they don't stick with me too long. I'll be hungry again soon."

"You think?" I teased her as I pulled my pancakes off the griddle and put a K-Cup in the coffeemaker.

"Oh. I miss coffee. It smells so good, but it tastes so bad right now."

"I'm sorry, babe. Should I not have it?" I did feel badly for her. We both loved our coffee, and even though she wasn't nauseated anymore, the taste of it was ruined for her.

"No. At least I can smell it and imagine it still tastes good." She put her plate in the dishwasher, slid her arm around my waist, and kissed me on the cheek. She started to clean up the griddle and batter bowl.

"I'll get it." I winked and pushed her away.

"Yeah. This is working out very nicely for me." But she ignored me and cleaned up my cooking mess in seconds, wiping the kitchen surfaces effortlessly. "I'm going to go dry my hair. You'll be ready to leave in ten minutes." It wasn't a question.

"I need to finish eating," I called to her back as she walked away.

"Okay, fifteen." And she disappeared.

Chapter Two

"Trigena, come on. You need to get ready," I called out to the workshop when I heard the table-saw motor stop running. I was pretty good at identifying power-tool motors, but it didn't really matter which one she was using. I knew better than to disturb her when there was the potential of a dangerous high-speed blade spinning.

"What time is it?" she yelled back.

"Almost six, and I told Dani we'd be there at seven. Come on."

"Damn it, K. I wish you'd ask me before you commit us to stuff like this. I have to get this done."

I stood in the doorway letting her rant. "Trig, you've been out here all afternoon. I want to see you. You'll finish it."

From where I was in the doorway I couldn't see her. Her shop was in our three-car garage connected to the house, but a panel she'd built in front of the door blocked the bulk of her workspace. She'd designed it to help cut down on dust in the house, but I'm not sure it worked. I was always cleaning sawdust off the kitchen floor. Even though I couldn't see her, I could hear her shutting everything down. Finally, she appeared around the panel and met me at the door. She was covered in a fine layer of sawdust and smelled like oak.

"How is it I work eight hours with Danielle and Justine every day, and they call you to make social plans?" She'd calmed down now that she was actually out of her workshop. Her intense focus was admirable but annoying as hell.

"They know you'll say no." I brushed a clean spot on her cheek and kissed her. "Now go get showered and dressed."

Trigena grunted at me and headed to the bathroom, but then she stopped and turned back around. She looked me up and down with admiring eyes, and her approving gaze filled me with confidence. The changes my body was going through could make even the most self-assured woman question herself. I couldn't help but smile at her reaction.

"You look beautiful. Is that a new blouse?" She walked back to me and placed her hands on my hips, held me at arm's length, and continued her appraisal.

"No, hon. The skirt is new. I don't know if you've noticed, but I can't quite fit into my other clothes right now."

"Hmm. All I noticed was how amazing you look." She winked. "We could stay here." She tried to pull me to her.

I held her at arm's length by her shoulders. "Trig, stop it. You'll get me all dirty, and we'll have time for that later. Besides, you'd still be out there in that shop if I wasn't forcing you to socialize, so go get changed."

"You're no fun."

"That's not what you were screaming this morning. You might have woken the neighbors." Since our house was nearly half a mile from the nearest neighbor it wasn't likely, but I liked it that I made her come so hard.

She smiled and kissed me before obeying my commands to get ready.

I sat back at the kitchen table, where I had some of the birth books Jules had given me and had been flipping back through some of the better ones. I read everything she provided, devouring information as fast as she provided it. I was completely sure about a homebirth, but Trigena was worried, as always. I had been feeding her every positive story our midwife shared with me, and I emphasized to Jules not to tell her anything that might scare her.

It was easy for me to imagine Trigena supporting me through the pregnancy. She would rub my back, hold my hand, and coach me through the contractions. I wanted her to wrap her strong arms around me and the baby as soon as he or she arrived. She was concerned about the homebirth at first, but Jules had been quite persuasive. She'd managed to bring Trig on board. I was surprised at how easily Jules had converted her.

I was prepared for a major struggle from the uber-conservative love of my life. She worried so much about everything that I hardly bothered thinking twice about anything anymore. My poor responsible girl overthought everything, and I could really do very little to ease her stress. Trigena loved hard. Once she cared about you, she built a fortress around you to protect you and keep you safe. Sometimes her overprotective, controlling behavior was hard to deal with, but mostly it was one of the main reasons I loved her so much. Not to mention her hot body. Since conceiving, all I could think about was wrapping myself around that sexy little thing.

❖

"Whoo..." I looked up as Trigena walked into the dining room with her black riding boots, tight skinny jeans, and a fitted red blouse with snug sleeves exposing her well-defined arms. Her long blond hair was flowing with loose curls—a dramatic transformation from the tough woodworker who'd entered the house a few minutes ago. "Staying here seems like a good idea now. You look great."

She kissed me. "Thanks, babe. I had to try to match my classy wife. What's this?" She picked up my sketchpad. I'd been doodling in my dream world while she was getting ready. "Is this what you want the baby crib to look like?" She looked from the paper down at me. "K, this is beautiful."

"You like it?" Trig was tracing the image I'd drawn with her index finger.

"Babe, I love it. I would've never come up with something like this." I could see her mind working, examining every detail. "I think cherry would be perfect...ahh...with some ebony inlay." Her excitement was contagious. She could build anything. If she could visualize it, she could make it out of wood, and she loved creating things.

"Really?" I've had that image of a crib in my head for years. I've wanted to be a mom for as long as I can remember, and in my mind the baby was always lying in the crib I just drew. I trusted Trig would make something beautiful, but knowing she liked what I'd always imagined my baby lying in felt so right.

"Yes, really! I'll need Janet to take a look to be sure I have the right ideas to make it structurally sound, but this is going to be perfect." She kissed me again. "I need to have you design more projects for me." She was still lost in her creative world. "I so envy your ability to put on paper or canvas the exact image you have in your talented head. You're good, babe—really good!" This had been a joke between us from a time when one of her contracting competitors had patronizingly referred to her work as good. Trigena is a perfectionist—good doesn't even come close to describing her work—so the word "good" took on a whole new meaning for us.

"Thanks, hon." I gathered up and put away all the materials in front of me, and we headed out to my Highlander.

"Me or you?" Trig pointed to the driver's door.

"You. I'll drive home. I'm your guaranteed designated driver." I rubbed my middle.

She took the keys from me and got into the vehicle. "Ahh, yes, another advantage of you being pregnant."

Chapter Three

Danielle opened the door and immediately wrapped Karrie in a big hug. "Damn, girl. You're still not showing at all and beautiful as ever. Pregnancy looks wonderful on you." She backed away and gave Karrie a once-over.

"Well, thank you, but I am showing." Karrie pulled her blouse tight across her midsection to show off her barely present belly.

Danielle couldn't resist touching the little bump. "Ahh, that's so cute."

"Hey, did you forget I was here?" I stood next to Karrie with my arm wrapped around her waist. Sometimes I felt exiled to the edges of Karrie's life and was wondering how much further away I might be after the baby was born.

"Oh yeah, you!" Danielle said teasingly and turned to give me a quick hug. "Pregnancy looks pretty good on you too. The girl who swore she'd never have kids."

"What?" Karrie looked from me to Danielle.

I gave Danielle the look—the one old friends can give one another that means, shut up now!

"You don't want kids? Trig?" Karrie looked at me with confusion all over her face.

"Hey, you guys, come on in," Justine yelled from the kitchen. "I have drinks poured and lemonade for our pregnant girl."

"Oh, shit. I..." Danielle stammered.

"K, babe...I want this baby with you. You know that." I squeezed her hand and led her into the house. "Dani, give us a minute please."

"Sure. I'm sorry." She turned and practically ran out of the room.

Tears had formed in Karrie's eyes, and she wiped at them with the back of her hand. She tried to release my hand, but I held tight. She pulled away. "Please let me go. Our friends are waiting."

I didn't let go, but I moved toward the kitchen with her. "Babe, I need to know you're okay."

"I'm fine." She stopped in the middle of the room and spoke without looking at me. "How could I be with you for ten years and not know you didn't want kids? How can I be almost four months pregnant with our baby, and I'm just now finding out?"

"Because it's old news. I love that we're going to have a baby." I spoke emphatically, probably trying to convince myself as much as her.

"Fine." She pulled away again, and this time I let her go.

When we walked in the kitchen, it was apparent Danielle had told Justine what had happened and the eggshells had already been sprinkled across the floor.

"Karrie." Justine ran over to give her a hug. She gave me an evil eye like somehow this was all my fault. "Here, hon." She handed Karrie a glass of pink liquid.

Justine punched me in the arm and handed me a glass of wine. "Why be a jerk?"

"Me?" I could tell this wasn't going to go well for me.

Danielle tugged me to the side of the room. "I'm so sorry. I had no idea."

"It's okay. We'll be okay." I knew it was true, but I also knew I had some repair work ahead of me.

Karrie tried to act as if nothing had happened. "So we need to talk about the baby room."

"Yes." Justine put some hummus and pita bread on the table. "Here, help yourself. Dinner's almost ready."

Danielle reengaged. "Are we going to do the guest room or your studio?"

Karrie and I answered at the same time with different answers. She said, "My studio" as I said, "The guest room."

"No, babe. You need your studio." I sounded more forceful than I intended.

"We need a guest room." She came back just as commanding. "Our families live too far away. They need a place to sleep when they visit the baby." She didn't look at me.

"Okay, well..." Danielle was obviously beside herself. I don't think anyone had ever seen Karrie or me mad at each other before. We'd fought before, and even though we weren't exactly fighting now, no one had ever seen us anything but in perfect sync.

As the evening went on, conversation came easier, but the entire night was strained. The only thing we really worked out was for the girls to come by in a few weeks and start designing a plan for the baby's room. I wasn't giving in to remodeling her studio, but I saw no use pushing that rope tonight when she was already upset with me, and certainly not in front of our friends.

❖

"I can drive," I said as she headed for the driver's door when we walked out of Danielle and Justine's house.

"I said I'd drive home."

"Okay, but I only had the one drink. I'm okay to drive."

"Fine." She stopped and turned back to the passenger side.

I pulled out of the driveway, and we rode in silence for as long as I could stand it.

"Can we talk?"

"What would you like to talk about, Trigena?" The emotionless response actually hurt.

"About what Danielle said and about how you feel."

"Listen, I don't know why you never told me you didn't want children. I've never made it a secret that I wanted them. I'd actually like to have two or three. You know this about me. Why do I not know that you don't want any?" Her voice rose with each word until she was almost yelling.

"Well..."

"Well?"

"You don't know because I love you, and I knew it was something you wanted, so I didn't want to...Well, it doesn't matter now because I want a baby." I was struggling, but I knew I wanted to want it.

"You thought you would lose me if I knew you didn't want kids, and you thought not telling me was okay? This isn't like compromising about the color of the bathroom. What if you hadn't changed your mind, and how do I know that you did? Maybe you're just telling me this now so I'll shut up," she said in a high-pitched, sing-song tone, and I got the point. "What about you? What about what you want?"

"I want you, and I want you to be happy." I looked over at her as I pulled onto the gravel road to our house, and she stared back, waiting. "And I want us to have a baby together."

"I don't understand. How can you change your mind? Your whole life you don't want kids, and now...now you do? This doesn't make sense." Tears started streaming down her face. "Damn it, I hate that I cry all the time—hormones!"

Karrie had definitely never been a crier, so seeing her like this made me insane. I wanted to fix it.

I pulled in our driveway and took her hand. I feared she'd pull it away from me, but I think she was completely drained. "Babe, when the woman you love more than life itself comes to you and tells you she's going to have a baby, all you can think about is how much you love her and the baby she carries for both of you." I paused, hoping for some response, but she just sat there. "I'm worried I'll suck at being a parent, but..."

For the first time since before we arrived at Danielle and Justine's, she looked me in the eye. "Please tell me you're not just saying that to make me stop crying—to make me happy." She sniffed and wiped her eyes on the back of her sleeve. "This isn't just about me. It's about us—this is our family."

"I'm telling you because it's true." Fresh tears ran down her cheeks. I wiped them away and kissed her. "Come on, babe. Let's go to bed." I just kept hoping something would happen to make it true.

Chapter Four

After the fifth ring, Trigena hollered from the living room where she sat in the middle of the floor with receipts, inventory sheets, and bank statements in small stacks all around her. "Are you going to answer that?"

It was the twentieth, and she always did her business accounting at the same time each month. She paid all the bills then too, so it was sometimes a stressful event—especially when she thought we'd been particularly economical, only to find out we'd exceeded our budget. Trigena rarely confronted me about how we spent our money, but I could tell when she was stressed out about it. She was way more restrictive with her own purchases. She would've allowed me anything, but she consulted me before she spent even a few dollars. She once asked me my opinion before buying a new saw blade.

Sometimes my regular salary helped her business when work was slow, and she hated that. I didn't mind though. In fact, I liked knowing I was contributing to her craft. She was so good at it, and she worked so hard. I remember, as hot as she was wearing her tool belt with a red bandana tied around her blond hair, her dedication and the efficient way she provided instructions to her crew had first attracted me to her. I could tell they enjoyed working for her and that she loved what she did.

I was completing my master's studies at a studio in Santa Fe when I met Trigena. Fate had brought us together really, because she hasn't had a job in Santa Fe since. It's too far to drive every day, but at that time she was just starting out and didn't want to pass on any job. John and Sarah Martin, the people I was renting a room from, had hired her to do a bathroom remodel in their master bedroom. When she came to the door the first day, she stopped long enough to introduce herself, but other than that I was able to get only a few words out of her.

The Martins had left me alone in the house to use their studio and to watch over the contractors while they were out of town. Had I known the contractor was a hot, sexy lesbian, I would've volunteered more readily. It had been more than a year since I'd even dated. My last girlfriend was a bad experience so I'd put relationships on hold.

I had so much work to do, and their studio overlooked a mountain view with a brilliant sunrise. After Trig introduced herself, I spent the rest of the week stealing looks at her between painting like a wild woman. I finished two abstract pieces of women laborers that I sold for large sums of money while she was doing carpentry work at the house. She was my muse and still is.

Cute and sexy, she became increasingly friendly and would ask me how my painting was going, but it wasn't until Thursday, when the rest of her crew was long gone and she knocked on the door of the studio, that I realized she'd even noticed me. It was late at night—almost nine o'clock. She still jokes sometimes about how long it took after everyone left before she finally got the nerve to knock on the studio door. I didn't even know anyone was still there until I heard her; she nearly scared the paintbrush out of my hand. She walked around the room raving about how marvelous my work was, and her charm and compliments won me over. Even if I'd wanted to, I couldn't have said no when she finally asked me if I'd like to have dinner with her that Friday night.

❖

When the phone rang again, Trigena just stared at me. She always got so absorbed in the paperwork for the four or five hours it took her each month, I was surprised she even noticed the phone.

I was cutting vegetables for stir-fry chicken, both of us home early. Trigena always left work before quitting time on accounting day, and I had only one class on Thursday afternoons. I knew she would be working at home today, and even though she would be busy I wanted to be with her. I wanted to make a nice dinner for her and at least be near her, even if she was too busy to notice until she finished.

"It's my dad."

She actually stopped and put the pencil she was using behind her ear, then looked over at me. I could see concern in her eyes. "Does he know?"

"I assume so. I'm not sure why else he'd be calling."

She adjusted the pillow she was sitting on, and the calculator resting on her thigh clanked on the tile floor. "Well, if he got the news, he's going to keep calling. If you really don't want to talk to him, you should turn off your phone."

"I'm going to have to talk to him eventually, I suppose." The phone stopped ringing just as I was about to answer it. I felt my shoulders relax and didn't even know I'd tensed up. At least maybe I could put him off for a while longer. Trigena and I could have a nice meal, and I would deal with him tomorrow.

"Mmm-hmm," Trigena grunted. She had already refocused.

The phone rang again almost immediately after I set it down. I picked it back up and looked to confirm that it was my dad. Trigena was staring at me with that what-are-you-going-to-do look.

I shrugged and picked up the phone. "Hello, Dad."

"Were you going to tell me you're having my grandchild? I have to hear it from your Aunt Carol?" He sounded hard and cold, real anger in his voice. As a child, I'd feared that sound so much.

"Nice to talk to you too, Dad." I was going for casual, but my reply just sounded angry and sarcastic in my head. Trigena was already up and seated at the bar stool next to the island like a sentry on guard duty waiting to defend her territory. She knew I would need her support—just stopping her work and sitting next to me gave me strength. Trigena was hyper-focused and could miss the little things sometimes, but she was always there when I really needed her—all of her, giving *me* that intense attention.

"Why wouldn't you tell me you were going to have a baby?" The anger was gone, and he actually sounded like he was about to cry.

"You haven't talked to me in over a year, and you made it clear then that you didn't want me to be a part of your life anymore. Why would you expect me to tell you what was happening in mine?"

Trigena and I got married after New Mexico legalized same-sex marriage, and I hadn't talked to my dad since. He'd not only refused to attend, but he'd told me if I married Trigena, he never wanted to see me again. I'd felt like a baseball bat had hit me in the chest. I couldn't believe he'd react that way, but he got his wish.

"I'd like to see you. I'd like to be a part of my grandchild's life, and yours too, Karrie. I miss you."

I turned my back to Trigena, not wanting her to see me if I started to cry. I hated that his words and his voice had such an effect on me. The flood of emotions poured over me, and I felt my face flush. "Dad, you wanted nothing to do with me. Now, I'm having a baby, and it's all supposed to be fine." My voice rose but didn't crack. I hurt, but I refused to cry. As soon as I finished, Trigena's strong arms were around me.

"Karrie, I was wrong. I shouldn't have done that just because I disagree with your life-style choice."

I full-out yelled. "This is not a choice or a style like which jeans to wear, Dad. This is my *life*, and if you can't embrace me and my wife, then you can forget about ever knowing your grandchild." I hung up and slammed the phone down on the counter. I even tried to walk away from Trigena's hold on me. I flailed a bit and pushed at her, but she wouldn't let go. I'd learned a long time ago that if she didn't want me to get away, it wasn't happening. Trigena was incredibly strong, so I stopped fighting and collapsed into her. She turned me around and held me close. I cried hard, big, sobbing tears, and she comforted me.

Finally, I pulled away. There were things I needed to be doing, and I wanted to be done with shedding tears over a man who couldn't open his heart to me and my only true love. We were happy, and we were starting our own family. I didn't need him.

"Babe, why don't you go lie down for a minute. I'll finish dinner." Trigena tried to lead me to our bedroom.

"No!" The word came out harsher than I intended. I was angry, but certainly not at Trigena—not even at my dad anymore. Him, I couldn't change. I was angry at me. How could I let him affect me still?

I was thirty-three years old. Trigena and I had been together since I finished my PhD twelve years ago. Because my mother had homeschooled me, I was ready for college at sixteen. My mom was Teresa James, an incredible artist. As much credit as I get for my paintings, I only inherited a very small percentage of her astonishing talent. I've just been much more prolific, primarily because I didn't have to be a wife to a demanding husband.

My dad was so worried when I went off to college so young, he sent my mom to live with me my first year in New York City. We stayed in a small apartment together, and I loved the time we shared that year. We painted and cooked together, the two passions Mom and I shared. It meant leaving Dad in Boston alone, and he hated to be away from us. Every Friday night he took the train to the city to be with us. He was a partner in a big law firm, and even getting away on the weekends was hard, but I was Daddy's little girl, so he made it every weekend.

From the time I was able to walk on my own, I was always with him. He even took me to work with him, probably way more often than the partners wanted, but he was the only black partner, and he brought in a lot of up-and-coming, wealthy, young black business clients. So they left Dad alone, and they could see when we were together there was no need even trying to tell him not to bring me. I was always good though. With a sketchpad and half-a-dozen colored pencils, I could stay busy all day. I had a little cassette Walkman, and Dad made tapes of all his favorite Motown hits. He'd put the headset over my ears and seat me at the corner of his massive oak desk, and I'd sit there working just like my dad. His secretary Jeanie brought me treats and watched out for me when Dad had meetings. I loved going to work with him. He made me dress in my best clothes—because that's what professionals did. I felt as important as I thought he was, and it gave Mom a break. We almost always came home to a new painting. She would have painted all day everyday if it wasn't for us.

During my first year of college my mom met Ida, a woman in the apartment upstairs from our place, and among the three of us, we somehow managed to convince my dad that I could stay in the apartment alone. Ida watched out for me, helped me with household chores, and we ate dinner together most evenings. Ida and I are still in contact, and whenever I go out East I stay with her.

I started dating a few guys while I was in New York, but I didn't feel right with any of those boys. I figured out why when I met Leah my senior year. I thought it was true love, and she broke my heart, but at least I finally knew who I was. I didn't tell Dad until I met Trigena. Mom had been dead for two years already, after a long struggle with emphysema. Because I waited to tell him until I met the woman I knew I wanted to spend my life with, I think he blamed Trigena. Like somehow she'd made me gay. He was never disrespectful to Trigena—she wouldn't have tolerated that—but it was clear he would never really let her into his life.

❖

Trigena moved up next to me, our naked bodies still entangled. I pulled her into a kiss. I was still recovering from the last of several orgasms and couldn't speak yet. I tasted the salty tang of my juices on her lips. Making love with Trigena tonight was exactly what I needed. She felt so soft and strong, and knowing how deeply she loved me made everything else disappear.

Trigena rose and lay on her side. She propped herself up on her elbow and rested her other hand below my extended abdomen. She was always rubbing my belly now. I thought people touching me would be one of the things I wouldn't like about being pregnant, but Trig's touch felt so right. It seemed like the larger my tummy grew, the more she wanted to be in contact with me. In addition to the love I felt, it helped alleviate any remaining fears I might've had about her not wanting kids. I was still apprehensive, but if the way she treated me was any indication of how she would feel about our baby, then I knew she'd already fallen in love with the tiny person growing inside me. I pulled her hand closer and tighter to me when I felt the baby kick.

"Woo." Trig just stopped and stared at my belly.

"I guess everyone's happy." I smiled at her. Watching her reaction to the whole pregnancy process was almost as much fun as going through it.

"Does that hurt?" Trigena asked.

"No. Not really. I think it could, but mostly it feels like an octopus wiggling around—a little uncomfortable sometimes, but right now it feels like…like…life."

She caressed my stomach and looked at my naked body. I might be worried about what she thought of how I looked, but I could tell she was admiring it. "You're so beautiful." She sat up next to me cross-legged. "Babe, can I talk to you about something?"

I could tell the heavy cloud that had subtly been present since I slammed the phone down hours ago was about to rain down. I knew when she went back to her paperwork that she'd put the subject aside only temporarily. She probably thought I needed a break from it. "Okay, Trig. I'm listening." I rolled over on my side and pulled the sheet over me.

"I realize it's not my place, and I know you'll do whatever you want regardless of what I say, but I think you should call him back. Both my parents and your mom are gone. He's the only real grandparent she'll have, so…"

"She?"

"I mean the baby."

"Trig, you said she. Do you want a girl?"

"I want a healthy baby. K, please stay with me—focus a minute." She smiled, trying to soften her directive.

"Okay, but later we're talking more about this little girl of yours." I squeezed the hand she had resting on me.

"Anyway. A person's history is important, and you know he would be a very good grandpa." She paused long enough that I almost spoke before she continued. "Babe, he asked. Couldn't we just talk to him? Maybe a baby would soften him a bit. I know you miss him." Trigena rubbed her thumb gently across my cheek.

I didn't want to cry about this after such a wonderful time with my wife, so I shrugged her away. "Is 'I'll think about it' enough for now?"

"Absolutely."

"So about this little baby's gender…" I moved her hand across my abdomen.

"It's nothing." Her cheeks reddened. "I just had a dream a few days ago and saw this dirty-faced little girl following me out of the woods. I can't remember the rest of it, but I can see her face and little curls clearly. I assumed we must have been on a camping trip." Trigena lay down next to me.

"Oh my God, Trig. I love that story. I know you'll take our baby camping." It was a happy thought. I was more worried about my risk-taking wife teaching our kids to use power tools than exposing them to any of her outdoor adventures, but most of all I felt good when I thought of the many things she'd teach them. "What if it's a boy?"

"Well, then I'll have someone to watch football with me."

"Hey, I watch football with you."

"Someone who cares what clipping is and doesn't have a sketchpad in her lap during the Super Bowl." She rolled over and turned on her alarm.

I laughed at the accurate description of my interest in football. "At least I know to cheer when Green Bay scores."

"You better." She flipped off the light.

"Trig, everything's going to change so much, so amazingly. I'm kind of scared, but what's scarier to me is never having a child. This is a dream come true for me, and I'm sharing it with you. Sometimes it's just too much to even believe."

Trig pulled me closer to her, and I laid my head in the crook of her neck. "I know this is your dream come true. It's going to be okay." Her soothing voice comforted me.

❖

I was surprised he picked up the phone after the first ring. "Hello, Karrie."

"Hi, Dad."

"I'm sorry about what I said. I have to learn when not to open my mouth." He spoke quickly, as if he feared I might hang up again.

"You might be too old if you haven't figured it out yet, but that's not why I'm calling. Trigena and I talked, and if you can agree to never discuss your thoughts about Trigena and me with the baby, then we want you to be a part of his or her life."

There was a pause, and I could hear him blow air out of his mouth before he said, "That's what I want, more than anything. And I'd like to see you…you and Trigena, before…soon…"

"Okay, then. You can let us know when you can make it out." I didn't really want to drag this out.

"Wait."

"What, Dad?"

"Do you know who the donor is?"

"Yes, we know."

"Is he black?"

"Why would you ask me that?" His question completely confused me.

"I just want to know if the baby will look anything like me."

"Trigena has blue eyes and blond hair. Don't you think we would like it to look a little like her?"

He laughed, and I tightened my fingers around the phone and gritted my teeth. "Karrie, you won't be having a blond, blue-eyed baby."

"Right." I took a deep breath and blew it out.

"Ethnicity is more than the color of a person's skin." He was preaching at me.

"Then why would you care if the donor is black? He isn't, by the way." I took a deep breath, but I couldn't stop. "It's because for you being black *is* about the color of a person's skin." My jaw tightened.

"Karrie, calm down. All I've ever said to you is dark-skinned people have a different experience than light-skinned people."

"You mean they have a more authentic experience."

"I mean it's harder. Come on. Do I have to give you a history lesson? Do you really believe America isn't a racist society?"

"I understand how it feels not to be a part of your own ethnicity. I didn't feel black or white."

"You were raised by a black father."

"And a white mother, and I never felt a part of either community." I raised my voice. I didn't want to be angry or hurt again. How could he always do this to me?

"Karrie, your light skin has afforded you a lot of privileges a darker person might not have gotten."

"You're assuming being biracial has made my life easier."

"I'm just saying that you don't really know what it's like to be black in this country."

"What?" I paused and caught my breath before I started yelling. This was supposed to be a makeup call. "Dad, how did we get here? Stop now." I paused, hoping he wouldn't say anything else. Thankfully he didn't. "Just let us know when you'll be here, and you need to thank my wife or I wouldn't be talking to you right now. Listen, if you don't think you can come here and be nice to Trigena—"

"I'm always nice to Trigena. She's a wonderful, hardworking woman."

"Okay, I mean...this has to be about the baby. Nothing else. You don't have to like my marriage, but you can't judge it and expect to be a part of our child's life. Do you get that? I won't make my child question where he or she belongs."

"Okay, you're right. Thank you, and thank Trigena for me. I'll have Jeanie call you when she's arranged for the tickets. She's so happy for you. She'll be excited to talk to you."

"Good-bye, Dad." I put the phone down and stood looking out the kitchen window.

Trigena walked in from the garage just as I hung up. "Are you okay?"

"He always does that to me." I turned to her. "He told me I have no idea what it's like to be black."

"K, you know that's not true."

"I've never known where I belong." The ever-present tears started flowing again.

Trigena pulled me to her. "You know where you belong."

Chapter Five

I hesitated before I knocked on Karrie's studio door. She never closed the door when she was working. She wasn't one of those artists who needed to finish a painting before she would let anyone see her work, but I was a bit concerned about disturbing her.

"It's open," she called out.

I walked into the small room intended for a bedroom. We'd pulled the carpet and put tile down for Karrie's studio as soon as we moved in. It wasn't the best room for a studio because it didn't provide much light or a view. Unfortunately, it looked out into the empty desert with one sickly pine tree standing alone like a solitary soldier on patrol. It was the best our house had to offer, though.

"Hey, babe. You okay?" It was only six in the morning when my alarm went off, and I realized Karrie wasn't in bed. She usually didn't get up until I did. She painted a little every morning, and I would kiss her good-bye and wipe a little paint off her face before I left. She had only one early class on Wednesdays. The rest of the week she could slow roll and make it in by ten. What was going on?

"I'm fine. I just couldn't sleep, and I didn't want to wake you. Is it six already?" She put her brush down and stepped back from the spot where her easel stood in the exact center of the room.

She didn't have a clock in the studio. She said it created some kind of weird pressure. It would've made me crazy not knowing what time it was, but Karrie had a pretty good internal clock and never missed anything despite her hatred for timepieces.

"Yeah," I answered, and looked at her painting. It was an Impressionistic-style painting of a woman and a little girl walking along a busy street. I've been admiring her work for ten years, and it still always amazed me. "It's beautiful, babe." I put my arm around her, and we both stared for a minute. Then I turned her toward me. "Is your dad keeping you awake?"

"Probably. It's okay, Trig. It'll be okay. I can't help but wish things were different."

"I know. I'm so sorry." I hugged her tight, and she relaxed into my arms. Our closeness felt nice. She'd been fighting me. She was struggling with her hurt, and I was an easy target.

"Can we just not talk about it? It is what it is, and we'll deal with him soon enough."

"Of course." I backed up to a stool I'd built for her. She always stood up when she painted, but I thought if she had a stool she would use it. She'd admired it appropriately and proudly carried it in here when I finished, but I'm not sure I've ever seen her sit on it.

"Don't you have to get ready for work?" She smiled at me.

"Yeah, ahhh. I wanted to talk to you about something first." I hesitated. I wasn't sure how this was going to go.

"Okay." She cocked her head.

"The girls are coming over tonight to work on the nursery design, and I wanted to talk to you about the guest room." Her expression turned hard.

"Trig, there's nothing to talk about. The guest room has a function, and we need a nursery. This room makes the most sense. I can set up in the front room or patio when I want to paint."

"But you paint every day. You need this," I said.

"Damn it, Trig. Why does everything have to be your way?" She threw her rag on the floor and walked past me.

"K, wait." She was in our walk-in closet and had already stripped out of her pajamas.

"Fine. Do whatever you want."

"I'm sorry. I...I didn't realize...I didn't think..." I knew I'd upset her, and I wanted to fix it, but I wasn't even sure what I should apologize for.

"Trig, we need the guest room. We don't need a painting studio. I'm choosing to be a mother. I can't be a painter."

Now I was mad. "Bullshit! That's your dad talking. Just because he cut off your mother's career...I won't do that to you. We're doing this together, and we'll both have our careers. We'll both be moms, and we'll help each other be the best moms and the best professionals. And nothing will stop you from being a painter. I won't let it!" She finished dressing while I ranted. I wasn't even sure she was listening.

And I was surprised at the words coming out of my mouth. First of all, I wasn't even certain I knew what it meant to be a mom. I had no siblings, so no nieces or nephews. This whole parenting thing was way outside my container, and it scared me to death. Secondly, I knew better than to mention her mom's limited career.

She pushed me out of the doorway with a strength I wasn't prepared for. "Don't talk about what you don't know." Karrie sat on the little loveseat in our bedroom and picked up her shoes.

"K...shit. This wasn't what I was going for. I'm sorry. I just want you to have the studio. You need to paint. I'm afraid if you don't have a place to go paint, you'll leave me."

"You're kidding, right?"

"Just listen one second, and if you disagree with me then I'll shut up, and we'll ask the girls to plan to convert the studio." I walked over and sat next to her.

"Okay, what?" She sat back and crossed her arms over her chest.

"I'll build the crib and the changing table just like we planned. There's room in there for a futon as well. We can get one of those really nice mattresses, and I can make everything match with your crib design. It'll be a beautiful set. Also the guest bedroom is closer to our bedroom so the nursery will be right beside us. Plus, knowing you, I can't imagine the crib will actually be in the nursery for the first few months." I winked at her. "Or years." She smiled at me. "K, I want you to always have your painting. You're good, you know?" I tried teasing a little.

"I am good, aren't I?" She took my hand. "I'm sorry I yelled at you."

"Oh, babe, I probably deserve to be yelled at once in a while. So can we convert the spare room instead of the studio?"

"I guess for now, but when we have two or three more we'll eventually have to use the studio."

"Oh, God. You're trying to kill me." I kissed her and started to get ready. I was behind schedule now.

She held on to my hand. "Can we just buy a futon? It would be so much cheaper, and I know you're worried about money. And we don't really need a changing table."

"Do you not know who you're married to? No daughter of mine is having cheap, store-bought furniture in her room." I went to dress for work.

❖

At the breakfast table, I finished my coffee and rinsed my cup. Then I went into the studio to kiss Karrie good-bye, but she wasn't there. A quick trip through the rest of the house confirmed it was empty. "Karrie, babe," I called out. I even opened the door to my shop and found it dark, but I called out her name anyway. I turned around in the kitchen and felt my heart rate increase. I picked up my phone as I headed for the front door. I was going to call RJ and Janet to let them know I'd be late. Just as I was about to get really scared, the front door opened and Karrie walked through. She was soaked in sweat, with a Camelbak hose hanging out of her mouth.

"Hello, Trig." I heard a voice on the phone I held to my ear while staring at my pregnant wife standing there flushed and breathing hard.

"Oh, hey, RJ. I'll be a bit late. Let Janet know."

"Everything okay?" he asked.

"All good. I just have to scold my wife for going for a run." I was staring at her.

"What?"

"Nothing. I'll be there in a bit." I hung up.

"Babe, what the hell were you doing? You scared the shit out of me. I couldn't find you."

"You know I go for a run every morning."

"You can't do that now. You're pregnant." I walked over to her like I thought I needed to help her.

"I'm pregnant?" She looked over at me with big eyes. "Oh, my God, what will we do?"

"Stop it." I almost laughed.

"What are you doing? Seriously, Trig, have you never known a pregnant woman?"

"Not one that is my wife. This can't be good for you."

"Jules said it was fine." She brushed past me, headed toward the kitchen.

I followed, talking to the back of her head. "You're kidding. She said you could go for three- to five-mile runs every day?"

She stopped and turned around so suddenly I almost bumped into her. "Yes. And I'm only running three easy miles most days. You have to trust me. I know my body, and I need this as much as I need to paint." She smiled at me.

"Shit…I can't win. I just have to worry about you twenty-four seven."

"That's your job. Oh, and making love to me. You have that job too." She kissed me, and I tasted the salty sweat on her lips.

"Hmm…the second job is so much easier." I put my arms on her hips and pulled her to me. "Maybe I could help wash your back."

"Get out of here. I know you're teasing. You already hate it that I made you late. Go. I'll take you up on that offer tonight." She pushed me away.

❖

"Hey, babe, are you home?" I called in the front door.
"In the kitchen."
"Justine and Dani are with me."
"Hey, ladies. I made chicken salad on pretzel rolls with fresh fruit and spinach salad. I know it's not too fancy, but I was craving chicken salad. Don't ask why." She was yelling from the kitchen while still working on dinner when we walked in.
"Girl, I'll eat your chicken salad any day. It's perfect for this crazy heat. Can you believe how hot it is for this time of year?" Danielle was first to wrap Karrie in a hug. Everyone at work knew about Karrie's chicken salad with grapes and apple slices. She occasionally made sandwiches for the whole crew.
"Hey, babe." I greeted her with a kiss.
Justine hugged Karrie. "Now that's a real pregnant belly. You're finally showing."
"I know. I just sort of popped out overnight." She rubbed her stomach. "So we should eat first. Trig, you want to open the wine?"
"None for us tonight." Danielle looked at Justine, who nodded.
"Iced tea then?"
"Let me wash my hands and face." I walked to the bathroom to clean up and returned to a discussion in full swing.
"Aren't you guys going to find out the sex?" Justine asked as she placed the plates on the table.
"No. We're going to wait and see. There's no health concerns, so there's no real reason for a sonogram. We'll find out when it gets here. Trig thinks it's a girl," I heard Karrie explaining as I entered the kitchen.

"Really? Interesting. I can see you two with a little girl, and Karrie, I bet you make beautiful babies."

Karrie smiled. "Thanks. I just want him or her to be healthy. I know everyone says that, but it's so true."

"Of course she's going to make a beautiful baby. Why do you think she's the pregnant one?" I kissed my wife and pulled out a chair for her. "Sit, babe. I'll get the rest."

"I'm pregnant because, after what I know now, you'd never even consider it." Karrie laughed, but not a soul spoke. The fear of bringing up a bad subject was too fresh. "Oh, come on. We've moved on." She touched my hand when I sat next to her.

"Right. Umm. Let's just eat, ladies."

"Yes, dig in," Karrie said.

"Karrie, everything looks great," Justine remarked.

"Thanks."

Danielle chimed in between bites. "So Trig tells us you've agreed to the guest room."

"Agreed? Hmm, more like gave in, but yes, as much as I hate to admit it, she's probably right." She looked over at me. "At least until we have more kids."

I rolled with it. "Yes, of course, until then."

We enjoyed a great dinner and made up for the last unfortunate get-together. Then I sent the girls into the guest room with Karrie to make a plan while I cleaned up. I trusted Danielle and Justine with any decorating project, and with my wife's great artistic eye, I knew it would be the most amazing nursery room ever, with no input needed from me.

"This is going to be great, Karrie. What do you think about us painting next week, Trig? We're done with the Fergusons' house, and we don't have anything for most of next week."

"Babe?" I looked at Karrie.

"Can we get the furniture out of the room by then?"

Justine jumped in. "We'll take care of that."

"Yeah. Justine's cousin needs a bedroom set. I meant to talk to you, but we were just planning to trade for the work. We'll give her the bedroom set, and they'll get the room ready for us," I said.

"Karrie, you know she insisted on paying us. We wanted to do it for a baby gift, but she refused," Justine said.

"Of course she did. You can't do that work for nothing," Karrie insisted.

"Yeah. I think it's just 'cause she wants to make us have to think of a gift for the baby. Anyway. Next week okay?" Danielle asked.

"Works for me," Karrie said. "I'm so excited to see it as a nursery."

"That just means I have to get my ass in gear with the crib and changing table."

Karrie poked me in the back as I was putting away the last of the dishes. "We still have time."

"We should get home." Justine pulled Danielle toward the front door. "Come on, Dani."

"She's right. Thank you so much for dinner, Karrie."

Karrie and I walked arm in arm with them to the front door. "My pleasure. I'll see you next week. Trig can give you a key, right?"

"Right," I echoed, and we all hugged. "See you all tomorrow for a scheduling meeting first thing."

"It'll just be me," Danielle said, and Justine nodded. "She has an appointment in the morning."

"Cool. Right. I remember. Good night."

The girls were gone, and Karrie and I were alone in our house again.

"Thanks for cleaning up."

"Thanks for dinner. Did you like what they came up with?" We walked back to the bedroom.

"I did. Oh, honey, it's going to be so adorable. She's going to love it."

"She?"

"You convinced me." Karrie smiled at me.

"What if I'm wrong?" I started for the shower.

"You're never wrong."

"Can I write that down somewhere?" I was stripped naked with the water running.

"Do whatever you want, but move over. I'm getting my back washed like you promised." She was out of her clothes in seconds.

I pulled her into the shower with me.

Chapter Six

"Hi, Dean Stone." I saw the head of our department out of the corner of my eye as I was sorting through slides for my next lecture. The class was only fifty minutes long, and I always wanted to show way more great works of art than time allowed. It was a challenge for me to select the best ones, so I was in the classroom early. "Are you looking for someone?" The older gentleman dressed in an expensive suit looked completely out of place in the undergraduate hall.

"Actually, Professor Gilmore, I was looking for you." He walked into the classroom wringing his hands and awkwardly moving around the desks. It had probably been fifteen years since he'd spent any real time in a classroom.

"Oh...okay." I'm sure the surprise on my face was apparent. "What can I do for you?" I had only spoken to the man about half a dozen times. It was always about my mother's paintings, and we'd never talked one-on-one.

"Congratulations on your pregnancy. You and your wife... ahhh..."

"Trigena." I quickly injected her name to avoid prolonging the awkwardness.

"Yes, Trigena." He paused a little too long. His strange behavior was heightening my concern about what he wanted. "You two must be very happy."

"Yes. Yes, we are." I had no idea he knew I was married to a woman, but he seemed okay with it. I was used to stereotyping older men into the same conservative category as my father, so I was a bit surprised.

"Is she going to quit working after the baby comes?"

"No." I had no idea where this was going, but the whole thing felt really weird.

"Oh." He just stood there looking at me, and I didn't know what to do. I was pretty sure there was no etiquette guide explaining proper behavior for when your senior boss confronted you about how to raise your child—assuming that's what he was doing. It sure felt like it.

I was only one year away from tenure, and while I had worried a lot about it the first couple of years, I pretty much stopped when I started getting calls from schools all over the country. Oddly, that was the one thing Trigena was never concerned about. She had absolute confidence in me as an artist and a teacher. My work, both my early stuff with my mother's influence and my master's degree portfolio, had been in a major traveling exhibit with great names—people I'd only dreamed of sharing an exhibit with.

Since I wasn't tenured, and I really loved working here, I refrained from stopping the conversation. Instead I just stood there waiting.

"Well, maybe you should reduce your schedule then. I mean after the baby comes."

"Yes. I've worked out my absence next term with Dr. Rainer. She's rescheduled and reassigned all my classes for spring semester, but I'll be back for a reduced summer schedule and ready for my full load next fall. She's okayed the schedule."

"I'm going to talk to her about reducing your next fall schedule by half as well. You can work part-time." He started to walk away.

"Dean Stone, I want to work full-time." I was so shocked I couldn't come up with anything more.

"The board will be meeting to discuss next year's faculty requirements tomorrow night. If you'd like to attend, you can bring up your concerns at that time." Again he turned away from me.

"Are you not happy with my performance? Should I be worried about my tenure?" I felt like I was taking a huge risk asking that question, but if I asked directly, then maybe I would get a direct answer.

"Professor, it looks like your students are arriving. We should talk about this with the board tomorrow night." He snuck out against the flow of incoming students and left me standing there in shock as undergraduates began filling up the room.

I rushed through a lesson I'd been so excited to teach and ran from the classroom to the assistant dean's office. Dr. Katherine Rainer had been a mentor and an inspiration for me since I arrived six years earlier.

I headed straight for her inner office, but her secretary stopped me. "Dr. Gilmore, the dean is in there."

I knew exactly why. I ran down the hall clutching my cell phone and using every ounce of strength I had to keep from crying and calling my rock. I needed to hear Trigena tell me everything was going to be okay. The last thing we needed now was to worry about our most stable source of income. We'd been saving for the last six months to be prepared for the time I was on maternity leave, but we were in no way prepared for me to take a dramatic cut in pay by being reduced to part-time.

I pushed my favorites list, and Trigena's picture came up on top. I started to touch the screen, but I turned it off instead. I couldn't call her at work; she hated it. She didn't want her crew to take personal calls, and she always held herself to a higher standard. The door to the ladies' room was just across the hall so I ducked inside and rinsed my face. I managed to keep myself from calling Trig and somehow pulled myself together. By the time I got back to Dr. Rainer's office, her door was open.

"Go on in, Professor. She's expecting you."

I nodded at her, even more confused now, as I rushed in.

"What's going on?" I was yelling, and I had to stop myself. Dr. Rainer wasn't the enemy here. "I'm sorry."

"Karrie, please sit down." Dr. Rainer sat dwarfed behind her large oak desk. She was a tiny woman with an elegant, regal look. Her hair was always perfectly styled and her clothes immaculate.

"Dr. Rainer…I don't want to sit. I have another class in twenty minutes. I just want to know what's going on."

She stood up and came around her desk and took my arm. She led me to one of the stiff wooden chairs in front of her desk and sat in the one across from me. "He's worried about your attendance and commitment after the baby comes. He…"

"What? That's ridiculous. I've missed only one class in six years of teaching. Doesn't he know who I am?" I stopped my rant, realizing what she was saying. "Dr. Rainer, that sounds a lot like discrimination."

"He would never say it like that, and he didn't say it to me like that." She gave me a look that made me know she was talking to me as a mentor and a friend, not as my assistant dean. "He wants to encourage you to go part-time so he can hire another professor. Apparently he has some negative experience from the past when one of his professors had a hard time returning to teaching after her baby came."

"This is crazy. I don't want to give up my career just because I want to be a mom. I still don't have tenure. He can just give it a try, and if I fail, he can relieve me. I don't want to go part-time, and frankly we can't afford it."

"He doesn't want to deny you tenure. He realizes you're a significant draw to the department. And your mother's exhibit is a gold mine for him. I actually think he believes this is the best way to keep you."

"Can't you talk to him? He'll be denying me tenure if he makes me part-time. I can't do this. I've invested six years here when I had countless other opportunities. I like it here. I've dreamed of following in your footsteps. I can't…" I felt a wave of emotion. I didn't want to cry, not here not now.

"Karrie, you should take it to the board like he suggested. I'll advocate for you. We'll work this out. Maybe he'd be happy with just one additional semester of a reduced class load." She sounded more like she was trying to convince herself than me.

I just walked out without another word, and she let me go. In the hall, I looked at the clock on my phone. I still had twelve minutes before class. I hit Trigena's number.

She picked up before I could think about what I was doing. "K, are you all right?"

At the sound of her voice I broke down and sobbed, barely coherent, "No, my…" Tears were streaming down my face, and students were filling the halls for the next class session so I took refuge in the ladies' room again.

"Babe, what's wrong? Is the baby okay? Are you okay? Please catch your breath and tell me where you are. I'll be right there."

Realizing how freaked out she must be at me crying and calling her at work, I took a deep breath. "I'm so sorry I called you and scared you. The baby is fine and I'm okay. I shouldn't have called. I…I just lost it and needed to hear your voice."

"It's okay, babe." She wasn't upset, but I could hear her relief. I'd really frightened her. "Tell me what happened." The ubiquitous Albuquerque wind that had been rushing in her phone stopped, and I heard her truck door slam shut.

I quickly reiterated the chain of events, and by the time I finished, I think she was angrier than I. "I have to get to class, hon. Thank you for listening. I'm sorry I bugged you at work. I love you."

"Listen, K, we're going to figure this out. Don't worry. I love you too, babe."

Just hearing her strong, confident voice gave me the strength to go to my classroom and make it through the rest of the day.

❖

By the time I got home, Trigena was already there with spaghetti and meatballs and Italian salad ready and set out on the table. "Hey, babe, I'm in here."

"You came home early." I walked over to kiss the chef. She even had most of the dishes washed. "I shouldn't have called you."

She dried her hands on the dish towel and wrapped me in a hug. I felt safe and loved. "If I've somehow given you the impression that work is more important than you, then I've screwed up. Today shouldn't have happened." She led me to the table. "What would you like to drink?" We often had a glass of wine with our dinner, so what to drink was a new challenge.

"Water's fine."

She filled two glasses with ice and water. She was so good at avoiding all the foods and alcohol I couldn't have while I was pregnant.

"Listen, here's what we're going to do." She paused and looked at me. "I mean I have a suggestion that I would like you to consider." She smiled.

"Thank you." I looked around the table and held her off for a bit. I just wanted to be in our home and not think about work right now. "This looks amazing. I'm so hungry. All I had time for today was a power bar."

"K! You can't do that. You have to eat." She served me way too much spaghetti.

"I know. It doesn't happen very often. Just on days like today." I started in on the salad. As good as Trig's spaghetti was, salad was what I really wanted.

"Can I tell you what I was thinking now?"

"Okay." I knew I had to let her talk or she was going to explode.

"Tell them you'll quit if you get cut to part-time."

"What?" I nearly spewed lettuce out of my mouth. "Ahh, yeah. First of all, I don't want to quit, and second, we can't afford that."

"Well, we can afford it for a few months, and they won't let you go. They know how good you are and what you bring to the department. It's like Dr. Rainer said, Dean Stone is trying to keep you in some convoluted way. You just let him know it has to be on your terms. He'll back down."

"Umm...so what if you're wrong? That's too big of a risk to take."

"Well, first of all," she was mocking me a bit, "I'm not wrong, and second, if I am, we'll move. You take your talent to one of the schools that has been recruiting you for the last six years."

"Trig, we can't leave here. Your work's here."

"I can work anywhere. And if we end up someplace where I can't get a contracting business off the ground, then I can go back to accounting. I still have some contacts and—"

"You're kidding me." I laughed.

"What?"

"You would shrivel up and blow away if you had to be shoved behind a desk indoors all day."

"Well...it won't come to that, but if it does, I'll do what's best for us."

I couldn't believe what I was hearing her say. As I started in on the spaghetti, I considered that she was probably right, but if they did let me go, I couldn't take her someplace where she couldn't build. She needed to build more than I needed to paint.

"Well?" she asked between bites.

"Maybe I could get something else here? I could go over to the community college and probably get..."

"No. Don't be ridiculous. He wins if you lose prestige. K, big-name schools have been calling you. Fuck him. You walk away to bigger and better. You're too good to be treated like that. I'll go with you tomorrow night. He won't have the support of the board. You'll see."

I finished most of the mound of pasta Trigena had put on my plate. She let me sit there soaking in her idea, but I knew she was getting impatient. "Okay. I think you might be right, and I know Dr. Rainer will speak for me, as will most of the rest of the faculty, but if we're wrong, and they let me go before tenure, I find different work here. We don't leave. Agreed?"

"Ahh...K, if we're wrong, we should take this chance to get you to one of those big schools worthy of your talents."

"No, Trig. There are two of us here. Soon to be three. This is where we belong. I want to raise our daughter here. This is our home. I'm happy teaching here."

"But would you be happy if you weren't teaching?"

"Yes. As long as I'm here with you." I was starting to sound corny, but it was true. "I used to think I wanted the Ivy League schools and the big art museums and fancy art shows, but that's not me. It's my dad's dream for me because he took it away from my mom." I could feel tears coating my eyes. "I have everything I want and more than I could've ever dreamed of."

Trigena moved her chair next to mine and pulled me to her chest. "I love you, babe."

Chapter Seven

I pulled out two ten-foot-long boards from RJ's truck. The beautiful rough-cut cherry, my favorite wood, was the color of a dark blush wine. I felt like a little kid in a toy store, so excited to start working on Karrie's crib design. It was just a piece of furniture, but building this was important. If I made it, maybe I would feel closer to the baby and perhaps understand Karrie's need to be a mom, but mostly I was thrilled with a new wood project. Karrie's design would take my skills to a whole new level, but with Janet's help, I could turn her beautiful art into a workable pattern. I couldn't wait to get started.

"This is gorgeous wood, RJ. Did you go through the whole pile for the best pieces?" We were stacking the boards in the corner of the workshop. As badly as I wanted to start preparing the wood today, I needed to let it acclimate in my shop. It would be next weekend's project.

"Actually, Doc had it all set out for me—all ready to load when I pulled up. He said I could go through the stack but challenged me to find better pieces than he'd selected. I think he threw in a few extra board feet." RJ winked at me as he placed two more boards on our neat pile. "The old man was disappointed you didn't come by the store yourself to pick it up. He's got something going for you, Trig." RJ laughed. Doc Thomas had been selling wood to me since I moved out here almost fourteen years ago when all I had was a circular saw and a hammer.

I'd walked into his hardwood store when I was still working at Klein and Son Accounting. I'd been assigned his account and was completing his tax paperwork. He'd asked if I could come by his office, said he was undermanned that day. I agreed. I'd do just about anything to get out of the stuffy building I worked in.

To reach his office, I'd had to walk through his massive warehouse filled with stacks of hardwood like multicolored wooden Tetrus blocks manipulated perfectly to fit. Amazing. When I left, he gave me more scrap pieces than I could ever use, and he's been giving me lumber ever since. I credit Doc for motivating me to make my dream come true and start my own business.

When Karrie came into my life, she sometimes went with me to pick out lumber—she loved beautiful wood as much as I did. And as much as Doc liked me, I think he fell in love with Karrie—they all do. K and I joke about it, but truthfully Doc was like a father figure to us. She asked him how old he was once—she could get away with stuff like that—and he said, "Somewhere between seventy and one hundred and seventy."

"He's too good to me. This is way more than I ordered. We need to take some of it back. I can't afford it, and I can't accept all this." I put my hand on the boards he was starting to pull from the truck.

"He told me you'd say that." He pulled one of Doc's business cards out of his pocket. "Told me to give you this when you started complaining and said he'd be personally insulted if this wood turned back up at his store. Shook his fist at me and said he'd hold me responsible if it did. So I ain't takin' it back, Trig."

I pulled off my gloves and took the card. In scratchy, barely readable pencil marks, Doc had handwritten a note to Karrie and me on the back of it.

Trig and K,
Please accept this small stack of lumber as an old man's gift to you and your baby. Yours, Doc.

I swallowed hard and tossed the card on my table saw. Karrie would cry for sure, but I had to keep it together while RJ was still here. "Damned old man. There's like eight hundred dollars' worth of cherry, the best cherry." I pulled my gloves on and grabbed two more boards.

"Oh, and he said the ebony would be here next week." RJ pretended to duck.

"Damn it. I told him to wait to order that until I was sure I could afford it."

RJ smiled and shrugged before pulling out the last of the boards. "There's nothing you can do about it, Trig. People just like you. We all try not to, but…we can't help it."

"Shit. Once I tell K, she's going to make him so much food he won't have to cook for a month."

"Maybe that was his motive. I'd do most anything for Karrie's cooking." RJ winked at me. "Hey, are we on for training on the weekend of the thirtieth?"

"Yes. I have approval from the boss." I nodded toward the house. "Do you think Natalie would want to hook up with K while we're out?"

"Actually, she told me to ask K to give her a call."

"Good. I know she'll be fine, but I don't want to leave her alone in the house all weekend."

"You worry about her way more than I worried about Natalie when she was pregnant. It must be a chick thing."

"Maybe you're just a jerk." I punched him in the arm as we set up spacers and stacked the last of the wood.

"Probably." He punched me back. "Are you going to announce the training session at the meeting?" He plopped down on the pile we just created, and I grabbed my stool and rolled it over toward him.

"Actually, I can't make the meeting. Can you announce it? And let them know there's only one session this season. If they miss it, then they have to wait till spring. I don't have time this year for individual training sessions." I passed him a bottle of Corona from the little fridge in the shop.

"Thanks. Good call. I'll announce it. Same plan as last year?"

I nodded while guzzling my beer.

"Why can't you be at the meeting?"

"K's dad is coming for an overnight, and we're all having dinner."

"Woo. How's that gonna be?"

"Well, I asked for it."

"What?" He leaned back on the stack of woods, ready to hear a long story.

"It's not that big of a deal. He called and wanted to be a part of the baby's life. I said we should give it a try. He's the only living grandparent the baby will have so it just seemed like the right thing."

"Hmmm…okay." He shook his head. "Hey, Janet says you're planning on taking the roof job after we finish up at the Fergusons'."

"We have to. Don't have anything else. It's bad karma not to take a job when there's nothing else. It could be weeks before something else comes up."

"What about the Hurst contract?"

"No word yet. We can't compete in the houses where they're putting in standard bathrooms, but I think we have a chance on the high-end custom jobs. It's just…well, we might not hear for a few more weeks. I also have a couple other bids out, so something should come in soon. And I pushed all the marketing again."

"How'd things turn out with Karrie's job? Are you worried about money?"

"RJ, I'm always worried about money. I have five people counting on me to keep them employed full-time. But the thing with Karrie's dean worked out just like we hoped. He stood up to recommend she go part-time, and she jumped out of her chair ready to give a big speech and put up a fight. All she had to do was say I don't want to give up my full-time class load. The chairman of the board spun around to the dean and said, 'See,

Charles. I knew it. Nothing to worry about.' He turned back to K and said, 'That's great news, Dr. Gilmore. Dean Stone was convinced we would lose some of the hours you were teaching.' It was all the asshole dean overreacting. I was so mad I wanted to pull the guy's ears off, but K got me out of the room as soon as it was all cleared up."

"Well, that's good then, right? You'll still have her income if things slow down."

"What's going on, RJ? You don't want to do the roof?"

"Trig, none of us do. It's not what we're good at, and we don't have what we need to do it safely. We lost you for three weeks last time because you take too many risks and fell twelve feet. It could've been much worse, you know?"

"It wasn't worse," I said in defense.

"We could all come over and knock out a bunch of outdoor furniture. That shit is fast and easy, and it always sells."

"Yeah, it sells in the spring, not in the fall, and seriously, we can't all fit in here and get any real work done. I can't pay everyone with money from a few sets of furniture. I can't turn this down. Janet too?"

He nodded.

"They sent you to talk to the stubborn old bitch."

He smiled at me.

I stood there a minute. He was right. I needed to get jobs that were better suited for our skills, and I shouldn't make them do work they weren't comfortable with. "Listen. I'll push the rope on those other contracts, and I'll beat the pavement. I'll go over and do the roof myself, and I'll find us some better jobs."

"The hell you will, Trig. That's not going to happen. Janet and Jason and I will be there Monday morning. The girls are working at your house, right? We're just trying to avoid anyone getting hurt. We sure as hell aren't going to send you out there alone. We support you and the decisions you make for the business. We just thought we should at least talk to you about it. Don't go all passive-aggressive on me."

I couldn't shake it that they were so disappointed in me. "RJ, what's going on?"

"Nothing. That's it. We just want to make sure we're safe. Does K know?"

The house door slammed closed behind us. "Does K know what?" Karrie asked.

Chapter Eight

"Does K know what?" I asked as I walked into Trigena's shop.

"Oh, hey, Karrie. Listen. I gotta go. Call Natalie so you two can make some plans while Trig and I are yelling at our trainees." RJ practically ran to his truck.

"Right." Trigena waved.

"Did you buy all this wood? It had to have cost a fortune." I ran my fingers across the top of the beautiful pile of lumber. There's something about the need to touch a piece of nicely figured wood. I understood why Trigena loved it so much.

"Well, actually, no." Trigena crossed her workshop and returned with a business card. "Doc gave most of it to us. There's enough here to do all the furniture for the baby's room."

I read the card as she spoke. "How much is all this? We can't accept it. It's too much." Doc's words and unexpected kindness overwhelmed me. I sniffed and wiped my eyes.

"I knew that'd make you cry. I had to get mad at him to keep from crying myself." Trig stood next to me, both of us staring at the huge stack. "I'm not sure of the value, but it's a lot. It's the best, too, but RJ said Doc told him he'd be offended if we took it back. He's right, you know. The best thing we can do is thank him and show him pictures of the furniture and the baby when she gets here." She placed her hand on my round midsection and smiled at me.

I nodded. "I'll make him some treats, and we should stop by sometime next week."

"I knew you'd say that."

"Oh, is that right? You don't know everything." I stuck my finger in her ribs.

"Oh no, you don't. Don't start something you can't finish." She held on to both my wrists.

"Fine. I give. Speaking of treats, dinner's ready. Come in and wash up. Are you done for the day?" I was hoping she was. I was finished painting and just wanted to spend some time with her.

"Ahh…well. I was going to finish some sharpening, but it can wait." She could tell I was ready for her to be done. I tried not to put too much pressure on her, but sometimes I was selfish and wanted some of her time. Mostly she felt the same way. I just had to remind her sometimes.

"Good. Thanks, babe. What was RJ talking about?"

"What do you mean?"

"He asked you if K knew? What was he talking about?" Trigena held the door for me to go ahead of her into the house, and she closed the large garage doors.

"Oh, nothing. We'll talk about it after dinner." She walked away toward the bathroom to wash up before I could say another word.

I put all the taco-making materials on the table.

Trigena walked back in. "What can I get you to drink?"

"I already have a Pellegrino, and I poured you some tea."

"Thanks, babe. I'm starving." She settled in to her chair and started serving herself.

"Trig, I want you to tell me what RJ was talking about."

"Oh, K, it's no big deal." Trigena didn't look up.

I just waited, watching her.

Finally, she turned to me and sighed heavily. "I took a roof-repair job for next week."

"Trigena! Are you serious? No." I sounded whiny, and I didn't want that. I was pissed. "You promised me you'd never do a roof again. You nearly killed yourself last time."

"I didn't tell you I wouldn't do a roof again. I told you I wouldn't if I didn't have to. I don't have any other work next week, and I might not have any the following one. I can't afford not to do it." She was angry now. "I told you this should wait until after dinner. You're overreacting."

I rose from the table and put my plate away. "Don't tell me how I'm reacting. Trig, you could've broken your back. You were off work for three weeks."

"That won't happen again. What are you doing? You need to eat." She was watching me put things away.

"I'm not hungry. You don't have to do this. You're just doing it to prove something—your stupid Midwestern pride."

"I'm doing this for us. I need to be working and making money so we have what we need."

"You want way more than we need. You want perfection. How about I want my wife to be alive and well to raise this baby with me. I can't do this alone." A wave of emotion came over me, and I knew I was about to cry. Trigena and I have had some fights, sometimes pretty intense because both of us can be stubborn, but I rarely cried when we fought until I got pregnant.

"Shit. I can't win!" Trigena put her own plate in the sink and spun me around. Tears had welled up in my eyes, and seeing my face took the fire out of her. She sighed heavily and tried to wipe my eyes, but I pushed her hands away.

"Don't touch me. I'm still mad. Do you ever think about anyone else?" I was full-on bawling now, and she just stared at me. "What happens to me if you get hurt?" She kept trying to put her arms around me or touch my face, but I kept pushing her away. "Fight with me, damn it. I'm pregnant, not broken."

Finally, she spoke softly. "I don't want to fight with you. Why are we doing this? I won't accept the work if you feel this strongly, but RJ and Jason are going to help me. Janet will be there too, doing all the work from the ground. I'll be very careful. It's a lot of money for not much work. I promise, babe." She looked at me sincerely. "Please eat something, K."

"You're worried about me eating. Augh." I was mad, and I guess I wanted to fight. "Fine, but don't do the work. I don't want you to do it." I wanted to see if she would really agree to cancel the job.

"Okay. I won't. I'll call Carl and see if he can."

We just stood in the middle of the kitchen in a standoff. She moved toward me again, but I walked away with a taco shell, sat at the table, and slowly filled it with meat, tomatoes, lettuce, and cheese. I looked over at her still standing there. "Call Carl then."

"Yeah. Okay." She walked to the front room to get her phone.

"Never mind. Don't cancel," I yelled from where I sat.

"What? Hold on," Trigena said. "What did you say?"

"I said forget it. Do the job if you want."

"Sorry to bug you." I heard her hang up. She walked back in. "Are you sure? I'll be very careful."

"Why didn't you tell me?" I demanded.

"I didn't want to upset you?" She said it like a question.

"How did that work out for you?" I just stared at her, and she said nothing to my sarcasm. "You knew it would upset me. We should've talked about it and then…well, maybe we could've come up with a solution before you committed yourself." I didn't look up but finally bit into the taco that I really didn't want. I'd been so hungry when we sat down to eat that I thought I should at least try to eat.

"You're right. I'm sorry. I was trying to protect you and make sure I had work."

I sat with the crumbling mess on the paper towel in front of me. "Stop treating me differently." Trigena didn't speak. She just stood there looking at me. "You can rub my feet, make me pancakes, and make love to me at my every whim, but don't treat me like I can't think just because I'm pregnant. We make hard decisions together, Trig. We always have."

"I'm sorry."

"Stop saying that. Do you agree with me or not?" I needed to know she understood.

Trigena came over and sat next to me at the high-top table she'd built for us after we bought the house. "I agree with you. I didn't realize that was what I was doing, but I can see that now. You're right. We make decisions together. If you really don't want me to do the work, I won't. And I won't do that again."

"I don't want you to, but I won't ask you to go back on your word. I know what that means to you. I just need you to promise you will be very careful. I can't do this alone. I need you, Trigena." The damn tears started flowing down my cheeks again.

"I promise, babe." She pulled me out of the chair and into a tight hug. She held me for a minute and released me and wrapped up my paper-towel mess of food. "Let me get you a plate and another taco."

"Thanks." I wiped my face and blew my nose, then sat back down and just watched her wait on me.

Chapter Nine

I was sitting at the kitchen table with my computer running AutoCad when the doorbell rang. I had dressed hours ago, so I could get some work done. I almost had the floor plan completed for the Hurst Homes' bathrooms. I received word last night that we had been awarded the contract for eight bathrooms in new homes in their development only two miles from our house. I was so relieved, and the timing was perfect. We would have the roof job done next week, and if I could complete the floor plan and send it over to Justine and Danielle before the end of the weekend, they would have time to create several design options by the time we were ready to get started. Leonard, Karrie's dad, was supposed to be arriving soon, but I didn't want to lose any time.

"Can you get that? I'm almost ready." I heard Karrie from the bathroom. She was worrying too much about her appearance, as she always did when her dad came for a visit.

"I got it, babe." I hit Save and closed my computer. I took a deep breath as I walked to the front door. This had the potential to be a very long night, and no matter what I did, I knew I would be viewed as a second-class citizen. When I first met Leonard, I resented the way he treated me, but I knew how much Karrie loved him and desired a relationship with him. She'd put me in front of him every time, probably driving the wedge between them even deeper. While I was grateful that she did, I felt a little guilty sometimes. It wasn't my fault that he wasn't in her life. It was his problem, but I was pretty good at being the diplomat when I tried. I wanted to contribute positively to the peace process, even if it had the same likelihood of success as the Israeli and Palestinian Accords.

"Good evening, Leonard. You're looking well." I opened the door wide for him to enter. Karrie and I had spent all morning cleaning our house. The effort we put into it might imply that our house was a mess, but between me being a bit uptight and Karrie being an immaculate housekeeper, our house rarely had anything out of place, yet we cleaned anyway. Karrie had set out small scented candles all over, and the whole house smelled amazing, like vanilla.

"Hello, Ms. Gilmore." He entered our house and looked around. "Where's my daughter?" he asked, and leaned in stiffly to kiss my cheek.

"She's finishing up. Leonard, when are you going to call me Trigena?"

"Oh yes, Trigena." He said it as if he was remembering some agreed-upon compromise.

"Hi, Dad." Karrie walked into the room wearing a beautiful cream-colored dress that hung off her right shoulder, exposing her elegant long neck and distinct collarbones that framed her sexy body. Just enough cleavage was showing that I couldn't help but let my gaze drift there. Then, suddenly possessive, I wanted to cover it. The linen dress hung perfectly over her stomach, with a cloth belt tied at the top highlighting her pregnancy. She clicked into the room standing tall on two-inch-high sandals.

"Babe, you're beautiful." I reached up for a quick kiss on her cheek. I was in casual slacks and a silk blouse with flats. I was way underdressed, and between her and Leonard, I would be looking up all night long.

"You're so pale. You need some sun. My gosh, you're really pregnant. I had no idea you were so far along." Leonard didn't move toward her. He just stood there staring.

"She's amazing." I took her hand. Karrie was one of the most confident women I knew, and most of the time I don't believe she even had any idea how absolutely stunning she was, but I knew she felt a little self-conscious about her body right now. The last thing I wanted was for this event to be derailed before it even started.

"Thank you, hon." She tightened her grip on my hand before releasing it and walking to her father.

"No hug, Dad?"

"Definitely, Karrie. It's good to see you. You do look beautiful." He seemed to find his senses and pulled her to him. He released her. "When are you due? I thought you just found out you were pregnant."

Karrie took my hand again. She always liked to hold my hand, but I knew what she was doing. "We're due in late January. I'm almost twenty weeks."

"Do you know the baby's gender yet?" he asked while we all stood awkwardly in the front foyer.

I answered quickly to help Karrie out. "No. We're going to wait and see."

"Why would you do that?" He glared at me.

"We don't want to expose the baby to any unnecessary procedures." I spoke up again since I too had believed a sonogram was necessary only a few weeks ago. Karrie and Jules had convinced me there was no need to expose the baby to the procedure since everything was normal and Karrie was so healthy and fit. I was now an advocate.

"That's ridiculous—ultrasounds are safe. People have been doing them for years." He looked disgusted with me. Leonard just couldn't refrain from giving his opinion, especially when it came to his daughter. "What if there's something wrong with the baby?"

"Nothing's wrong with our baby, Leonard." I spoke calmly, but Karrie didn't.

She dropped my hand and moved a step closer to him. With her heels on, she looked him right in the eye. "What if there is, Dad? What would you have me do if we were to find out something was wrong with the baby?" She paused dramatically. "Terminate?" Her voice was elevated from the start and grew louder as she finished.

"Ahh well. I..."

"Exactly." She seemed satisfied and stepped back. "Are we going to eat or not?"

"We can all ride in the Highlander." I spoke and walked around Karrie to get the keys.

"I'm parked behind you. We'll take the rental. It's a Lexus."

I couldn't help but wonder if Leonard thought the Highlander wasn't good enough for him or his daughter.

I looked at Karrie to see if this was one she wanted me to fight. She shrugged, and we picked up our purses. I sent them out, quickly blew out the candles, and locked up.

When I got out to the car I was discouraged to see Karrie had climbed into the backseat. I opened her door. "Babe, wouldn't you be more comfortable sitting in the front?"

"No, I'm fine," she insisted.

I climbed in the front. My stubborn wife was making this more difficult than it needed to be, but I couldn't do a thing about it.

We drove in silence for longer than I could endure. "Leonard, are you still taking clients?" He kept saying he was going to retire, but I think the firm will have to push him out the door or he'll never leave.

"Yes."

That was all I got by way of response from the sophisticated black man sitting next to me. He wore a perfectly tailored, dark-gray, double-breasted suit with highly polished black wingtips. I had seen Leonard only about a dozen times, mostly when he came to visit, and once when Karrie took me to Boston with her, but I'd never seen him in anything but a suit.

I decided to sit quietly since my attempts at conversation had gone nowhere.

"How's school, Karrie?" he finally asked.

"It's good, Dad." I heard the upbeat tone in her voice. She was pleased when he asked about something that meant so much to her.

"I wish you'd think about coming back East. So many places want you, and you could really make a name for yourself." He peered in the rearview mirror.

"Dad, this is my home." The positive tone was gone.

"She's making a name here, Leonard." I should've kept my mouth shut, but I was so proud of my amazing wife. "She's got a show scheduled for November in Santa Fe. She's been painting like crazy. She's done some great work—very different style. You should come in and see it after we finish dinner." I felt her kick the seat.

"I'd love to see her work. She never wants to show me."

"Because you never think it's any good, Dad."

"That's not true. I know how good you are. Your mother always said I knew nothing of art, but I know how talented you are. I just want you to always do your very best."

Karrie didn't speak. I almost felt the temperature drop in the car. I didn't understand how two people who were family could keep pushing each other away so hard. I couldn't believe the woman I loved and knew so well could be so closed. I never wanted to hurt her like he had, because I could see the potential of her icing me out like she did him. She'd built the outer shell so thick she couldn't let him in. She refused to let him hurt her again. Or at least that's what she hoped for, but I knew he could hurt her repeatedly.

We drove the rest of the way to St. Clair's Bistro and Winery in silence. I held the door for Karrie when we arrived and leaned near. "Babe, I know this is hard, but please try to be open to him."

"Trig, you don't know about this. You fix everything else, but you can't fix this."

I nodded and closed her door before taking her hand and meeting Leonard at the front of the car. We were seated immediately and given wine menus. St Clair's had some of the best New Mexico wines, and Karrie and I enjoyed it very much.

"Why did we come here? Karrie can't drink."

Karrie started to speak, but I interrupted. "I chose the winery. They have very good food, and I thought you might enjoy one of our local wines."

He grunted. I knew he thought there was no way New Mexico could have any wine he would want to taste. So he asked for an iced tea. His loss.

After we had ordered, we were all silent again. Only a few patrons were in the restaurant on a Wednesday night so there was nothing even to distract us from our discomfort. I wanted to tell them both how stupid they were acting, but the words Karrie had just spoken in my ear were still fresh in my memory.

Finally, Leonard asked, "Have you picked out some names?"

Karrie looked at me, and I looked wide-eyed back at her. I wanted her to talk to him so I sat quietly. "No, Dad. We haven't thought much about names yet. Trigena believes we're having a girl so I have some ideas, but we haven't discussed them."

"So your doctor agrees with not having an ultrasound?"

"Dad, we're having a midwife deliver our baby," Karrie said.

I think my adrenaline shot up to a new high as I felt the anxiety of this discussion. I was really hoping this topic wouldn't come up.

"A midwife? Well, aren't you going back in time, when there are so many advances to help with the delivery?"

Karrie handled it. "Dad, they come out the same way regardless of what advances are used. Please don't ask any more questions about our choice for how our baby will be delivered."

"Karrie, at the risk of making you angrier at me—"

"Then don't risk it, Dad. Could we just enjoy a meal?"

"That sounds like a great idea," I said as I watched our tall, skinny waiter coming toward us with bread, but Leonard couldn't resist.

"You keep saying our baby. Ms., I mean Trigena, surely you understand this is not your baby. This baby is my daughter's and some donor's, whom she probably barely knows. It will have none of your genetics."

Karrie actually screeched, but I grabbed her hand and spoke quickly. "Mr. Holbrook, Karrie and I are married, and I know you don't like that, but we are. The baby is ours. It will be loved by two mothers." I paused, thinking of all the things I wanted to say and finally settled on one. "There's more to family than DNA. We're going to have a beautiful family with a lot of love and support."

"Dad, we can leave right now. I can't sit here and let you judge and criticize us. Trig, let's call a cab."

"Wait, babe—one minute, please." I turned my full attention to Leonard. "We asked you here tonight so you could see your daughter, who is going to have your grandchild. You asked to be a part of his or her life, and after discussing it we agreed that we wanted our child to know his or her only living grandparent. I heard Karrie tell you that if you couldn't accept us, then you couldn't be a part of our child's life. You don't have to like that we're married, but you have to let go of your judgments. We're happy, and we're having a family of our own. We don't need this. Please think about it. Karrie and I will be on the patio in the back. If you want us to join you for dinner, please come out to get us. Otherwise we'll take a cab, and we'll consider this finished."

"Wait—"

"Give us a few minutes outside," I insisted, and helped Karrie out of her chair and headed for the patio on the east side of the restaurant. Karrie was practically running in front of me.

When I reached the door, she let it slam in my face. I realized then that I'd overstepped again. I went out and met her at the rail.

"When are you going to stop doing that?" She didn't yell, but she was gritting her teeth.

"I don't know. I'm sorry. I just wanted to salvage things."

"Trig." She stopped abruptly before changing her tone. "You can't bring back your parents by trying to include my dad. I know you want to be the glue that binds us, but he left me a long time ago. He wants me to be the little girl that sits on his lap and does whatever he wants without thought. He won't let me be me. He doesn't even want to know me. He wants me to be my mother. I loved Mom dearly, but I'm not her. I'm my own artist, I'm a teacher, I'm about to be a mother, and I'm your wife. This is not about me being too stubborn to work things out. I'm not saying I don't contribute to the difficulties to some extent, but he won't change."

I just stared at her. I had no words. I think I knew she was right. I looked out over the vineyard in front of us, letting my eye follow the perfect rows of grapevines up the slope.

"Trigena, look at me." I turned back to her. I was worried that she might start crying, but her eyes were dry. "We're happy. I love you so much, and I love our life. I don't have time for the negative, unproductive parts of my life anymore. I'm done with this, and I'm not going to try anymore."

Out the corner of my eye I saw Leonard walking toward us. "Babe, your dad."

She turned around and waited for him to approach her, then spoke. "Dad, we're going home. I'll pay for our meals. I hope you have a safe flight home. Good-bye, Dad." She said each word clearly and emotionlessly, as if she had recorded a speech and played it back to him. Then she took my hand and started walking toward the cashier.

"Wait, Karrie. I'm…"

"Good-bye, Dad." She left him standing there.

At the cashier's she put two hundred dollars on the counter and pulled out her phone. "Hey, Justine. I'm so sorry to bother you. Can you please do me a big favor?" She was ahead of me talking, and I couldn't hear the rest of the conversation.

Justine arrived within minutes of her call and didn't ask a single question. I sat in the back and listened to them talk about

Karrie's dress and how lovely she looked. At home, Karrie changed into a pair of shorts and a tee shirt—just as sexy as the dress. She started the grill and got out two hamburgers.

"Hey, this is my job." I took the plate of meat from her and went out to grill the burgers.

She came out with a Corona in one hand and iced tea in the other. She handed me the beer and sat in one of the chairs of the patio furniture I'd built when we first got together—long before we moved to this place.

"I should refinish this. It's starting to look bad." It was getting pretty dark out; we could barely see how bad the wood actually looked.

I flipped the burgers and sat next to her. "I was thinking I'd make some new stuff one day."

She smiled at me. "In your spare time."

"Yes, then." I kissed her. "You okay?"

"Better than ever."

"Hmm...I don't believe you, K."

"Believe me. It's what's right, and I'll always have my memories."

I looked closely to see if she was going to cry. "You looked beautiful tonight. You still do."

"Well, then, I'll expect some reward later." She smiled and looked up at the sky full of stars.

"That's my job." I bent over to kiss her and felt her tongue explore my mouth. A flood of desire filled my body. I wanted her far more than I wanted a burger.

Chapter Ten

When I finally decided to enter Trigena's shop, no motors were running, but by the time I rounded the panel, Trigena had turned on the planer. I contemplated stopping, but using the planer was slow work, and it could take several minutes before she would shut it down. So I covered my ears and stood in the opening of the shop waiting for Trigena to notice me. I think she has an instinct for when someone else is in her space because she looked up almost immediately. Even with her industrial dust-collection system, a cloud of wood particles was floating through the shop, creating a haze that made me feel like I was looking through dirty lenses.

Trig held up one finger and continued feeding the coal-black board through the loud machine, then flipped off the motor when it came out the other end.

She pulled off her goggles, respirator mask, and ear protection and walked over to me. "Hey, babe. Let's get you away from this dust."

With both hands on my shoulders she started guiding me out of the shop. "Wait—I want to see it." I turned out of her grip and headed over to the crib, which looked complete to me. "This is amazing. It looks just like I've always imagined it." I turned to give her a hug, but she held me back.

"I'm filthy, babe." She stood next to me as I admired it. "You really like it?"

"I love it. You're the best." I watched her smile as I ran my fingers across the smooth surfaces, appreciating her hours of sanding and precision woodworking. "Is it done?"

"No. It's only dry-fitted together. I'm working on the ebony for the inlays. Here and here and across the rails." She pointed to the grooves she'd cut to receive the black wood she was working on. "I can't believe you're almost finished. It seems like you just started."

"It's gone together perfectly. I can hardly believe how easy it's been. It's your awesome design." She winked at me. "Now let's get your pregnant self out of this dust." She let me run my fingers across the top of the crib frame one more time before guiding me back into the house.

"Did you realize it was eight thirty?" I asked her when we entered the kitchen.

She was already gulping down a full glass of water. With a quick glance at the clock to confirm the time, she began apologizing. "No. I had no idea. I totally lost track. I promised to make dinner. I'm sorry, babe. You must be starving. Let me wash up really quickly, and I'll get something started." She headed for the bathroom.

"Wait. I am starving, but that's the only reason I knew what time it was. I lost track too. Go shut down the shop and get in the shower. I ordered takeout from The Rose Garden. I'll go get it."

"No. I'll get it. I promised you dinner."

"Trig, do what I tell you for once." I leaned in for a kiss and grabbed my keys. "I want to show you what I did today when I get back. Don't go in the studio until I get home."

"You're pretty demanding tonight. I guess that's what I get for making you starve—Hangry Karrie."

"I'll be right back." I headed out. Chinese wasn't Trig's favorite, but I loved it, and it was quick and easy. At this late hour on a Sunday night, we didn't have a lot of other options, and quick and easy was a must.

❖

I entered the house with two large bags of food. It was way more than we would eat, but we could have left-overs tomorrow.

"Hey, babe." Trigena called back as she entered the kitchen with wet hair, wearing shorts and a tee shirt. I couldn't help but notice she was braless.

"You look relaxed."

"I am." She smiled and crossed the room to take the bags out of my hands. "I'm exhausted. I had no idea I'd been out there for so long. And starved. Thanks for getting the food. I owe you a big, fancy dinner."

"What's new?" I teased her as I got plates and pulled out our chopsticks.

"You're right. I could never pay you back for all the great meals you make me."

"Well, maybe we're even since I'm not likely to start building furniture for you." We sat at the table and started exchanging little boxes of food.

"When do I get to see this work you did today? You've built it up now, you know?"

"Let's eat first or I might pass out."

"Mmm-hmm." She agreed with a mouth full of food.

"Remember, I'll be late Monday, Tuesday, and Wednesday this week. We're starting student shows."

"I should come down and see them one night."

"You want to?" I was surprised. Trigena loved my work but rarely was interested in looking at other art.

"Yeah, I do. I'd like to see what your students are doing. And I want to support you."

"Are you sure you don't just want to watch over me? You don't generally enjoy these shows."

"Hmm…well, could I help some way?"

"No. There's nothing you can do, and really, I just need to be there to meet students' family and friends. You don't have to worry. I won't be doing any real work, but if you want to come I'd recommend Tuesday night. It's the only night all the work will be on display, at least most of it." I did like it when she showed up and I could have her by my side.

"Okay. I'll take off a little early and meet you in your office at, like, five?" She smiled. She seemed actually excited.

"Five works."

"And don't you forget, I'll be leaving Friday, probably before you get home for the training session with RJ. Did you call Natalie?" Trigena reminded me of her search-and-rescue training session. I was secretly dreading it. I didn't mind being alone, but I always worried about her. Few people know as much about survival as Trigena. She's spent as much time training and learning survival techniques as she has learning to work with wood, but I still worried.

"I did. We're going to take her kids swimming and then order pizza and watch a movie on Saturday. I won't stay there, though. At this point, I prefer my own bed." I was starting to get big enough that comfort was becoming a bit of a challenge. It concerned me, because it would only get worse, and sleep had always been an issue for me. I didn't need it to be more difficult.

"Good. At least you won't be alone all weekend."

"Trig, you worry too much. I have so much work to do, I might not even notice you're gone, but it will be nice to see Natalie."

"Oh, really. You won't even notice I'm not here? Hmmm." She started cleaning up our mess. "There might be some things you'll miss." She took my plate as I finished my last bite.

"I might miss someone cleaning up after me."

She looked at me wide-eyed. "Well, then that's something. Come on. I want to see your painting. You already saw what I spent my day working on."

I sat at the table not moving. "It's really beautiful, Trig. Thank you."

She walked over to me and pulled me out of the chair into her arms. "You don't have to thank me, babe. I'm just so glad I could make it look like your dream."

We stood there holding each other for a few minutes. It'd been a busy weekend for each of us, and I missed her touch. "You feel so good."

"Mmm. You too," she whispered in my ear.

"Come on." I led her to the studio and opened the door. I had three new paintings set up on my easels. It was a series that had come to me late last night while I wasn't sleeping because the baby was extremely active, and I couldn't get comfortable. All of the paintings still needed some touch-ups before I would be completely satisfied, but the basic image was clear. The first picture showed a small girl at a well pulling a bucket of water out of it. It was bright and cheery, with spring colors all over. The next picture focused on a woman putting a child to bed in a cabin. It was darker, and out the window fall leaves hung in a tree that was getting bare. The final picture depicted an old woman in a rocker on the porch of the same cabin with a blanket over her and a dusting of snow on the ground. I was very pleased with the results, but I questioned my judgment sometimes. As much as I appreciated Trigena's kind words, I didn't really trust her as a critic because I honestly can't ever remember her saying a bad thing about anything I've done. She did once tell me she didn't like some of the abstract work I did a few years ago, but she still told me it was beautiful.

"K, wow. You did all three today. These are magnificent. No wonder you lost track of time. I love the colors. The blues are so brilliant. Babe, I think these paintings are the best you've ever done." She stood staring at each one, moving slowly back and forth, taking in each piece.

"Oh, come on, hon. I was hoping to hear your abundant praise, but the best...really?"

"Well, I never pretend to be an art critic, but these have... they have...ahh...emotion. I can feel them." She remained focused on the pictures, not even looking at me.

"Trig, now you're going too far."

Trigena moved to my last painting and stood staring at it. "This one, it's so dark...it's...is it bad? It's really familiar to me. Is it somewhere we've been? Do I know her?"

"I'm not sure if it's some place I remember. I saw it the most clearly, and I was able to reproduce the exact image I had in my head. I painted it first this morning. I don't know why, but it concerns me since it's so dark and cold. I don't know exactly—it's just what I saw."

"I don't know where it is, but I think I've been there, or somewhere that looks very much like it. I can't get over how familiar it feels."

"All three are the same place, you know?" I pointed out what I thought was obvious.

"Wow. I knew these two were the same." She pointed to the last two paintings. "But the perspective change here is so dramatic, I didn't realize it was the same place. These are really great, babe."

I pulled her away. "You always know how to make me feel good. Come on. Take me to bed."

"I'm not just making you feel good." She followed me to our bedroom.

We both went through our nighttime routines and climbed into bed. I groaned as I crawled in next to her.

"You okay, babe?"

"I may have stood up too long today. My back's feeling the new distribution of weight." She turned over and placed her hand on me and rubbed my belly.

"Turn over on your side. I'll rub your back."

"Oh, thank you." I rolled over and let her massage my lower back. I couldn't help but make little noises expressing my pleasure. "I might miss this too."

"See. I'm worth having around."

"What do you think of Sophia?"

"Well, I don't know who Sophia is so..."

"Trig, seriously. For a girl's name." I explained, even though I knew she understood what I meant.

"Hmm...well, I don't love it...but I could think about it. You like it?"

"I was thinking about names today, and Sophia and Olivia kept running through my head. I couldn't even think of other names."

"I like Olivia."

"Really? I like it too, but I didn't think you would."

"Why?" she asked me.

"I don't know. It just didn't seem like something you'd like."

"I wonder what that means, that you would think I wouldn't like a name. Maybe you don't know me as well as you thought you did." She tried tickling me, but I just leaned close to her for more. Her touch felt so good. "What if it's a boy?"

"It won't be."

Chapter Eleven

I was finishing washing the dishes I'd used to make dinner when Trigena finally came busting through the front door. "I'm sorry. I'm sorry, I'm so late," she yelled from the foyer. I heard her boots hit the floor, and she ran into the kitchen. "She's not here yet," Trigena declared and sighed heavily. She tried to kiss me.

"You're filthy." I pushed her away. I didn't want to be mad, but I couldn't help it.

"Listen K, I'm—"

"No, you listen..." I stopped myself. "We'll talk later. Go get in the shower and hurry. She'll be here any minute, and you're a mess."

"Okay. I'm sorry." She took off for the bathroom, still rushing.

As soon as she was out of sight, the bell rang. I hurried to the door to greet Jules. Knowing it would be her made me feel a little better. I relaxed my tightened jaw and opened the door. I loved talking to Jules and learning as much as I possibly could about what to expect from the birth. As excited as I was, I was also scared. When I thought about the actual birth, I felt a tension in my chest and fear that I couldn't do it. But Jules was so reassuring. My mantra from her was, "Millions and millions of women have had a baby before you. You're a strong, independent woman. You'll do just fine."

Seeing Jules smile when I opened the door helped me forget how frustrated I was with Trigena.

"Hi, Karrie." Jules leaned in for a hug and then examined my middle. "Look at you. You finally have a little belly."

"Come in, come in." I backed up out of her way as she rolled her small case in with her. "It doesn't seem little to me." I rubbed my abdomen.

She laughed. "In a few more weeks you'll think this is a tiny belly. How do you feel?"

"Really good—no more morning sickness, so Trigena is trying to fatten me up, and I have a lot more energy." I headed for the living room.

"Good for her. That's exactly what she should be doing." Jules followed me. "Is Trigena here?"

"Yes. She was running late. She'll be right out." I was careful not to display my anger. We were good at keeping our issues just between us. "Here. Have a seat. Can I get you anything? Tea, Pellegrino, orange juice? I also have an extra stuffed green pepper from dinner—ground turkey, fresh tomatoes, rice. Are you hungry?" I headed for the kitchen, divided from the living room by only a short wall.

"That sounds really good, but I ate before I came over. Just water would be great." Jules started unpacking items from her bag. "Should we go ahead with some of the technical things while we wait, or do you want her to be here for everything?"

"You're going to want me to pee, right?"

She nodded.

"Well, okay then, I'll go do that. I need to go anyway—always." That feeling of a full bladder was a new constant in my life. "Trig will probably be out soon. You want me to leave it on the back of the toilet like before?" I crossed the room with a glass of ice water.

"Yep. You got it." She handed me a sample cup.

"I'll be right back."

When I returned, Trigena was already in the room. She'd just entered with bare feet, wearing shorts and a tee shirt, and I overheard her apologizing.

"Hi, Jules. Thanks for coming so late in the evening. I'm sorry I was late. It was a tough day. We lost almost all our work today when a ceramic-tile bathroom wall slipped. It was almost complete. We had to take it all down before it cured. How are you?"

"It's all good. I just got here. I'm doing well. Besides work, how are you?"

I walked up and stood next to Trigena. "That was fast."

She tentatively wrapped an arm around me. "Yeah." She smiled at me, and I let her off the hook and gave her a quick kiss.

"Okay, ladies, let's see how this mama and baby are doing. Let's get your blood pressure, your favorite thing. Go ahead and lie down, Karrie." She moved off the couch to make space for me. "I want you as relaxed as possible, and we'll measure that little belly of yours." Jules went about feeling and measuring my abdomen. "Has your little person been really active?"

"Yes, very, especially at night. I think she's going to be a runner."

"Jules, that reminds me. Karrie said you told her she could keep running every day. I'm a little concerned. She's running five miles some days. Is that okay?" Trigena couldn't resist asking, but I'd told her she should.

Jules looked down at me on the couch. "How do you feel when you run?"

"Great. I love it."

"No pain or discomfort?"

"No. I can tell I'm carrying a little more weight, and I'm going slower, but I don't feel pain."

"Trigena, as long as she listens to her body and feels good, it's fine for her to exercise. She's a runner so that's what she should do." She looked back at me. "You need to listen to your body though. When it hurts, don't do it."

"I feel hyper aware of my body right now, so I'll listen."

"You probably won't feel comfortable at all when you get into the last month or so, but trust yourself." She looked back at Trigena. "Your worry is good. Be protective. That's okay."

"Your measurements look fine, a little on the small size, but you have a small frame."

Trig jumped in again. "She misses a meal now and then at work. I'm worried about her not eating enough."

"Trig, seriously, you're a tattletale." I squinted at her from my vulnerable prone position on the couch.

"You could make her some good hand-held snacks so she'd always have something to eat quickly when she didn't have time to eat well at work." She smiled down at me.

"Yeah. I could do that. Right? Like what should I make?" Trigena was actually excited. She liked to be given a task so she could feel like she was contributing.

"Hon, I have plenty of snacks and stuff. I'm doing better. Please stop worrying."

Jules wrapped the blood-pressure cuff around my arm, then stopped in the middle and started talking to Trigena. "Have you read the book I gave you?"

"Yes, cover to cover. It answered a lot of my questions."

Without me even knowing it, Jules had finished taking my blood pressure and pulled off the cuff. "Looks good, Karrie. I'll go dip your urine and be right back." She packed a few things back in her bag.

"I didn't even know you took the blood pressure." I sat back up on the couch.

"I try to sneak it in, so I don't get a false reading. You get a little stressed when you know I'm about to do it, and we've had a few high readings that concerned me a bit. It's all good now, though."

Trigena teased her with our joke. "You're good." We exchanged a knowing glance.

Jules looked at both of us. "I'm missing something, I think." She walked out of the room.

"K, I'm sorry. I—"

"Trig, I don't really want to talk about it. I just want to say one thing. Try to imagine how I feel when you show up late for an event so important to me and our baby, especially when we schedule it around your activities." I stopped.

"K. I was here on time, and it was a matter of a whole day's work lost. We can't afford that."

"Exactly." I hated it that she always had an excuse more important to her than the baby. "Right. I said I don't want to talk about it."

"How can you not consider what this means to my work?"

I just looked at her as Jules reentered the room.

"Everything looks great. You're doing so well." She looked between us and then cocked her head at me. "Everything okay?"

"Yes. I was just scolding her for ratting me out," I lied.

"What other questions do you have for me, Trigena?" Jules sat back on the couch across from Trig.

"Most of my anxiety is about the birth. For now, I just want to make sure I'm doing everything I can for Karrie." She lowered her eyes as she looked over at me.

"Are you cooking for her and giving good massages and helping even when she doesn't want you to?"

"She's great." I wanted Trig to know, as angry as I was about her being late, I did appreciate all she was doing. "You should see the crib she's building."

"I'd love to." Jules continued packing her bag. "Trig, the birth classes will probably answer most of your questions, but don't hesitate to ask me anything. Oh. I haven't asked you if you would like to catch your baby."

"I can do that?" she asked.

"Trig, that would be great." I hadn't even thought of it.

"Really?" She cocked her head at me and looked over at Jules. "I don't want to mess something up or drop it. It'll be slippery, right?"

"I'll be there, and I'll help you," Jules said.

"Hon, I'd like it if you did." I moved next to her and took her hand.

"Okay. I'm a little scared though."

"Don't worry. It'll be fine. Now can I see that crib?" Jules stood up with her bag all sealed and ready to go. "Do you have any other questions?"

"I'll take you out through the shop and hold off on the questions until after the birth classes. Umm...I do have one for now." She looked at me, and I was immediately scared of what she was going to say. "Umm...Karrie...umm...we are...Should we... what about sex? Is sex okay? I'm loving it, but I'm scared of hurting her or the baby." Trigena struggled through the question.

"Great question." Jules had a way of making everything an acceptable subject. "I have to resort to my stock answer. As long as it feels okay, then sex is always a good thing." She smiled at both of us. "Karrie, do you have any bleeding or cramping afterward?"

"No bleeding, though I do feel a little cramping after an orgasm, but it's not bad."

"That sounds normal. And you might even have a little bleeding, but again, as long as you're doing what feels right, you'll be fine." She touched Trigena's arm. "It's your job to make her feel good. Sounds like you're doing fine."

Chapter Twelve

"Hello, Ms. Gilmore. You look nice." K's twenty-something TA, Ashley, greeted me with a little too much excitement. "Dr. Gilmore's expecting you." Ashley has been with her for four semesters. She'd been to our house for a couple of different department events that Karrie hosted last year. After one particularly long and challenging semester, Karrie and I took her out for dinner, but I didn't know her that well. Karrie thought a lot of her and her artistic talent, so that was good enough for me. I appreciated anyone who could take some of the workload off my wife, especially now that she was pregnant.

"She better be expecting me." I spoke sternly and looked seriously at the young woman, until I saw concern in her eyes, and then I smiled. She gave a bit of a nervous laugh and glanced back at her computer. K told me I intimidate her students, so I made a habit of seeing if I could get a reaction. I tapped my knuckles on her desk as I walked past. "Just kidding, Ashley, and please call me Trigena."

"Of course, yes, Trigena. Go on in." She seemed to relax a bit.

I walked to the doorway of Karrie's small office. As university professors' offices go, it was actually not too bad, and unlike most academics' offices I'd been in, it was organized and clean. One wall had bookshelves floor to ceiling, and while most of them were filled with art books, one shelf in the middle held only photos of her and me. On the wall behind her small modular desk was a good-sized window that looked out onto the quad. She'd moved into this office on her first day, and I always wondered how she was so lucky, as a brand-new professor, to get such prime real estate. Opposite the bookcase hung her degrees from Columbia and Yale, surrounding one of her mother's paintings, which held a place of honor.

When Karrie and I first met, I knew she was finishing a master's degree, but I had no idea she'd gone to Columbia for her undergraduate degree. And then when I found out she was attending Yale for her master's, I was so intimidated I almost didn't ask her on a second date. Justine and Danielle encouraged me to ask her out again after I raved about how amazing she was every time I talked to them. I finally called her a week after our first date, and she was so mad at me for waiting so long I think she almost said no.

When I told her this little blue-collar, state-school-educated girl didn't think I could hold my own with an Ivy League graduate, she was really pissed. She gave me a lecture about judging her like she knew I didn't want to be judged. So when she started working on her PhD, I just rolled with it. I've never discussed her education, and she's never mentioned mine, not that there's much to talk about, but I was secretly very proud of my brilliant wife, and I admired her diplomas every time I saw them.

I stood there taking in the familiar décor. Karrie was deeply absorbed in something on her computer, so I just waited for her to notice me.

"Hey, hon. How long have you been standing there?" She looked up at me with a big smile. I loved this woman so much and often wondered how I'd gotten so lucky to be with her, but now I worried that a child would take away what we shared.

"Hey, beautiful. Not long."

"Ashley!" She yelled to the outer office. "It's your job to not let anyone sneak up on me, not even hot chicks."

"Sorry, Dr. Gilmore," Ashley yelled back, then stood next to me in the doorway. "I thought you were expecting her."

"I'm kidding, Ash. Get out of here."

"No, ma'am. You told me when I started here that I wasn't to leave until you did, and you still have a long night ahead of you."

"You'll stay tomorrow night. I have another helper tonight." She winked at me.

"Are you sure?" Ashley asked with hope in her eyes. Karrie usually came home at a decent hour, so Ashley was lucky in that respect. Some TAs spent sixteen-hour days with their professors. But I knew working for my wife couldn't have been easy. She had a standard so high that very few could even come close. From what I could tell, Ashley did pretty well, but she likely spent many extra hours researching long after Karrie had gone home just to come close to K's demands.

"I'm sure. Go before I change my mind."

"Thanks, Dr. Gilmore. Good night Ms...ahh...Trigena."

"Good night, Ashley," Karrie and I said in unison.

"Are you hungry?" I held up the Subway bag I had in my hand.

"I'm starving, but that's not what I want." She cleared off her desk, putting pens and papers in desk drawers. She didn't look up.

"Oh...I could get something else or we could go somewhere, but I thought you didn't have much time." I was surprised. Karrie usually liked Subway sandwiches, and I don't think I'd ever known her to not be appreciative of whatever I brought. She wasn't one to complain or be picky. I was a little hurt, but when she looked up at me, I could tell that no food substance I could purchase would satisfy her hunger.

"I've been waiting for you all day." She stood up behind her desk. "Close and lock the door, please," she directed me as she turned and closed the blinds behind her.

"Yes, ma'am." I followed her instructions and tossed the sandwiches in the chair in the corner of her office.

She walked toward me, and I met her in the center of the small space. After she took my face in both her hands and kissed me, I opened my mouth to accept her tongue and quickly entangled mine with hers.

I pulled back for a breath. "Are we in a hurry?" I wanted to know if we had any time constraints.

She was breathing heavily. "They'll wait for me."

"Mmm…Who wouldn't?" I pulled her back to me and felt her soft lips on mine, then moved my hands under her blouse and began to caress her soft skin, lingering on the curves of her stomach before I moved up to lay them on her breasts. She pushed my hands to my side away from her and untucked my shirt with a quick jerk. She slid her hands to my breasts and cupped them as she continued to kiss me. I kept trying to touch her, but each time she pushed me away. Karrie was sometimes the assertive one, but not usually, and rarely was she so controlling. I finally gave in and left my hands resting on her hips, which she would allow if I didn't move them.

Once she was sure I was going to stay put, she pushed my blouse up and reached behind me, and in one quick movement she released the fastener on my bra, which gave her easier access to my breasts. As she lightly massaged them, pleasure rushed through my whole body. I felt a gentle pull at each nipple as she rolled her fingertips across them. It was so exhilarating I pushed into her for more.

Karrie's hands moved to my waist and unbuckled my belt and unfastened my pants by touch alone. She continued to kiss me, moving to my neck and shoulders. She pushed my pants down and immediately started working on the buttons of my blouse, which fell to the floor with my bra tangled in it. I stood before her in a pair of black-lace panties, self-conscious about being nearly naked in the room where she met students all day long. I glanced back at the door to confirm it was shut and we were alone. It was thrilling to be here like this, but a little scary as well. Karrie grabbed my face to return my attention to her.

In a husky voice she asked, "Worried the principal will catch you?" She pushed me toward the little leather sofa under her diplomas. I remember asking her why she needed it when we'd lugged it across campus and up two flights of stairs, but I was glad now for the effort. I sat down and tried to pull her toward me, but she just pushed me into the sofa. It seemed wise to obey. She shoved her slacks and panties down in one motion and began to unbutton her red-silk blouse slowly, rocking gently as if to music in her own ears. Before she removed her blouse she reached behind her and with one hand unfastened her own bra and slid everything off together. My beautiful wife stood naked before me. From my vantage point I had a perfect view of her labia exposed through her short, silky pubic hair. I wanted her so badly. I rose to kneel before her to taste her sweet juices, my own body flooding with wetness.

She backed away from me. "No. Don't you understand this is my show?" I sat back down and just stared at her. I had no idea her pregnant body could turn me on so much. I took her in from head to toe. Karrie's sexy shoulders and elegant posture highlighted her long neck. Her plump breasts were silky smooth, the curves of her dark skin appropriately proportioned with her small, round belly. The dark skin of her legs accentuated her shapely runner's thighs. My wife was an exotic woman, and the pregnancy brought out all her striking features like the glow of a star.

As much as I was enjoying the gorgeous view, I couldn't stand not touching her. I reached for her again, and again she pushed me back and kneeled in front of me. She pulled me forward so my buttock was at the very edge of the sofa.

"What are you doing?" I smiled at her.

She pushed my upper body back against the back of the sofa. "I want to taste you," she said through deep breaths as she began kissing and lightly licking my stomach. She inched down me, not missing any bare flesh. I felt a rush of pleasure at my crotch and knew I was soaking wet. I wanted her to touch my clit. I pushed myself up to her. When she reached the waistband of my panties, she rose and pulled them slowly down my legs and tossed them to the side. She moved from my belly button to the top of my shaved mound with kisses. When she reached my clitoris, a flick of her tongue shot a shiver through my groin, and I jerked. I felt her tongue sink deep inside me and rose to meet her. With both hands on my hips she forced me back against the smooth leather. I tried to sit still and enjoy the erotic pleasure, but it took every ounce of my strength not to rock with her pleasing rhythm. Just when I thought it couldn't get any better, she slid one finger inside me and filled me with an overwhelming desire. She moved slowly in and out, and I couldn't keep from moving with her. The building climax was impossible to resist. Just as I was sure I would come she stopped and pulled out of me. I cried, "No. Please don't stop."

"Beg me," she commanded as she briefly looked up at me, before she went back to teasing my engorged clit.

"Please, babe, please. I need you inside me."

She stopped abruptly and looked up with an evil grin. She spoke in a sultry voice, "What do you want, Trigena?"

"I want you to…fuck me, K." I practically yelled at her.

She smiled and returned to providing me with an irresistible rush of pleasure—a decadence I couldn't get enough of. She slipped two fingers inside my wet vagina, and I shuddered at the intensity. "Yes, babe," I called out to encourage her touch. She obliged my longing and began to move more quickly, in perfect pace with my need. She stopped again, and I ached for her to move inside me. "Please. Please," I gasped. I was so near climax I could barely speak.

Karrie inserted a third finger, and the fullness she provided was all-engulfing. I nearly exploded immediately from the sensation, but she stopped moving and rose again to meet me, kissing me quickly on the lips. She panted in quick breaths, "Touch me Trig, I'm so close. Come with me." I reached between her legs and slid two fingers between her wet labia. We stroked together gently at first, and then she pushed hard against my hand. We called out with pleasure in unison as we climaxed together, then held each other in the continuing aftershock. I felt her pussy tighten around my fingers as my own contracted around hers. She relaxed on top of me and rolled to the side. We lay spent together, legs and arms intertwined.

"That was amazing. You're amazing." I held her close with her head on my shoulder. "I love you, Karrie."

"Mmm...I love you, Trigena."

I leaned over and pulled her on top of me so we were lying across the sofa. She felt so good—her flesh against mine. I felt so close to her, I never wanted to move. It couldn't last long; we had things to do. But for now, we needed a few minutes for our strength to return before we could even consider getting dressed and making an acceptable appearance at her show.

Chapter Thirteen

I was reviewing student art proposals when Ashley knocked on my door. I motioned for her to come in.

"Dr. Gilmore, Dr. Simmons is here," she announced from the doorway.

"David, come on in," I called from behind my desk. As he entered, I got up to greet him. We hugged, and he dropped his eyes to my stomach. I was still getting used to people staring at my belly. The shirt I wore fit tight and left nothing to the imagination. He hadn't seen me in a couple of months, since school started. He worked in the engineering building, on the opposite side of campus from the art building, so we didn't cross paths much.

"Wow, Karrie, you're really pregnant." David just stared.

"Yes, David, I am. Did you think Trigena and I were joking?" I laughed at him.

"No, of course not." I had managed to break his trance, and he gazed back up at me. "You look great."

"Thank you. Please have a seat." We sat in the two hard wooden chairs in front of my desk. "To what do I owe this unexpected pleasure? Is Martin doing okay?" David and I had met three years ago when we were assisting a very talented student majoring in both art and engineering. He was having some financial issues, and we managed to get him a scholarship.

"Martin is doing great," he answered and sat looking down at his feet. David was a handsome, confident man, so his behavior was out of character.

"Okay. Did you just stop to say hi? We could hook up for lunch or something. Trig would like to see you. Maybe we could plan a dinner date."

"Ahh...Karrie...I...ahh...I've been thinking, and I'm not sure I can do this." He glanced at my stomach, and a rush of adrenaline pumped through me. I had this overwhelming desire to just run away from him—anything so I wouldn't have to hear what he had to say.

"Do what?" I swallowed hard.

"I don't think I can sit back and pretend the baby you're carrying isn't mine." He spoke loudly, and he emphasized each word clearly, as if he thought I wouldn't understand. David had found his confidence.

I jumped up and closed the door. It was unlikely anyone heard him, but Trigena and I didn't want anyone to know who the donor was, especially since he was a friend. And up until a few minutes ago, I didn't think David wanted anyone to know either.

"What are you getting at?" I was so scared of what he might say, I steadied myself with the chair when I returned to where he was sitting.

"I'm not saying anything yet, but I would like to talk to you and Trigena about some options so maybe I could play some part in the child's life." David stood up. He was over six feet tall, so even with my heels on I had to look up at him. His deep-blue eyes stared into mine.

David had seemed like the perfect donor. He was smart and kind, and best of all, he was single with seemingly no roots—even a little wild. He wasn't at all interested in marrying or having kids. David was active and fit; I'm sure most women would find him extremely handsome. I had mentioned to him one day that I wanted to have kids, just as a topic of conversation, and he'd offered to be a sperm donor for us. His confidence could present itself as arrogance, so when he started describing all his attributes, I was turned off at first. But the more I thought about it, the more I knew he was right. Before I said anymore to him, I presented the idea to Trigena. It took a lot to convince her, but when she met him, and they hit it off immediately, I think she was sold. But when he told her he wasn't interested in kids, she was finally convinced it would be okay. On the drive home, she asked me only one question. Would he honor his word? I was sure he would, so I answered, unequivocally, yes.

I couldn't believe what I was hearing. I slid back down in the chair. "You said you didn't want anything to do with the baby." My palms were sweating, and my heart felt heavy. I felt like I'd just been pushed off a fast-spinning merry-go-round. I couldn't get my balance.

"Karrie, I'm not trying to make this hard on you and Trigena. I'm just feeling like this isn't right. I'd like to talk about options," he said, acting calmer now. I think he had to get past the hard part of breaking this new situation to me.

"David, I can't believe this. We don't want you to be involved. Trigena wants to raise her on our own." I'd gotten in such a habit of calling the baby her, it just slipped out.

"Her? You know it's a girl?" He smiled.

"No. We don't know. We just think it is. David, I don't like this, and Trigena is really not going to. She's going to spin through the roof." I gripped the arms of the chair.

"All I'm asking is that we talk about it. I don't want to interfere, but maybe I could help and be a male role model. I'm not a bad guy, and how could it be bad to have someone to help out sometimes? I just feel like it isn't right for me to pretend I know nothing about it."

"You didn't feel like that six months ago. You assured us you didn't want any part of being a parent. What changed?"

"I don't know. I just feel this way, and I thought I should talk to you about it. I don't want to do anything legal—"

"Legal? What are you talking about? Do you think you're going to fight us for this baby?" The grip I had on the chair ratcheted up. I leaned toward him and raised my voice. "What the hell, David? Are you serious?"

"Karrie, calm down. No, no—I don't want any of that."

"But you're considering it? You've talked to someone already." I stood up and paced the ten feet across my office.

"I talked to Dr. Zinn. I just asked him some questions."

"Dr. Zinn? Did you tell him I was pregnant and you felt you had some right to my child?"

"Karrie, let's talk with Trigena. I don't want to upset you."

"Too late, David. This is ridiculous. Trigena told me we should have a contract. I trusted you. I trusted your word. If you're serious about this, I'll call my lawyer, and we can have them meet."

"No, that's not what I want. Please just think about it. Maybe we can come up with something. I'm not saying I have the answers. I just want you to consider my side of this."

"The only thing I can think is the man who told me and my wife he wanted nothing to do with children was a liar, and we're going to have to deal with my mistake of trusting you." I turned to him. "You should go. Send me an email telling me who you would like my lawyer to contact."

"Let's just meet with Trigena. The three of us can talk about it."

"Do you think because the two of you could talk about how to construct a building and some mutual woodworking projects that she's going to be all sympathetic to your change of heart? You don't know her. I assure you my reaction to this is nothing compared to the wrath she's going to rain down on you. This won't end well for any of us. David, you agreed. You volunteered to assist us. We could've gone to a sperm bank. I can't believe you're the man I called a friend." I spun around and stopped in front of him. "Go now."

"Karrie, I…I don't…I'm sorry." He stood looking at me.

"Good-bye David." I kept my composure until he closed my office door, and then I fell to the floor in tears.

Chapter Fourteen

I heard my phone ring from the open truck windows when I was carrying in plumbing supplies. I was about to blow it off and return the call when I got done for the day, but as I walked into the house I couldn't stand not knowing if it was Karrie. I took the materials in to RJ and Jason and went back out to the truck. Sure enough, my phone showed a missed call from her. My heart raced, and I quickly hit the button to return the call.

"I'm sorry, hon." I heard Karrie's sweet voice, and I could tell she was barely holding it together.

"K, what is it, babe?" My voice cracked, and I squeezed the phone tight.

"Trig, I'm so sorry to call you at work again."

"K, please. It's okay. Just tell me what's wrong. Are you okay?"

"He wants to be a part of the baby's life." Karrie started crying, and I could hardly understand her.

"Babe, what? Who?" I couldn't process what she said until I stumbled through the *whos* and *whats*, but then it hit.

"David," she said into the phone at the same time I yelled his name back at her.

"Trig..."

"I'm on my way. I'm going to give that son of a bitch a piece of my mind." I started the truck and continued to rant into dead air as the Bluetooth connected to the truck. I knew she couldn't hear me, but I didn't care. I just needed to yell.

"No, don't come here." I could tell she wasn't crying anymore. "Please, Trig, stay there. I'll be home in just a few minutes. I called our lawyer, who encouraged me not to do anything. She needs a lot of information, and then she can look into what rights he has and what we can do. Please don't come here. Talking to him could just make things more complicated. I just needed to talk to you. Tell me you're still at work."

I sat with the engine running, trying to process. "We should've had a contract." I knew I was throwing it in her face, but I couldn't help but think how complicated this baby was. And it was getting more complicated with every new day.

"I don't need to hear 'I told you so.'"

"But I'm right. What are we going to do? We can't afford a lawsuit, especially not one we can't win." I slammed my fist on the steering wheel.

"Trig, this isn't helping. I'll see you at home."

I had managed to help her stop crying by making her really mad. I was pretty good at that these days, but I was mad too or just overwhelmed, and anger was the only way I knew how to express my reaction.

"K, I'm sorry. I'm just…I'm scared. We don't need this." I couldn't help myself. I wanted to blame someone.

"No, we don't, but we got it. I'll see you at home."

"I'll meet you there." I heard her phone click.

When I pulled up to our house, the driveway was empty. I was surprised Karrie wasn't home yet. I just sat in my truck. My anger hadn't seemed to dissipate; if anything it felt more intense with each passing moment, like a volcano ready to erupt. It didn't do any good to be mad at Karrie, but I was. I couldn't help but blame her. In addition to being the one who wanted to have a baby in the first place, when we had the perfect relationship with just the two of us, she had been so sure David wouldn't want anything to do with us or the baby. All the while I was insisting on a contract. Even Jules had encouraged us to have some documentation in place. There was no harm in formalizing things, she said, but Karrie didn't want to do that to a friend. Fuck. Friend, my ass. "Lying piece of crap" were the only words I had for him now. I still felt like hitting something; the muscles in my arms felt like rubber bands stretched out too far. I wanted to beat on something, but I could tell from the throbbing in my right hand that I was already going to have a bruise on the base of my hand from repeatedly striking my steering wheel.

Just as I was contemplating the fact that I couldn't be angry at Karrie and expect to be effective at solving this issue, she pulled up. Even though she was parked right next to me, she didn't look over. She got out of the car without acknowledging me and headed for the house. She was weighted down with a backpack over one shoulder, her leather briefcase in one hand, and a lunch bag in the other. I got out and hurried up next to her to take some things out of her hands.

"Hi, babe," I said as I approached. She looked over at me and released the bags to me, but she didn't say a word. She just unlocked the door and went into the house.

I sat on the bench next to the door and kicked off my boots, then took her things to the kitchen. She was already changing her clothes in the bedroom. When I walked in she covered herself; seeing her do that felt like she'd stabbed my soul. She didn't feel comfortable exposing herself to me when we were angry with each other. I felt like I had a right to be mad at her, even if it wouldn't help anything, but I couldn't understand why she was angry at me.

"Are you going to give me the silent treatment, or are we going to talk about this?"

She spun around so quickly, I actually jumped back. And she yelled, "Why would I want to talk to you? The person who's supposed to love me the most is too busy placing blame to take any positive action toward some type of solution." She paused and headed toward the door and then turned back again. "I messed this up. This is MY fault. I wrongly trusted someone. Are you happy now?" She left me standing half-dressed in our bedroom.

I realized I wasn't contributing to a solution. I was acting like an idiot. She was sorry and felt horrible for the situation, and she totally blamed herself. I finished changing into a pair of shorts and an old tee shirt, then entered the kitchen, where she was preparing dinner.

"I'm sorry. This is not your fault. It's David's. Trusting someone is not wrong, but betraying someone's trust is. I'm scared, K, and I acted stupid. Please talk to me so we can figure this out together."

She didn't look at me, but she spoke calmly. "The lawyer is going to call me tomorrow. There's really nothing we can do tonight."

"Okay. Umm...then will you let me make dinner?"

"I got it. Why don't you go out in the shop or something?" She continued to cut basil, but she did glance over her shoulder at me. That was a start.

"What are you making?" I stepped closer and touched her back. She tightened at my touch, and a tinge of pain pricked my heart.

"Pesto chicken with mixed vegetables."

"Are you going to grill the chicken?"

"Yes."

"I'll do that." I looked around for the chicken and saw it marinating in a bowl in front of her. She handed it to me.

After I took the bowl and headed for the back patio, I heard her say, "Thanks."

Outside, I scraped the grill clean and warmed it. When I had the chicken on the grill, I sat down on the bench and looked out over the desert. I couldn't help but wonder why she stayed with me sometimes. I always put so much pressure on everyone. I felt heat in my face and my eyes watered. I rarely cried, but I just wanted to sit in a corner and bawl like a child. Then I could wait for someone else to handle everything—to be responsible. I was scared of what it would mean for David to be a part of our life, but I was terrified that if I didn't unwind I was going to push away the only thing that ever really mattered to me. I heard the back door and quickly wiped my face.

"Here." I turned to see Karrie holding a glass of wine.

"Thank you."

"Were you crying?" She had started to go back in but came back and sat next to me.

"No. I was just thinking how sorry I am to be so hard to live with. I'm sorry I get so mad."

Karrie took my hand. "Trig, we have to stop this. We never used to fight. You're worrying too much and making things so much harder than they need to be. You push me away sometimes or scare me away."

"I know I'm sorry. I'm—"

"Stop saying you're sorry." She dropped my hand and avoided my eyes.

"But I am."

"Then stop getting so mad. This thing with David is scary, and I was the one that put us in this situation, but whatever happens, we still have a family. We can do anything together, Trig. Have you forgotten that?"

I shook my head. "No, you're right. I just have to let go. As long as I have you, I'll be okay." I couldn't help wondering even as I said that if I could love the child she was carrying enough to be a good mom and what would happen to us if I couldn't.

"You have me. You'll always have me." She leaned into me and I held on tight, afraid somehow she knew what I was thinking.

Chapter Fifteen

I was walking back to my office from my morning class when I heard Trigena's voice in my office. She was talking to Ashley, and they were laughing about something. I immediately quickened my pace at the sound of her voice. I thought sure when she kissed me good-bye this morning I wouldn't see her again until Sunday night when she returned from the training session. She was planning to work until noon and then pack her gear for the trip to be ready to leave in time to get up the mountain before dark.

"Trig, is everything okay?" I interrupted the laughter that came from the College of Fine Arts open reception area where five TAs sat. It was the waiting area for eight art professors and the gateway to my office. Once a semester got started, there was a steady flow of students through the reception area each day, but it was usually pretty quiet. Hearing all the TAs laughing was rare. Trigena must've told them a story. She was a great storyteller, but she had a reputation of being intense, even with my regular students, so someone had broken through her tough exterior. The soft, vulnerable side of her was what I fell in love with, and I hadn't seen that side much lately. I loved her strength and confidence, and I was always proud to walk beside her with that tough shell wrapped around both of us, but the fact that she'd closed off so much lately, even to me, scared me.

"Yeah, babe. I came to take you to lunch." Trigena stood and greeted me with a kiss. We had made up last night, but the stress of David's visit was still very fresh and certainly not going away, so I was surprised at her cheery mood.

"I didn't expect you." I walked past her to my office, and she followed me.

Ashley stopped me. "Dr. Gilmore, I checked your calendar. You don't have any appointments until two thirty."

"What?" I stopped and glared at her.

"Trigena asked me to check your calendar." She transitioned from happy girl to serious TA instantly.

"K, I just wanted to know if you had time to go eat with me." Trigena spoke quickly to cover for Ashley.

"Oh, okay. I wasn't expecting you."

"Should I go?" she asked as she closed my door behind her. I was so surprised to see her and the mood of the reception office, which was normally casual and happy, was so loud and goofy, it had thrown me out of my comfort zone in my own territory.

"No, no. I'm sorry. I…ahh…I was focused on work. I'd love to go to lunch with you." I put down the classroom materials I still held in my arms.

"I'm sorry, babe. I should've called. I wanted to surprise you. I thought you'd like it."

"I do. I'm glad you're here." I walked over to her, and we hugged. "You're just in such a different mood. Last night…"

"I know. I'm so sorry. I lose track of what's important sometimes. I want to be part of the solution. I don't want to make anything harder on you. We'll work with the lawyer, and we'll fight David the best we can." She held both of my hands and squeezed them when she said "we."

"Okay. Good. Right?" I was still skeptical, and we were definitely not in sync with each other, but it was nice to see her smiling, and some of the stress that was weighing her down seemed to have lifted at least for now.

"Route 66 Diner?" she asked.

I nodded, and we left my office. "I'll be back in about an hour, Ash."

She smiled at me, and I think I saw her wink at Trigena as we walked out. Somehow in the few minutes while I was still in class, my wife, the intense scary bitch, had endeared herself to the staff of TAs. I knew how she did it. She did it to me.

❖

Trigena was gone when I got home. I knew she would be, but I held on to the hope that she would change her mind. I had no reason to believe that possibility, since at lunch she was telling me her training plan and giving me a list of GPS coordinates of the locations where she expected to be throughout the weekend. I knew she would be safe. It was only a training session. There was no real danger, and she would always have RJ there with her, not that she needed someone. Trigena knew everything there was to know about outdoor survival. Each year she managed to convince me to go on a short backpacking trip. Even this spring before I knew I was pregnant, she dragged me out. I'm not sure why I always dreaded the thought of it, because as soon as we get on the trail I always love it. I think that's what motivated her to keep after me when I initially turned her down each time. After she finally lured me out into the woods, she always showed me some new and interesting trick. She would emphasize survival techniques to me, as if she thought I would ever go out in the wilderness without her. One thing she made clear, though, was her healthy respect for Mother Nature.

The truth is, as much as I generally worried about her until I got her back home safely, I was more worried about me tonight. After we had a wonderful lunch together, during which we even reconnected a bit, I asked Trigena to drop me off instead of wasting time finding a parking spot and delaying her departure even more. From the street where she let me out, it was a short walk to my building, but on the way I tripped and fell flat on my face. Worse than that, I fell on my belly. I skinned my knee badly, and blood flowed down my leg like a red stream, but at the time I was more relieved to see Trig's truck was long gone. I was initially more concerned with the embarrassment than my well-being or even that of the baby. I was sure everything was fine. I had just been a klutz—a word not usually associated with me.

Of course Ashley made a big fuss of getting my knee cleaned up and bandaged, but neither of us was worried beyond the bloody knee. But as the day went on I began to feel worse and worse. I was weak and lethargic and a little sick to my stomach. I hadn't felt sick for over a month, almost two, so I was convinced it was associated with the fall. I was getting a little worried, but I wanted to give it some more time. Maybe I was just in shock.

I entered our empty house and went straight to the bedroom to change out of my work clothes, pulling on a pair of pajama pants and one of Trigena's old University of Illinois tee shirts that had so many holes in it I'd begged her to throw it away. I'd left my middle exposed, because the shirt was too tight to be comfortable around my expanding middle. It felt like home and made me miss Trigena even more, but wearing it made me realize why she didn't want to throw it away. It was part of us. The truth is, I wore it more than she did now that it wasn't fit to wear in public. As I stepped into my slippers, I was gripped by an intense pain in my lower abdomen. It felt like someone had grabbed my uterus with two hands and wrung it out like an old rag. I had to stop to let the cramp pass.

When the pain had mostly subsided, I went to the kitchen and made a peanut butter sandwich. I wasn't hungry and didn't really want to eat anything but thought perhaps that was part of the problem. It was almost seven and had been several hours since we ate lunch. I took the sandwich and a small glass of milk to my recliner in the living room. Trigena would have scolded me for eating only a sandwich, and had she been there she would've probably made me some soup or something healthy. I settled into my chair and stared at the sandwich that now I didn't want. I forced myself to take a couple of bites, but my stomach churned. I sat it back on the end table and tried to relax.

It must've worked. I woke up later and realized my crotch was wet. I pulled myself forward in the chair, and the same extreme pain shot through me again. This time it was a hard punch in the gut. I called out to no one and sat still—too scared of the returning agony to move. Finally, I pushed myself into action. Whatever was going on wasn't right. I needed to call Jules. The pain had dissipated, and I went to the bathroom. When I pulled down my pajamas I saw bright-red blood in my panties. My heart rate increased, and I shook with so much fear I had to steady myself by holding onto the sink. I pulled my stained pants back up and went in search of my phone.

Without hesitation I punched my favorites. Jules was second only to Trigena on the list. I'd put her above Danielle and Justine and Ashley the minute we agreed she was the right midwife for us. Trigena and I both loved her.

I pushed the button and listened closely as the phone rang and rang. Finally, a very long message came on explaining all the possible scenarios a pregnant woman could be experiencing. "Jules, it's Karrie. I'm bleeding, and I'm really scared. If I don't hear from you soon I'm heading for the hospital." I didn't want to go there if it wasn't serious. There was too much to explain to the traditional medical-care professionals when you chose a homebirth. I wanted to avoid that if I could, but I was terrified. There was a lot of blood. With my phone in hand, I walked slowly back to the bathroom, and fortunately the cramping had ended. I changed my clothes and cleaned myself, then put on a maxi-pad to determine if I was still bleeding. I had to tell myself to breathe. I felt myself holding my breath and had a pressure in my chest I couldn't shake.

I picked my phone up and looked at the screen. Perhaps I'd missed Jules's call. I walked slowly back and forth across the smooth tiled floor of our master-bedroom bath. I was sure sitting still or even lying down was the right thing to do, but when I tried it I felt like my skin was too tight. I couldn't stand it. I had to move. I waited. I sat on the side of the bed. I paced the bathroom floor, and I waited some more, all the while flipping my phone over and over in my hand, ready to connect at the first noise from it. Every couple of minutes I pulled my pants down to see if there was more blood. I saw only a little, but the sight of it each time I looked sent a new panic straight to my heart.

I'm sure it had only been a few minutes, but it felt like hours. I pulled my favorites up and hit Trigena's number. It rang one time and went to voice mail. She was out of cell-phone reach. The coordinates to the location where they were taking the new volunteers were in my purse from lunch, with notes she had included from her and RJ's training plans. I knew some of the other volunteers and could call them. Trig had the list of the entire group in a folder we shared on our home network. Any one of them would go get her for me, but I didn't want to overreact. I hung up the phone without leaving a voice mail. I didn't trust myself to stay calm, and the last thing I wanted to do was scare her again. It seemed to me that pregnancy had turned me into a panicky drama queen.

I paced some more, but when the pain began to creep back across the side of my body, I punched Danielle's number. "Hello, K. What's up?"

I couldn't help it. I burst into tears. "Dani, can you and Justine come over?" I sobbed into the phone.

"Of course. Are you okay? Where's Trig?" I heard her in the background instructing Justine to get the keys.

"Trig's doing survival training with RJ. Dani, I'm scared. I'm bleeding, and I can't get ahold of Jules."

"We're on our way."

Chapter Sixteen

Lunch with Karrie was the best idea I'd had in a long time. I initially felt the tension I had created from my tantrum the previous day, but soon enough things between us felt right again. We just had lunch with no discussions of anything stressful—no baby, no baby daddy. It was good to enjoy each other's company and spend a few minutes together just like old times before I left for the weekend.

My entire world always felt off balance when Karrie and I were fighting—that sick feeling in the gut that nothing could soothe. I couldn't think or carry out even the simplest tasks when she was angry with me. Knowing things were okay made the ride up the mountain much more enjoyable. I would've been worrying about making things right with her and fixing the David problem, but instead I was thinking about how beautiful she looked sitting across from me at lunch. When I kissed her good-bye, I felt a pull to stay home this weekend. I was going to miss being with her.

"This is a beautiful drive." Terry Jacobs observed the changing fall leaves. I was driving with two of our new volunteers, Terry and John Jacobs, a married couple in their thirties.

"It is." I agreed. "I love being up here in the fall. In addition to the beautiful scenery, it's cooler here in the fall. It must be much different from where you're from." Terry and John had grown up in the South and had come to Albuquerque for work about a year ago.

John spoke up. "It doesn't look that different. It's just so much dryer here. It's hard to get used to. I think we should be pretty prepared. We just need to know a bit more about the mountains around here. Mountains are the one thing we don't have in Texas." They seemed to be pretty knowledgeable about survival techniques and had been in volunteer groups before.

"RJ and I'll give you some good info during this quick weekend session, but the more time you spend up here, the more familiar you'll become with the area."

"The boy with RJ, he seems inexperienced," Terry said.

"I'm hoping he surprises us, but if not, he'll catch on quickly." RJ followed us with Mark Kline, an airman from the nearby air-force base. He seemed pretty green despite his air of confidence—a young man's arrogance.

"Where will we be camping tonight?" John asked.

"A nice, quiet spot. You'll like it." We were headed first to our favorite training spot. RJ and I had stumbled on it during a hiking trip one summer, and we'd been using it for training ever since. It was secluded and had a variety of resources available for the initial training. "Then we'll be doing a long hike to a second location, and it will be the trainees' job to navigate back to the vehicles." Tomorrow we would spend most of the day hiking in farther, or so it was meant to appear that way to the volunteers. RJ and I would take them on a long winding hike that turned out to be a circle, bringing them less than a mile from our base camp site and our vehicles.

If any of them realized where they were, we would always treat them to a special meal on the way home. I was hopeful that the Jacobses would figure it out. It was a trick, and we didn't always use it, but I'd planned it that way for this session so I could go back to the truck and drive down the mountain for cell service. I wanted to call and check on K Saturday night. I didn't think I could stand not knowing if she was okay. Besides, it was a good lesson for the volunteers. It was easy to walk in circles in the woods and not realize it.

❖

"That was a short trip." Mark jumped out of RJ's truck and stretched when we reached the campsite.

"Okay. Get your gear. We're actually going on a quick navigation hike to your campsite." RJ pulled his day pack out and waited impatiently while the volunteers got their backpacks. "Gather around. I'll get you all oriented, and then we're hitting the trail. We'll review some basic ground navigation."

"We're not camping here?" Mark hefted his pack on his back.

"RJ and I will camp here. You'll find a good site," I said as I pulled camping equipment out of the truck, including a huge tent.

"Did you bring your own hotel room?" Terry was teasing.

"When you're on the training team you can bring yours." I smiled at her. "You better get over there, or RJ will leave without you."

RJ took the volunteers to their campsite while I set up our camp. RJ and I didn't sleep in the elements anymore when we were training volunteers, at least on nights when we could avoid it, so I set up our big four-man tent. We let the volunteers use whatever they felt comfortable carrying on their backs, but we made them hike in with their gear. RJ had more fun with this than I did. He would often make them walk in circles until someone threw something out of an oversized backpack. Usually two or three miles was good enough to get someone to shake out a few heavy, useless items.

If they couldn't carry something, they couldn't use it. It depended mostly on their experience level, but if they dropped something, RJ or I would haul it back to the trucks so they wouldn't lose anything valuable. Often they learned to team up to share gear and food to lighten their loads. They seemed to absorb that lesson quickly. RJ and I always brought enough food for them to have something to eat if all else failed, but we certainly didn't give in to them unless they became desperate. During a weekend training session, no one was in danger of starving. We were more concerned with someone getting too cold or dehydrating in our dry environment.

I was cooking the steaks on a grill set over the campfire coals when RJ walked out of the woods. "Did you get them all settled?" I asked him as he sat on the log across from me, his face flickering and distorted behind the flames. We always made the fire way bigger than necessary so the volunteers could use it to warm up if they got too cold in the night.

"Yeah. I think the Jacobses are pretty prepared, but I did get one prize from Terry." He pulled a large hardback book out of his backpack.

"Are you kidding me? What was she thinking?"

He turned it over so I could see the title. "*A Mountain Survival Guide*," he announced. "I guess she thought she could study." He laughed and flipped through the pages. "Maybe I should read it."

"How'd the navigation lesson go?"

"Good, but they had no idea how close they were to our campsite when I stopped, until I pointed it out to them. I'll be surprised if they know where they are tomorrow."

"They know their way back here?" I asked. I hated to get up in the night and go check on them, but RJ and I always took turns trekking out to their campsite at least once each during the night to make sure they were okay. He and I would worry if we didn't. Even though they were only about five hundred yards from us, we didn't want to lose anyone or have anyone get injured. It wasn't cold enough for frostbite yet, but the overnight temperatures would get pretty low, so hypothermia was a possibility if someone was exposed too long.

"Yeah. After I pointed out the landmarks and the direction they were all pretty embarrassed." He poked at the fire. "Those smell amazing. I hope they don't smell them." He hitched his thumb in the direction of the volunteers' campsite.

I turned the meat over. "They had good bags? And some food?"

"Actually, that kid had mostly military MREs in his bag and a government-issue sleeping bag—plenty warm. The Jacobses had subzero bags and a tent they carried between them—real light, fancy thing. They also have on nice clothing. You noticed Mark wore mostly cotton and jeans. I think we need to get his jeans wet tomorrow, so he can see how hard it is to get those suckers dry. I have a pair of pants that will fit him. They may be a little short, but he won't have to walk around camp in his skivvies all night."

"I think these are ready." I pulled the steaks off the grill. "K made us a salad too. It's in the cooler. If we don't eat it she'll be pissed, and since she also made us a pie, I think we better eat the salad."

"I won't argue with that, but if I can't get my ass out of the tent to go check on the campers tonight, I'm blaming your wife." RJ began shuffling through the cooler.

We finished eating, cleaned up every scrap on the ground, and got ready to turn in. Since we weren't returning to this exact spot, RJ and I would break down the tent and use only our backpacks tomorrow. We wanted things to be as simple as possible when we got up before dawn, so we could start on our hike tomorrow. We had to do land navigation—more advanced than RJ's quick lesson—shelter, food, water, and first aid tomorrow. It would all be introductory training, with hands-on projects going on all day while we hiked, but it would be a starting point.

The volunteers would have more training each month in the classroom, but the best training would come when they were assigned to a team on a real rescue mission. When we were lucky enough to have seasons where no one got lost in the state, we did some group training sessions and put new folks with veterans for more advanced training. This weekend was as much for RJ and me to evaluate skills as it was for them to gain skills.

❖

"We're going to camp here." I dropped my pack. I considered myself to be in pretty good shape, but I was beat. We'd hiked nearly ten miles in about six hours, with a quick stop for lunch and lessons along the way. We even had each of the volunteers build a shelter. It was rare that we ever had to stay out overnight on a rescue, but it was a useful skill. The mountains contained plenty of excellent materials to use for building a quick shelter to provide protection from the elements. I could tell all the volunteers were exhausted too, but we didn't have to stop for anyone so they were in decent shape as well.

Mark was the only one who was pretty unhappy. RJ had waited to near the end of the trip to cross the creek at the widest point. We could have just stepped over it in plenty of places, but he placed a log and asked who wanted to cross first. Mark, of course, took the bait and started the balance-beam act across the stream. After only three steps he slipped in.

"Can anyone show me where we are on the map?" RJ set down his pack and pulled out the map. Terry and John joined him.

"Mark, get out of that wet gear. RJ, give him your extra pants," I directed. I actually felt pretty bad for him. The water was only about two feet deep. He didn't fall down into the water, so only his shoes and the bottom of his pants were wet, but the last mile and a half must've been extremely painful.

RJ pulled the pants out of the bag and tossed them to him. "Here. Go change into these, and I'll get a fire going so we can try to dry your shoes."

He looked at me desperately. "Do we have a long hike tomorrow?"

"No." I should've made him tell us where he thought we were first, but it was clear he had no idea. I saw no reason to stress him more. "The base camp is just over that ridge not even a mile."

"Oh, thank God. My feet are all blistered. I'd never make it on another long hike." He went behind a tree and changed while I started on the fire.

I heard John having a V8 moment. "Damn. I thought I was keeping pretty good track of where we were."

Mark approached the fire. "Put your boots and socks by the fire. Put on a couple pairs of socks to walk around the campsite in," I instructed him.

"I only have the one pair. I was trying to pack light." He looked embarrassed.

I pulled out two pairs of socks. "Mark, we need to do some basic instructions about gear. You haven't done too much backpacking, have you?"

He shook his head. "I went with some buddies once, but we hiked only a couple miles from the campground. I'm not really prepared. I just thought this sounded kind of cool." He nodded thanks for the socks.

"It is cool, but if you're serious about it, you need do some in-depth reading and invest in some quality gear."

"Yeah. Would you help me? I'd really like to be on the team, if he doesn't disqualify me." He looked over at RJ setting up the tiny tent he and I would share tonight.

I laughed. "We don't disqualify any volunteer. We're happy to have anyone who wants to learn. I'll get you a list of required items and a list of desired ones. They're more luxury items. I'd start with the required stuff. It can get pretty expensive. Most of the volunteers have old stuff they're selling so you should check at the next meeting. We hikers are gear junkies, and we're always buying the latest new lightweight item."

"Cool. I'll be better prepared next time."

Terry and John finished putting up their tent and were getting ready to cook some dehydrated meals.

"Hey. I have like six more MREs if you guys want one."

"What flavors have you got?" John asked. "Some of those things are pretty damn good."

While Mark spilled out his pack and spread out the MREs, I carried my gear over to the tent RJ had just finished securing. "Hey. Mind if I head over to the truck and call K?"

"I'm surprised you're still here. Go check on her."

"Thanks." I smiled at him. I was glad he wasn't giving me a hard time for worrying so much. He would have definitely been worrying if it was his wife. "Give me a couple hours."

"Take your time. We'll be fine."

I took my water bottle out of my pack and hollered over to the group. "I'm leaving you in RJ's capable hands. Don't piss him off, or he'll put your shoes in the fire."

Mark laughed. "I don't doubt it." The three volunteers had bonded over shared MRE packets.

I took off down the hill in a slow, steady jog, made it to the truck in about fifteen minutes, and headed down the mountain toward Amanda's tackle shop. It was a little store on the way up that had a few fishing and camping supplies and, best of all, cell service. It was only about ten miles from our campsite. I turned on my phone and went into the store while I waited for it to start up and access the satellite. Spotting the ice cream case, I contemplated whether I could get back to the campsite with some bars before they melted.

My phone pinged and the screen lit up with four missed calls: one from K, two from Justine, and one from Jules. I dropped the ice cream bars back into the case, my heart in my throat. I saw one voice mail, but I ignored it and hit K's number. It went right to voice mail.

"Shit, shit, shit." I fumbled with my phone to listen.

"Is everything okay?" The middle-aged bearded man who was stocker, janitor, clerk, and owner of the store called from behind the counter. He recognized me from the many times he'd seen me in the store, but we'd never exchanged names. I think I heard someone call him George once.

"I don't think so," I called back. I was waiting for voice mail to connect. He came around to the aisle where I stood and looked around for a problem. I pointed to my phone; he nodded and walked away.

My voice mail connected and I heard Justine's voice. "Hello, Trigena. Give me a call as soon as you get this message." I banged my thumb on the Off Hook button and scrolled for Justine's number, every nerve in my body on high alert. Panic made my chest hurt and my arms feel weak.

"Hi, Trigena." She spoke like nothing was wrong.

"Justine, where's Karrie?" I yelled at her.

"She's here with Dani and me at your house."

"What's going on? Why are you there?" I was still yelling and panting, trying to get air in my lungs.

"Trig, calm down. She's going to be okay."

"Justine, damn it." I yelled again and noticed the store owner staring at me, so I lowered my voice and, through gritted teeth, demanded answers. "Tell me what happened and let me talk to K."

"Trig, she fell yesterday after you left, and later in the evening she started bleeding. She couldn't get ahold of Jules so she called Dani. We came over and took her to the hospital. They kept her overnight for observation and to run some tests. She was pretty shook up. We just got her home a few hours ago. She's asleep right now. She's resting for the first time since she called us."

"I'll be home as soon as I can get there. Why didn't someone come get me? She had all the coordinates for where we were going to be. Shit!" I was walking toward the truck, planning to speed all the way home.

"She's okay now, and she didn't want us to bother you. Dani kept trying to persuade her to call someone from the group, but she kept telling us no. She said she'd worried you about too many things during this pregnancy already."

"You don't do what the pregnant lady tells you to do, you get me!" I was standing in front of my truck and yelling again.

"She was upset enough that I left you a voice mail. She threatened to kick us out of the hospital if we did anything else to contact you. Trust me, Trig, if the doctor hadn't said she just needed to rest, I would've come to get you myself." Justine sounded like she was apologizing.

"I'm scared. Are you sure she's okay?"

"She's scared too, but all the tests indicated she and the baby are fine. She'll be upset if you come home now."

"I can't stay up here now. I'm on my way." I got in the truck and started it.

"Trig, where's RJ? Is he with you?"

"Fuck! RJ and the group. Shit I...I got to...listen...I'll figure this out, and I'll be there as soon as I can." If I drove back and hiked back across to the campsite, it would take me an additional hour to get home. If I left from here I could be home in about ninety minutes—before dark. But I couldn't leave with RJ not knowing where I was.

I got out of the truck and went back into the store, where a young man about twenty was standing by the counter checking out with a few groceries. I interrupted him. "George, right?"

The clerk looked up with a scowl on his face. "That's right. I'll be right with you."

I ignored him. "Do you know anyone who'd be willing to take a message up to a campsite? I have to go home." There was a lodge next to the store, and I was hoping maybe he knew someone familiar with the area who could make a trip for me. "I'll pay." I pulled out my wallet. "Seventy-two dollars. It's all I have right now, but I'll pay more. I can leave my gear as—"

"What campsite?" the young man asked.

"At the end of Fire Road 405 there's a barely discernable dirt road that leads to a big open area. My buddy's tan Chevy pickup is sitting there. To the northeast of that site about a mile over a ridge is a group of four people camping. They'll have a pretty good-sized fire."

"Can you get there on a dirt bike?"

"Yeah. There's not a path, but if you take it slow when you get over the ridge you should see them."

"I'll go. My bike is in the truck, and I know where 405 is. I was just going to head to a campsite myself. Maybe I'll just stay at your base camp."

"Oh, you're a lifesaver. Here." I held out the cash in my hand. "I'll get you more money if you want."

"No way. You look like you'd do the same for me." He smiled a big, perfect, white smile under his scruffy face.

"I would—for sure. Thank you." I couldn't imagine what I must look like. My hair was probably in a rat's nest from the hike today. I knew I must smell as bad as I felt. I was planning to take a quick dip in the creek when I got back. And my clothes were covered in dirt and mud from a fall I took during the hike. I just nodded and ran out toward the truck.

"Hey, ma'am." He caught me as I was starting my truck. "What is it you want me to tell them, and what's your name?"

"Oh yeah. Shit. I'm not usually such a wreck. My name is Trigena." I waited.

"I'm Trevor." He held out a big dirty paw of a hand, and we shook.

"My wife is pregnant." I paused a minute, scared of the reaction. I probably could've gotten the message to RJ without outing myself.

He didn't flinch. "Cool."

"Seems she fell and had to go to the hospital."

"Shit, Trigena, You better get your ass home."

"Right. So there's a big dude in the group—beer belly." I held my hand out over my stomach. "His name is RJ. He and I were training a new group of search-and-rescue volunteers. Just let him know I'm heading home." I was shifting from foot to foot.

"Get going. I'll take care of it. He doesn't have a gun, does he?"

"Well, yeah, he does, but he won't shoot you. Trust me. He'll invite you to camp with them."

"Right. Good. Okay, go, go."

I climbed in and headed down the mountain.

Chapter Seventeen

When I woke up, Trigena was staring down at me with wet eyes, still wearing grimy nylon pants and a sweat-stained tank top. She held her favorite hiking shirt in her hand.

"What are you doing here?" I spoke softly, still trying to find my voice from sleep. I tried to raise up to hug her, but she put a strong hand on my shoulder and held me in place.

"Don't talk. You should go back to sleep. I'm sorry I woke you. I just needed to see that you were okay. I was so worried about you. I thought I was never going to get home." She started to sit on the edge of the bed but looked down at herself and stood back up.

"I'm going to kill Justine." I raised up to meet her kiss. "Honey, you stink."

She laughed, and I could see a wave of relief come over her. "I'll get in the shower now. I just had to see you. I sent Dani and Justine home."

"You brought the group back? I told them not to bother you. I knew you'd end the trip."

"RJ's still up there. We finished the big hike, and I came down to call and saw Justine's message. Don't be mad at her. I was already pissed that she didn't have someone come get me." Trigena was stripping out of her filthy clothes. "I gave you all those coordinates for a reason."

"Don't put those in the hamper," I reminded her. "I won't be mad at either of them. They were here in seconds after I called. I just didn't want to worry you again." She balled the clothes up and threw them in a pile next to the door to take to the laundry room, then looked at me for approval. "Don't you know that's my job?" She leaned in for another kiss.

"I do know, but I'm afraid your job is going to kill you or ruin us. What happened to your face?"

"I got a little too friendly with a tree. Is it bad?" she asked.

"Well, it's going to leave a mark for a few days." After wiping clean a spot on her face, I could tell it had looked worse than it was. Once she got some of the dried blood and dirt off, it probably would just be a little scrape across her cheek. "Now get cleaned up. I'll get you something to eat." I started to get up to fix her something to eat.

"What are you doing?" Trigena came running over to the bed. "Lie back down."

"They said I just needed to take it easy. I'm not bedridden."

"Let me get showered, and I'll fix us something to eat. Then you can tell me everything that happened while we have dinner in bed. Please, babe. Let me take care of you. Justine told me Jules scheduled an ultrasound for Monday afternoon. Shouldn't we do it sooner to make sure everything's okay?"

"No. Everything's fine, hon. The doctor said so. The ultrasound is at three. Can you meet me over there?"

"I'm taking you." She jumped into the shower. I still felt tired and a little sore, so I obeyed her instructions. I was so glad she'd come home, even if it really wasn't necessary.

❖

Trigena and I spent all morning lying in our bed with our laptops, clicking away at the keyboards. After Trigena had fed me and put me to bed last night she got up early, did laundry, made breakfast, and brought all my schoolwork to me in bed. We split a chicken panini, and I fell right to sleep while she worked beside me. I'd been dozing in and out for the past couple of hours, always happy when I woke up to see her there beside me. I knew it was driving her crazy to be stuck in bed, but it was nice. When we first started dating we would occasionally spend all day in bed, making love and watching movies. I couldn't remember the last time we'd done that.

"Hi, babe. You're awake." She smiled down at me. "Do you need anything?"

"You can go work in the garage." I felt a little guilty keeping her away from the work she wanted to do.

"Well, I actually snuck out and left a note and your phone in my spot." She held up a slip of paper and phone. "You were out."

"Really? I thought I was just dozing. I didn't realize I fell asleep so deeply."

"Yeah. I put a coat of finish on the crib. I came in and you were still sleeping, so I milled the wood for the changing table."

"What time is it?"

"After six. Are you hungry?" She kissed the top of my head.

I looked around to see that the room was dim with the setting sun. "Well, I guess I must've needed a nap."

"You did."

"Let me fix us something. I want to exercise a little." I began to get up, and she stopped me.

"K, let me."

"Trig, you're running out of dishes that you know how to prepare," I teased her.

"I called Dani and she gave me a recipe. I marinated some chicken in a chipotle sauce and was going to grill it and make some rice. We have spinach salad and fruit, so see. I can be resourceful."

"Are you kidding me? You did all the work in the shop and marinated chicken while I was sleeping? Wow." I was amazed at how hard I slept.

"Well, actually I put the chicken to marinate while I was making lunch."

"Trig, thank you for taking care of me." I truly wanted her to know how much it meant to me.

"Babe, did you expect anything less? Of course I'd take care of you." She frowned at me.

"No, I…I just really appreciate you. You're good to me—to us." We both looked at my belly.

Trigena's eyes filled. "I'm just so glad you're okay. You scared me." She spoke through tears and wiped her eyes.

I held out my arms and she relaxed into me. I think I felt the world lift off her shoulders. "Honey, we're okay. It's going to be okay. I'm so sorry I made you worry…again."

We lay together for a few minutes, and then she looked up at me, dry-eyed. "I love you, babe. Now let me fix you something to eat."

"Okay, but I won't eat in bed again. I'm getting out and sitting with you while you grill."

She agreed but wouldn't let me walk by myself. She wrapped her arm around my waist and helped me out to the patio, then ran into the house, only to return seconds later with two pillows. "Now stay put," she directed me.

Monday morning was much like Sunday, only I insisted on getting up and working at the table. Trigena made breakfast and sat with me most of the morning, but before lunch the call to go to the shop was too much for her to ignore. She worked on the changing table until nearly two, when she came in.

"Are you ready, babe?" She came out dressed in jeans and a royal-blue blouse. Her wet hair was braided, and she held my purse in her hand.

"Trig, it only takes fifteen minutes to get there, and the appointment with the doctor's not till three."

"Oh." She set my bag on the table and got a drink of water and paced around the kitchen island. "Will Jules be there?"

"Yes, hon. She's meeting us there. Please sit down and check your email or something. We'll leave in fifteen minutes."

"Okay, yeah," she said as if I'd just presented the greatest idea in the world. I let her click away at the computer while I went to put on makeup.

As soon as I entered the kitchen she pounced on me, again with my purse in hand. "Are you ready now?"

"Yes. Let's go." I walked behind her to the car.

We drove in silence to the clinic, and finally I couldn't stand it. "It's going to be okay."

"I know." She looked over at me.

Jules was sitting in the waiting area when we entered. "Hi, ladies. How's everyone?" She gave us hugs.

"This one is about to go crazy." I pointed to my wife. "Or make me crazy."

"Trigena, I'm sure everything is going to be fine. We'll see your little baby in just a few minutes." She smiled at us. "Victor is great. He'll take good care of you. I signed you in already. We can sit for a minute, but it won't be long. He's on schedule." She pointed to the hard, black plastic waiting-room seats, and we all sat down. Trigena grabbed my hand and pulled it to her lap. She squeezed it tight.

"Hi, you must be Karrie. And Trigena." A barrel-chested, athletic man greeted us with a firm handshake and a big, white smile. "I'm Victor. Are you ready to get a picture of your baby?"

"Yes." Trigena nearly yelled at him.

"Okay. Follow me. Jules, you're coming too?"

"Ladies, would you like me to go in with you?" Jules asked.

"Of course. Come on." I motioned for her to follow us.

I lay flat on my back with a big blue glob of ultrasound jelly plopped on my belly. After the initial shock of the cold goo, I relaxed and waited for Victor to adjust the machine to get a picture. Trigena hovered over me, waiting for something to show up on the screen. Jules stood by patiently at the end of the exam table.

"Here we go, ladies," Victor announced.

A black-and-white blob showed up on the screen like a Rorschach print that only health professionals could interpret.

Trigena squinted at the machine. "Is that the baby?"

I turned my head to look closely, trying to make out the image. I could see what had been showed to me dozens of times by expectant mothers. Like every time before, I couldn't tell exactly what I was seeing, but it did look a little like a fetus. "Is she okay?" Trigena squeezed my hand.

"Your baby looks great, and there doesn't appear to be any placental abruption, just as your doctor predicted. Since you're not cramping or bleeding anymore, I think it's safe to say everything's fine."

"She looks good, doesn't she?" I asked Victor, wanting someone who knew what the heck they were looking at to tell me what they saw.

"The baby looks perfect, but you're not having a girl." He pointed to the screen. "Sometimes the way the baby's positioned makes it hard to tell, but this baby is clearly a boy."

"A boy?" Trig stared at the screen, scanning for the evidence Victor was pointing out. "Are you sure? It's supposed to be a girl."

"Oh." Victor looked surprised. "I thought this was your first ultrasound."

"It is." Jules put her hand on Trigena's shoulder. "Sometimes our instincts are wrong. He's very well formed, and everybody's just fine."

"Yeah, yeah. That's all that matters." Trigena smiled. "A boy." She leaned down and kissed me.

Chapter Eighteen

We finished early on one of the custom bathrooms in the Hurst homes, and I didn't want to get the crew started on the next house so late in the day, so I sent everyone home early. I drove the short distance to our house and opened the garage. I'd nearly finished building the changing table, and the strong smell of cherry wood flooded out. I just needed to put the runners on the drawer and do some sanding. The days were getting pretty chilly now, but with the sun shining into the shop, I could work in shirtsleeves without the heater.

The crib was ready for inspection, but I still had it in the finishing room because I didn't want to expose Karrie to any off-gassing fumes. She kept begging me to let her see it. The last look she'd had was before I put the accents on and finished it.

I planned to do just a little bit of sanding and then go clean up and have dinner ready for her. She was seven months along now and getting tired after standing most of the day. I'd been working long hours lately and was never home in time to beat her to dinner preparation. But when I heard the Highlander pull up, I couldn't believe it when I looked at the clock. Four hours had passed.

"Hi, hon. What are you doing home so early?" Karrie walked into the shop.

I was covered in a fine coat of dust from sanding, so I carefully pushed her back. "Babe, it's really dusty in here."

"You just don't want me to see the crib." She kissed me.

"Well, yes, but I also don't want you breathing a bunch of dust." We walked to the front of the house and entered through the main door, and I pushed the garage-door button to close the shop. "I lost track of time." I sat on the bench and started taking off my boots, and Karrie plopped down beside me. "I was going to fix dinner."

"Nice try. You lost track of time. Hmmm…sure, you did."

"Let's go out. We've been saving like crazy and working way too hard. I want to take you out." I held her hand.

"Oh, babe, I don't mind cooking dinner. You know I like to cook."

"I know but…for a change. Come on. I'll get showered and be ready in fifteen minutes."

"Okay. Where would you like to go?"

"You choose. I'll give you time to think about it while I'm getting ready."

"Okay, get." She pushed me off the bench.

❖

"You figured it out?" I returned to my beautiful wife sleeping on the couch. She hadn't even taken off her shoes, but she was curled up as if she was out for the night. I picked up the phone and tiptoed into the front room to call Dion's pizza place. I ordered our favorite Dion's Special with New Mexico green chilies. As I placed the order, I felt Karrie's hand around my waist and her belly against my back.

After I hung up I turned to face her. "Is that okay? I didn't mean to wake you."

"It's perfect."

"I was going to let you sleep while I went to get it." I held her next to me.

"You feel so good, honey. I don't think we've stopped moving in weeks. I just like being in your arms."

"I like you in my arms." I paused for a second. "I just can't pass up the work that's coming in. I'm trying to get all these bathrooms finished because we have a huge kitchen remodel when we get done. It's in the Northeast Heights."

"Trig, could you stop for just a minute and actually hold ME—like you love me."

I heard real anger in her voice and knew I'd rambled on about work when all she wanted was for me to love her.

"Stop worrying all the time. Just be with me for one second." She pushed back and looked at me with sad eyes. "I'm glad you have more work, but you always get work. You've never been without it for long enough to be concerned. Everything's going to be fine."

I pulled her close to me again and buried my face in her hair. "I'm sorry. I love you, K. I lose focus sometimes."

"I love you too, Trig." She leaned into me. "Even when you lose focus."

I held her until she finally released me and said, "Aren't you going to go get pizza?"

"Yes, yes, I am." I rushed out to the truck.

❖

"How do they do this?" K said through a mouth full of pizza. "This is the best pizza in the world."

"There might be some Italians who would disagree with you, but it is pretty good stuff."

I insisted Karrie stay seated while I cleaned up our plates and put the remaining pieces in a plastic container. I was planning to take her to bed early for a relaxing body rub. Just as I was finishing up in the kitchen, the doorbell rang. "Are we expecting anyone?"

"At eight on a Thursday night? No." Karrie looked toward the door as if it were a foreign object.

"Probably someone selling something. I'll get rid of them." I walked across the room and opened the door to see David standing in front of me.

"Hello, Trigena." He greeted me as if nothing had happened.

I tensed from head to toe and clenched my fists. "What the hell are you doing here?" I pushed him back and exited the house, closing the door behind me.

Chapter Nineteen

When I heard Trigena yell and slam the door, I rushed through the front room and grabbed the door to join her outside. I didn't really think she would do anything stupid, but I knew how mad this situation with David had made her. I was concerned she would say something she shouldn't. Our lawyer had told us not to communicate with him at all. I knew she was drawing up some papers to get him to withdraw all parental rights, but since I hadn't heard from her, I wasn't sure of their status. She had prepared Trigena and me for the possibility of him refusing to sign and having to then come up with some kind of compromise with him.

I grabbed the door but couldn't get it to open. I tried the lock and found it wasn't locked. Trigena was holding onto the handle. I pulled again with more force, and she released it. I stumbled back a bit but caught myself, and the scene I opened the door on scared me. David was backed up against the rail of our front porch with his hands raised, trying to talk, and Trigena was yelling at him. An adrenaline rush caused my shoulders and arms to tense up, and panic filled my chest. I felt light-headed and held onto the wall to steady myself.

"Get off of my property before I call the cops. If you want to communicate with me or Karrie, you talk to our lawyer." Trigena had moved within a few inches of his face. "You have some nerve showing up at my house. You lying sack of…"

"Trig, stop. Please stop." I was finally able to speak.

Trigena turned, wide-eyed. She was surprised to see me there. "K, go back inside."

"No. Wait. Please." I just stared at her. I still felt off balance, and she must have seen it, because she came to me and took my arm. "Let's just listen to what he has to say." I looked over at David, who also seemed surprised at my appearance.

"Please, just give me five minutes." He took a tentative step forward. "I realize I've been wrong."

"What!" Trigena's voice was still angry and loud, but she didn't let go of me.

"Let's go inside and sit down." I was trying to create a more comfortable situation for everyone, but mostly I just wanted to get off my feet.

Trigena nodded. I could tell my appearance took some of the fire out of her. She opened the door and led me to the love seat in the front room, a small area in our entryway that we rarely used. Trig had even considered a couple of different options to remodel to make better use of the space, but it was perfect for this situation—invite someone in the house but don't make them feel too welcome. David had been in our home before at a time when he was made to feel very welcome. I was sure the significance of being relegated to our sitting room wasn't lost on him.

Once I was settled on the love seat, Trigena sat on the sofa next to me at the edge of her seat, as if ready to pounce. She stared up at David and nodded to the chair across from us. He sat down tentatively and then began to speak, looking down at his hands.

"I was wrong to think I should be a part of your child's life."

"You're damn right you were," Trigena said. I put my hand on her thigh to calm her, and she spun around to stare at me.

"Trig," I said, pleading with my eyes for her to give the man a break. The room remained silent until I finally said, "Go on, David."

"Oh yeah...I...I realize you would've never considered me as a donor if you had suspected I might be interested in being a part of the baby's life. I understood that when you asked me." He paused as if trying to find the right words. "I guess I just thought, maybe I could play some part."

"How exactly did you think this would work?" Trig interrupted him again, with sarcasm in her voice.

"Trigena, I know. I wasn't thinking. You and Karrie want a family, and I agreed to help you. I'm going to honor my word. I never meant not to, really. I'm not sure what I expected, but I understand how I upset you both and how I was wrong." He stopped and finally looked over at both of us.

"Okay?" I said, unsure of how to go on. "So you won't be going to court for shared custody?"

"I never intended to do that. All I really wanted was for the baby to know I was her father and to help out or be involved in some way."

"That's what you don't get…" Trigena elevated her voice.

"So you don't want that now?" I patted her thigh again.

"No. I understand it doesn't fit into your family plans at all. I hope you might still invite me over as a friend, and I might meet your daughter as a friend of the family." David looked down again.

"How can we trust you?" Trigena asked.

"I signed the contract your lawyer sent, and I sent it back in the mail before I came over. I'll never identify myself to your daughter. I swear." He was staring at Trigena now.

"Thank you, David," I said and took Trig's hand in mine.

"Yeah, thanks, David." She squeezed my hand. "We've been friends for several years. I'm sure we can continue to be and have you to our home to meet our…well, son, actually."

"Oh, I thought you said you were having a girl." He looked back at me.

"Well, turns out we were wrong."

"Congratulations." He paused, seeming to look for some kindness in Trigena's eyes, but she only stared back. "I'm sorry for the stress and problems I've caused. I should go." David stood up, and Trigena jumped to her feet. We followed him toward the door. "Good night." He raised his hand in a wave.

Trigena flipped on the exterior lights, and we both said good night. She pushed the door closed behind him and turned to me and picked me up.

"Trig, put me down. You're going to squash me and the baby." I was laughing.

"Can you believe that just happened? Did that just happen? Did he just say he wasn't going to interfere? He signed the contract?" She was speaking so fast I couldn't get a word in to answer her. "K, this is so good. One giant stress is gone."

"I know. I know. He did the right thing."

"We are so done with that guy." She wrapped me in a hug again. "He's the last person I'm going to let near you and the boy."

I gently pushed her away. "Trig, really? You won't let him see him as our friend?"

"K, are you kidding me? He's proved we can't trust him. I won't take that risk again."

"He made a mistake, and he corrected it. He'd be a good role model for a boy. Are you planning to punish him now? He came to us to apologize." I couldn't believe what she was saying.

"Listen, K. I don't want to talk about this right now. We disagree, and you can't change my mind. He put us through too much. I don't want to fight." She walked away, leaving me standing in the foyer.

Chapter Twenty

I had about two hours to rest before everyone started showing up. I'd been cleaning and decorating the house and even preparing most of the food, with strict supervision from Karrie. It was New Year's Eve, and every year since we'd been together, she and I had hosted a party on that holiday. Karrie had tried to make a unilateral decision to cancel, since she was only two and a half weeks away from her due date, but I insisted I could and would do all the preparation. We didn't have a lot of social events at our home, especially not parties, and the fifteen or so people who attended every year knew each other well. It had become a tradition, and I didn't want to let it go.

"Do you think I can trust you not to go messing around and being on your feet if I go lie down for an hour? I want to be able to stay up until midnight." I was teasing Karrie, but I was truly concerned she would overdo it if I didn't keep an eye on her. I'd just walked out to the garage for a second to return the stepladder I'd used for decorating, and she was up folding more napkins. "Seriously, how many napkins do you think we're going to need?"

"I just want to be prepared." She smiled and continued grabbing more as I escorted her to our bed. "I'm fine. You lie down."

"I won't lie down and get that valuable rest I need if you don't come with me. I don't trust you." I continued to lead her away.

She gave in and put the stack of extra napkins back into the pantry and followed me to the bedroom. "Fine."

I heard her light little snores before I fell asleep.

❖

"Are we the first to arrive? It is our goal to be first each year, but Justine was taking way too long to get ready tonight." Danielle had started in as soon as I opened the door.

"Dani, you're thirty minutes early to a party you're supposed to be fashionably late for—of course you're first."

Danielle laughed. "I know. We just came to help." She gave me a quick hug and walked straight to Karrie. "Oh, girl, I bet you'll be so glad when he finally gets here. Why are you standing? Sit down and give us instructions. We work for your wife. We know how to do what we're told." She turned to see if I got the joke. "Trig, the place looks great."

I'd worked most of yesterday evening and today on decorations while multitasking the baking and cooking. Bright, primary-colored streamers hung from corner to corner of every room in the house, with streamers dangling from them. Each room also had several helium balloons resting against the ceiling, and little silver New Year's party sprinkles were on every surface.

Justine came in behind her with her arms full of a chocolate sheet cake. "What are you doing with a cake? I made one." I shook my head in mock irritation.

Justine looked at Karrie. "Umm…I thought…I…"

"I asked her to bring it." Karrie saved her and walked over for her hug. "Thank you, Justine, but her cake looks amazing."

"What? You didn't think I could make a cake? I'm so insulted." I knew she had every right to question my cooking skills. I'd burnt or misread recipes so many times I deserved their skepticism.

Karrie came over and wrapped her arms around me. "You've been amazing, hon. I had no idea what a great party planner you are."

"Come on. Let's get the *second* cake in the kitchen. Besides, she won't sit down and rest if we don't make her, and as much as she wants this little guy to get here soon, I'm sure she doesn't want it to be tonight." I rubbed her eight-month-pregnant bump.

"You're crazy, girl. Why did you host this year?" Justine asked as she followed us to the kitchen. "We offered to take over."

"I didn't do a thing." Karrie nodded to me. "Trig wouldn't let me, and she insisted that she could do it at our house. I tried to bow out. I assumed we could get a bye this year."

"It wasn't so bad, and I love New Year's Eve. I couldn't let you guys take over the party. We might never get it back." I pushed Karrie to the chairs at the bar. "Sit, babe. What have we forgotten? Anything? Except I refuse to fold more napkins."

"What about napkins? Looks like you've got plenty here." Danielle turned from the punch bowl. "I could mix this now if you want."

"Exactly." I gave Karrie an I-told-you-so look.

She ignored me and started giving Danielle instructions about mixing the punch. "Don't forget to set aside a pitcher for me before you put in the Everclear."

"Can we see the crib?" Justine pulled Karrie out of the chair toward the nursery. "We keep hearing about it."

"She finally let me see it last week." They all walked out, leaving me with the punch.

Within the hour the whole group had arrived—all my work gang, three of Karrie's peers in the College of Fine Arts, our neighbors from down the street, and two of my regular clients. As the night went on, I watched closely to see that Karrie wasn't getting too tired or doing too much. I'd had no idea how much I would love taking care of her. I think I liked her being pregnant;

it made her just a little bit more vulnerable. I stared from across the room. But being pregnant led to a baby. As it got closer, I was somehow pushing the idea out of my head, like maybe if I didn't think about it, Karrie wouldn't actually have a baby.

I know my rage over David disturbed Karrie, but I was surprised at how intense it was. I didn't want to discuss it with her, but I thought hard about how I'd wanted to kill him, to do anything to get him away from her and the baby—the baby he had a biological claim to and I didn't. Karrie also had a biological connection, so where did that leave me? But Karrie is my wife. That's the most important thing to me, and anything that threatens our closeness, my place next to her, well—I just can't handle it.

And when I was honest with myself about fearing that David would somehow weasel his way into my family and stake a claim to the child my wife was having, I had to add that I was afraid the baby, and then my wife, would prefer him. I was afraid I wouldn't be a good parent, and David would be. Even without David in the picture, I was afraid. The baby would take up Karrie's heart and focus. I would be the inept outsider. Everything would change. Maybe David wouldn't be a concern, but my insecurity was growing as the day approached when it would no longer be just Karrie and me.

Karrie was having a great time, smiling and laughing with our friends and discussing her excitement about the new arrival. I just continued to push the thought out of my head, and I moved away from the conversation when it was all about the baby.

Before I knew it I heard RJ and Jason yelling for everyone to be quiet. "Hey, everyone. Listen up. It's almost midnight. Less than a minute."

I spotted Karrie and moved quickly across the room. It was our tradition to go out on the patio and share our first kiss of the year. She was looking for me too, and I met her in the middle of the room.

"Come on, babe." I pulled her out the back door. The patio was lit up with Christmas lights and tiki torches. "I love you so much." I held her belly in my hands.

"Thank you, Trig. You're so good to me. You've truly taken care of me. I love you too."

I heard the countdown through the open back door. "Eight, seven, six…"

I pulled my beautiful wife to me and kissed her. "Happy New Year, babe."

Chapter Twenty-one

"Trigena?" I called from the bedroom. I had no idea what time it was, but she was already out of the bed. I waited for a few minutes, sure she would come trotting in to see what I wanted, but she didn't. I slowly got out of the bed. I'd slept all wrong; my back was killing me. I walked around the house, and she was nowhere. I looked at the clock—almost two.

I couldn't believe I'd slept all day. Most of our friends had left the party by two a.m. Only Danielle and Justine had stayed until Trig pushed them out about three, but I'd climbed in the bed as soon as the door was locked. I remember waking up around nine and thought I would get up in an hour or so, but I never dreamed I'd sleep all day. I don't think I'd done that since I was an undergraduate.

I finally found my phone, and then I saw Trigena in the backyard. She was cleaning up from the party. Our friends were pretty tame, but they had left a few plastic cups and paper plates outside that would blow through the desert if she didn't throw them in the trash. She also wanted to put the lights away. I could tell as I walked through that she'd spent most of the day in the house cleaning. I'm embarrassed to admit she actually did a better job than I would have. I hoped she was doing a little nesting of her own. As I looked around at our shiny little house I couldn't believe I'd slept through it all.

I walked out into the crisp January afternoon. The sun was shining, as it did most of the time in New Mexico—one of the many reasons I loved it here.

"Good afternoon," Trigena yelled from across the lawn.

"Why didn't you wake me?"

"I wanted you to rest." She walked across the lawn holding a trash bag. The wind was pretty mild today, so she'd been able to collect everything before it went sailing onto the West Mesa. She kissed me and wrapped me in a one-arm hug. "Want some breakfast or lunch or dinner?" We laughed.

"I really can't believe it's two."

"You must be starving. Come on."

"No. I'll get something. You're in the middle of this. I'll get something to eat and put on some clothes and come out and help you."

"I'm almost done. I'll fix you something, then finish, and we can curl up with a book." She was already pushing me inside.

"Trigena Lynn Gilmore. When was the last time you sat down and read a book?"

"Hey, I read."

"Yeah, you do. You read accounting statements, you read building plans, and you even flip through the pages of a woodworking magazine now and then." I was trying to be funny, but I could tell I'd gone too far.

"I just thought we could spend some time together, but I have some work I can do in the shop. What do you want to eat?" She was washing her hands.

"I was joking. I'm sorry. I'd love to spend time with you, doing whatever you want to." I tried, but she wasn't going to let it go now.

"I'll make you some eggs. Do you want some turkey sausage? We have some left in the freezer."

"Trigena, look at me."

She turned around, holding two eggs in her hand.

"I'm not hungry. Talk to me. Why are you so angry?"

"I'm not angry. I'm trying to fix you breakfast. You *are* hungry, aren't you? You haven't eaten in like fourteen hours."

"Why did you keep referring to the baby as *my* baby last night, not *ours*?" As soon as the words came out I wished I hadn't said them. It must've been on my mind and the tension in the room had caused a fission reaction that was about to go nuclear, and I was the one who pushed the button.

"I did not," she snapped and spun around and broke both eggs into the skillet.

"Yes, you did." I waited for her to counter, but she didn't even turn around. "What's going on? Are you still questioning this? It's too late, in case you haven't noticed. I'm having a baby and very soon."

"K!" She did turn around this time and threw the skillet in the sink when she did. "Would you let it go?"

"I can't let it go! If you don't want this baby, we've got to figure something out."

"Like what? What are we going to figure out? You're having a baby."

"We! We are." I was yelling now.

"Oh, you can do it, but I can't?"

"What?" I wasn't tracking, and my confusion took some fire out of me.

"You just said it. You just said, in case you haven't noticed, *I'm* having a baby." She was backed up against the stove with her arms folded in front of her chest.

"You know what I meant."

"Well, then you know what I meant when I said it."

I just stared at her for a minute. I'd clearly lost that round, and I was the one who started it. I got up and walked over to where she stood and put my arm on her shoulder. She jerked away as if something repulsive had landed on her.

"I'm sorry. I..." I backed away. "I'm just scared of what happens to us if we don't both want this and why it keeps coming up."

"You keep bringing it up." Trigena turned and pulled the pan out and started scrubbing the egg off. She didn't say what I wanted her to say. I just wanted her to make me believe she did want this as badly as I did.

"Trig, do you want to be a mom?" I waited for much longer than I wanted to before she turned and looked at me. She started to speak, but her phone rang and she ran to it, leaving me standing there waiting. A pain in my chest moved slowly up to my throat, and for a second I couldn't breathe; then the tears began to flow. I walked to our bedroom and started the shower.

Chapter Twenty-two

I ran to the phone and away from my pregnant wife begging me for some reassurance I couldn't give her. I couldn't even lie now that reality was so close. My hands were shaking when I picked up the phone. I didn't even look to see who it was.

I heard a panicked voice on the phone. "Trig, I've been calling you all afternoon." It was Aaron from the search-and-rescue team.

"What is it?" I asked, trying to focus my attention on him.

He spoke quickly and explained the situation without taking a breath, finally ending with, "I need you to go, Trigena."

"No. There's no way. I can't." I had never once said no to a SAR mission, but as confused as I was and as much as running away sounded good, I couldn't leave Karrie, especially now. I had to try to repair this situation. If I couldn't make her believe I wanted this role as a mother and make myself believe I could do it, then our marriage was at risk. "No. I can't. K's due in two weeks. I can't go up there."

I stood listening as Aaron went on and on; mostly he was repeating himself. All he really knew was that there was a lost child, and while he had a full team of people on the way up the mountain, he didn't have anyone with any leadership training.

"RJ can do it. Have you talked to him?" I sacrificed my friend.

Aaron explained that he'd called RJ, and he was waiting for me. RJ had never been through the leadership training, and they couldn't assign him the responsibility. If he took charge of the team and something happened, there could be all kinds of lawsuits, not to mention loss of life.

"I just can't. I'm sorry, Aaron. You have to find someone else." I turned away from the window and found Karrie standing across the room in her robe. I had no idea how long she'd been there.

"What is it?" she asked. She was so calm I was surprised.

"Hold on," I said to Aaron. "Lost kid in Carson Mountains," I told Karrie.

"You have to go." It was all she said before she turned and walked away from me.

"I'll call you back, Aaron." I hung up and chased my wife.

"Karrie, listen. You could have a baby any day." I spoke to her back as I followed her to our bedroom.

"A baby you don't even want." The calm woman was gone and angry Karrie was back.

"I want the baby. Karrie, I want what you want."

"Stop it!" She spun around from the pile of clothes she was moving from the hamper to the laundry bag, busying herself with menial tasks. "Trigena, would you just stop it?"

"What?" I said as calmly as one can ask a one-word question. I didn't want to fight, but I was having a hard time figuring out what to do to stop doing just that.

"Stop saying what you think I want to hear. I don't want you to want what I want. I want to know what you want. That's something I should've known years ago. It all feels like a lie—a lie just to keep us together."

"It's not a lie, but if I'm doing something for you to keep us together, then why is that so bad?" I asked honestly, not knowing exactly what I'd done wrong.

"How about if you tried doing what you wanted and trusting that we—you and I, Trigena, two people who love each other very much—could work through it." She sat down on the edge of the love seat in the corner of our room and looked up at me. She was still angry but not yelling now.

"You want to be a mom, and you want kids. I want you to be happy." I walked over to sit next to her, but after I spoke she jumped up. Still, I couldn't just say to her, I want to be a mom with you. I knew it wasn't what I wanted, but at this point I didn't even know why anymore.

"You're doing it again." She walked away into the master bathroom. "Go up to those mountains and find that missing child and think about what's happening with us. Then come back here, and together we'll decide whether I'm going to raise this child alone."

"What? Why are you saying that?" I tried to approach her again, but she backed away. "We're a family, K."

She walked out of the room toward the kitchen.

"Will you stop walking away from me?" I asked. I was trying not to be angry, but I was struggling. Everything I said was wrong, and I was getting mad at her.

She pulled out some food from the refrigerator and started preparing things. "Please just go up there. Listen to me. I'm trying to work things out myself, and I'm mad. I'm mad at myself because I never knew what you wanted or didn't want. How could I not know?" I tried to interrupt her but she went on. "That child in the mountain needs someone to find him or her, and we need some time to think. If you come back from this SAR and can't look me in the eye and tell me you truly want to raise a child with me, then we have to consider some options that will work for us."

"Karrie, stop talking like that. I'm not leaving—not now—and I'm never letting you go." Tears were streaming down my cheeks, and I wiped my sleeved arm across my face.

"If you don't go, then I'm going to leave the house for a few days. We need some time, and if you don't think you do, then fine! I do." She looked up from her food preparations. "Why not go find a child while we're taking some time? I'm making some food for you and RJ."

"I…I…How can I focus on finding a kid if you're talking about leaving me?"

"Call RJ and then call Aaron back. They need to know you're going to be there."

I stood there watching her pack plastic bags with food.

"Trig. Please just go. You know there's no one else who can do it, and it'll be good for you."

I couldn't believe I was doing this, but I didn't know what else to do. I picked up the phone and called RJ.

Chapter Twenty-three

"Trig, seriously. Why aren't you packing your gear?" I was working hard to just help her get ready and not be angry. Regardless of how I felt right now, I loved Trigena more than anything, and this was serious stuff. If we didn't focus she might forget something that could save her life or someone else's.

"I can't go with us like this—fighting. And you're about to have a baby. They'll find someone else." Trigena had gone back out to the yard and was stacking the last of the lights. I followed her.

"Number one, I'm still two weeks away. If you go up there with the rest of the team, you'll find the kid in twenty-four hours. And number two, how is this not driving you crazy? There's a child up there lost. This is what you do." I stood my ground as she locked the shed and pointed in the direction of the house.

"Come on in, Karrie." She took my arm. "It's cold out here. We can talk in the house."

Once she closed the back door, I started in again. "What happened? Why is a kid lost on New Year's Day?" I was really refocused now. I couldn't imagine how a child got lost in the woods in this weather.

"I don't know all the details, but it seems a lady called in and said her neighbors went on a camping trip. They were supposed to have returned on New Year's Eve, but they didn't come back.

I don't know why. Aaron just said a kid was missing. The lady apparently said the whole family went."

"They went camping up there in January? Who would do that?" The temperatures up north probably barely made it to thirty in the day, and the nights were in the teens. I couldn't imagine anyone camping like that.

"Some people like camping in the snow," Trigena answered. I was distracting her. I could tell she was really starting to think about the missing child.

"They took a kid? How old?"

"Karrie, I don't really know. I didn't get all the details because he needs to get the other team members notified and up the mountain. We only have a few folks who live that far north, and they'll have to get things set up for the rest of the team. It's going to be dark in an hour or so. They won't be able to start until morning. It doesn't sound good."

"Trig, you need to go," I insisted. "Call RJ. He'll want you up there."

"No. I'm not leaving you."

"Sit down." I motioned her to the bar stools next to the island. "Just listen, okay?" She shrugged and finally nodded. "There's a kid lost up there in freezing weather, maybe a whole family. You're good at finding people. If they have a chance at all, you could improve it. The base camp will only be four hours or so from here. Even if I go into labor while you're gone, you can be back here before I have the baby. You're going to go crazy worrying about your fellow team members and about the family if you don't go."

She shook her head, but I said, "Go up there. Help them set up and make the teams. Do whatever you can for seventy-two hours, and then come home. We both know if you don't find them by then, it's probably too late anyway, but at least you'll know you've done what you can. Besides, I need some time, and you need to find out whether you can do this." She started to interrupt me. "I mean really do it, not just tell me you will and then be miserable. You'll kill our relationship, the one based on trust and love and honesty." I'm sure my sarcasm came through in the last comment.

"Why are you pushing me to go? I already know what I want. You and the baby are my priority." Trigena took my hands.

"Don't make me mad again. I'm not kidding. I'm leaving if you don't." I raised my voice with each word. "Call RJ, please." She put her phone on the island when we sat down. I pushed it toward her.

She gritted her teeth and shook her head at me. "There's no arguing with you, is there?"

I shook my head. "A child is involved. I'd want you looking for mine." As much as I wanted her to go up into the mountains and think, I also knew she could help. She had an instinct for finding people.

She picked up the phone. "If I call and he's already gone, then we won't talk about this anymore and you won't leave."

I just looked at her and nodded at the phone. I was pretty sure RJ would be waiting for her.

Chapter Twenty-four

I scrolled for RJ in my contacts, pressed the off-hook button, and waited for him to pick up. I did want to go see if I could help, but I didn't want to leave Karrie. I knew where I needed to be right now.

"Hey, Trig, want to meet me over here? I already have most of the stuff in the truck. We'll just transfer your personal gear." RJ spoke quickly, panting between words. I heard him grunt before I heard a loud clank through the phone.

"RJ, you there?"

"Yeah, yeah, I'm here. I dropped the phone. I'm trying to do a little multitasking. I could use your hands." He continued to breathe heavily.

"I'm worried about Karrie. She's due in a couple of weeks. The baby could come any day now. Did they assign you as incident commander?"

"Oh, shit. I totally lost track of time. Is she really due that soon?" He said it more as a statement than a question. "I don't know who's been assigned IC. There's a real shortage of information. That's never good."

"Dude, you were here yesterday. You didn't notice she's about to have a baby?"

"I don't pay attention to stuff like that." I heard the radio in his truck come on too loudly. "Are you sure you can't just come up for a couple of days and get us set up? I don't know who's supposed to be in charge, and if someone hasn't been assigned I've never organized a search before. If we don't find them in a few days, they probably aren't coming home. It's seriously cold up there, and a Pacific Northwestern storm's on the way." The phone died for a second, and I could tell when his Bluetooth reconnected.

"Where are you going?"

"I'm completely out of gas. I have to fill up. I can send Natalie over to stay with Karrie."

"I'll come help you get things packed."

"No. I'm packed. I was just waiting to hear from you. Aaron said he was calling you."

"I…I just can't leave Karrie." I felt her hand on my shoulder. She was standing behind me as I stood looking out the front window. I turned to see her appealing to me with her eyes.

"Go up there," Karrie whispered.

"Okay. Listen, RJ. I'll go up for an overnight and help you all set up for daylight tomorrow. I don't have a thing packed, so come over here when you get filled up. I'll follow you so I'll have my truck there. You know where the incident base is going to be set up, right?"

"Yeah. I have coordinates. It's supposed to be a private residence. Some volunteer has a cabin in the woods."

"Okay. I'll start packing. Ask Natalie to call in on Karrie tomorrow."

"Of course. See you in about twenty minutes." RJ hung up.

"This is crazy." I stared at my wife, put my hands on either side of her belly, and then pulled her into a quick hug. She pushed me away, and my heart leaped into my throat.

"What do you need me to do to help you pack?" Karrie backed away and looked at me.

"Nothing. I…what am I doing?" I started toward the shed, and she followed me quickly.

"I'll go get your toiletries and thermals. Is your bag in the nursery-room closet?"

"I can get it. Just…" She was gone.

I pulled out my winter bag. It had my subzero sleeping bag, ski pants, my Sorel snow boots, hand warmers, space blankets, and pretty much everything necessary to keep a person warm or get someone warm. I grabbed my backpack from the top shelf. It had everything else in it, from flashlight and fire-making material to shovel and first-aid kit. When I returned from the training session I'd debated about repacking it. I was planning to just leave everything out and repack in the spring, sure I wouldn't be going out this winter with a pregnant wife. As I pulled it down, I was glad I'd decided to repack. I dragged everything to the front of the house, where Karrie stood with my duffel bag packed nearly full.

"Stop!" She was carrying it to the truck. "Put that down. I'll get it."

"It's not that heavy. It's mostly clothes," she yelled back at me but did as I asked and left the bag next to the front door. She'd finally pulled on a jacket; it was cold and getting colder as the sun set. I was in a tee shirt and just beginning to feel the chill. All the rushing around had been keeping me warm.

"Babe, I'll be back tomorrow night, okay? I promise." I picked up the bag she'd packed. "What the hell did you put in here?"

"Everything you need. I've seen you do this enough times. All your thermal gear, lots of socks, your Gortex and two fleece linings. I also found six dehydrated meals left from your training session. Your winter gloves are in there, and I put three fleece hats on top, but I only saw the one turtle. I thought you had a few of those. I think that's it. The rest is in your pack, right?"

"Damn, babe. You're good." I kissed her cheek. Wow, she let me touch her. "Now get in the house. I'll be right behind you."

"Let me know if you need anything else."

"I need you to get in out of the cold." I tried to smile, but I was stressed. I appreciated her wanting to help, but it was destroying my mental focus. She shrugged and went inside. She knew me well enough not to take my remark personally.

• 173 •

I pulled my laminated checklist out of my backpack side pocket and went down the list. I wasn't sure what Karrie had included in my duffel bag, but she'd seen me do it many times both for real and for training. The items she listed off sounded pretty comprehensive, and I trusted her. I double-checked the items in the winter bag and scanned the top of my backpack. I'd just packed it so I felt confident I had everything.

Finally, I put the list back in my pack and returned to the house. I entered to the wonderful smell of hot coffee.

She handed me the coffee. "Oh my gosh, you're freezing." She grabbed both my hands in hers. "I filled both thermoses in case RJ doesn't have any."

"Thanks, babe." I sipped the coffee. I knew things weren't fixed, but at least we were working as a team again. Someone else's emergency had distracted us from our struggles.

❖

RJ pulled up in our drive exactly when he said he would. "Hey, Karrie. How you feeling? Natalie said to tell you to call if you need anything. I think she said she'd contact you and stop by tomorrow, if you were up for it."

"I'm fine. Just huge." Karrie rubbed her stomach. "I'll touch base with her tonight, and we'll make some plans."

"Good, good, that's good. She'll like that." RJ was practically wearing a hole in the carpet pacing because of his nervous energy. "I'll wait in the truck."

"I'll be right out." I closed the door behind him. "Okay, babe. I got to get going or RJ's going to have a heart attack."

"I know. Go up there and find that child. Please be careful, okay?" She pulled me closer.

"Now, you can't be worrying about me after you insisted I go." I ran my fingertips across her cheek and through the strands of loose hair that had fallen from her ponytail. "Call if you feel even the slightest tingle, okay? If my phone doesn't have service, get in touch with Aaron. He'll have the base-camp sat phone, or he can radio. I'll be home tomorrow night."

"Trig, go up there and do what you need to do and figure things out." She tapped my head with her index finger. The stress of our fight flooded back through me, and I felt that pressure in my chest again. I nodded, not knowing what to say.

"I'll be fine. You be safe, okay? I love you. Now get started, so you'll have time to get some rest tonight before you have to start in the morning." She brought her soft lips to mine and pulled my upper lip between hers. I didn't want to go. Things weren't right with us, and leaving felt so wrong. I pulled her close and held on, but she pushed me away and toward the door.

I walked to the truck. The sun was almost completely down now, and it was getting really cold. RJ had started my truck to warm it up.

He hollered from his window. "I have the route in my GPS."

"Hold on." I ran to the backseat of the truck and pulled out the two-way radios and ran over to his truck. "It'll be easier than phoning all the time. Go ahead. I'm behind you."

RJ took off from my house and drove much faster than he should have. Even though I knew basically where he was going, I wasn't sure of the final destination in the mountains, so I followed closely. If we got too far apart I'd lose radio contact, and once we got in the mountains our cell service would be spotty. The roads were dry and clear most of the way, so there was no danger, but we couldn't do anything today so there was no reason to risk an accident. A good night's rest before we started tomorrow made sense though. And we were both anxious. It was always like that when someone was missing, but it was worse knowing a small person was lost. I was hoping the child was still with the parents. I had so little information that I had no idea what I was walking into, but thinking about it kept me from worrying about Karrie and me.

I'd hung up with Aaron so quickly, I didn't really give him time to tell me much, and when RJ showed up, we were both so anxious to get on the road, I didn't even ask him what he knew. I didn't know which other team member had been called. I assumed no others were from the Albuquerque area, or we would've carpooled. It required too much talking over an open radio to find out now, and I'd find out soon enough. One thing I knew about search and rescue was that no matter how much you thought you knew when you started out, things always changed or were wrong from the beginning.

"Hey, Trig." RJ's voice crackled over the radio.

"Go," I called back.

"I'm going to stop up here for a quick break."

"Copy." I was actually relieved to hear that. I didn't know how much farther we had to go, and I really needed to stop. The coffee K had made was having an effect.

I followed RJ into a little twenty-four-hour truck stop with a filling station next to it and pulled up to one of the two pumps. I climbed out and yelled over to RJ, "I'll be right in."

He nodded and walked inside. The place was all lit up so it was obviously open, but the exterior of the building looked like it was more suited for a demolition crew than patrons wanting food. I think it had once been covered with white paint, but so little of it was left, it was a tough judgment call. The door appeared to be hanging with only one functioning hinge. I watched RJ pick it up and move it out to get in. Replacing the hinges wouldn't have done the trick, though, because the door frame was cracked and rotten. One of the six panes of glass had been replaced with a piece of plywood.

Had I been alone or with Karrie, I would've been a little scared to pull up to a place like this, but with RJ, I wasn't worried and actually wished we had time to have some crispy bacon and eggs. It reminded me of the greasy spoons I used to go to with my dad when I was a kid. On Saturday mornings before we worked in the shop or went horseback riding, my dad would take me to Slagle's, the local diner. We'd have pancakes and drink coffee together, then go home and play all day. I remember one weekend when I was in high school that he and I built a trunk for me to hold all my stuff. I still have that wooden trunk out in the storage shed. He passed away a couple of years later, and I still miss him.

It was freezing up here, and the wind cut through me. I shivered when I got out of the truck and rushed to the pump. It was an old-fashioned one with the flip handle on the side. I grabbed my jacket out of the truck to go in and pay before I pumped, because there was no slot for my credit card. I felt like I'd fallen backward into 1970. Just as I was about to run for the door, I heard a voice through a speaker over my head. "Go ahead and pump, ma'am. The gentleman who just came in gave me his card to hold for your gas."

I called out, "Thanks." I had no idea if the voice could hear me or if there was a button someplace I should be pushing.

I hurried and got the gas pumping and grabbed my gloves out of the truck. The handle of the pump was so cold it stung my hand. The gas started slowly, dripping into my tank. It was so slow RJ was finished and standing next to me stomping his feet to keep warm before it had even run in five gallons. "Hey, grab my credit card when you go pay."

"It might never get full at this rate." I watched the analog numbers click past slowly, as if the cold air had caused the cogs to freeze. "How much farther to the incident base?" I turned to him and swayed from foot to foot to keep the blood moving.

"GPS says about forty-five minutes, but Aaron said the snow was heavy up there. We might run into some bad conditions that'll probably delay us." He glanced at his watch, and when he did, I pushed my coat sleeve back and looked at mine. It was almost nine o'clock. If we were lucky we'd be there in an hour or so. I was hoping our volunteer's cabin was occupied and warm when we arrived.

"Do you know who's going to be there?"

He shook his head. "I have no idea what we're getting into. I just know a family with a mom, dad, and two kids didn't show up this morning when they were supposed to."

"Two kids?" The pump clicked.

"Yeah." RJ shrugged as he headed back to his truck. He tapped the radio attached to his hip and said, "Call if you need me to slow down or anything."

I nodded and went in to pay. I returned with his credit card. "I just paid with your card."

"Good. I probably owe you for something." He smiled.

"I'm kidding, you know." He nodded, and I ran back to my truck to get out of the wind and back on the road.

After less than fifteen minutes' drive, we hit some packed snow, but it was still passable. I shifted into four-wheel drive for some extra traction.

"Trig, did you put it in four-wheel?" The radio clicked.

"Did you forget who's with you, old man?"

"Right, sorry."

He was nervous and just trying to watch out for his team—of one.

Most of the rest of the ride was uneventful but slow. I kept thinking about my wife and how I'd screwed up. I was struggling with which part I'd messed up the most—not telling her I didn't want kids or not being able to convince her that I wanted them. I agonized over how I could come to terms with this. I couldn't live without Karrie, and that thought scared me to death, but how was I ever going to be a good parent? And did I even want to try?

It took us nearly seventy minutes of slow, careful driving, but when we reached the location on his GPS, we were relieved to see a large, modern cabin. The place was surrounded with motion-sensitive floodlights, and they were all popping on as we pulled up. The lights brought out an old bearded man in flannel and blue jeans. He stood tall on his porch and waved us in.

As RJ and I walked toward the porch, the bearded man called out to us. "Good to see you folks. I'm Thomas MacDonald. Everyone calls me Mac. Me and my son, Trevor, live up here. We're part of the volunteer team. He's out getting supplies and won't be back until late tonight. You're the first to arrive. Bring in whatever gear you need, and I guess you all get the bedroom since you're here first."

RJ smiled, and I was suddenly very happy he'd gone so fast. I felt bad, though, since I wasn't going to go out with them tomorrow, or at least not for long, so I decided to let someone else have the bed.

We gathered up our personal gear and returned to the house. My wish had come true. It was toasty warm inside, heated with a fireplace in the center of the cabin. There were two small bedrooms on the opposite side of the chimney, and the rest of the cabin was wide open, with a tall ceiling and a loft above the kitchen. Mac guided us to one of the bedrooms.

"This is my son's room. He put on new sheets before he took off. He'll sleep out in the shed as long as you folks need the space. There's a stove and a cot out there. He'll be comfortable. I'll go out and start the stove before he gets back."

"RJ, you settle in here. The next dude to arrive will bunk with you."

"I can't take the bed, Trig. You take it." RJ backed out of the room with his bag hung across his body.

"RJ, seriously! I'm leaving tomorrow, and you might be up here several days. Get over your chivalry and take the bed. Besides, who knows if there will even be other chicks coming up, and it'd be a waste." He just stared at me as I pushed him back in. "Mind if I set up in your loft up there?"

"Anywhere's fine, ma'am." Mac pointed to the thick, solid oak stairs that led to the loft. They were steep but sturdy. I'd have to remember how steep they were in case I had to go down to the bathroom at night.

"Please call me Trigena, Mr. MacDonald."

"Only if you call me Mac." He laughed, his stomach jiggling as he did.

"Thanks, Mac. I will."

"Now, you get yourself all set up. I'm afraid we only have the one bathroom, but the plumbing's good and the hot-water heater is big and our propane tank is full. I'll put some coffee on for you two while you wait for your friends." He said it like we were all meeting up for a slumber party and not a life-or-death search-and-rescue mission.

"Ah...Mac." I stopped him as he was starting down the stairs. "Do you have any information about the lost family?"

"A bit. Come on down when you're finished, and I'll tell you what I know."

I rolled out my sleeping bag and sorted through my bag. My amazing wife had thought of everything. I probably wouldn't have packed pajamas, but she included my red-plaid flannel PJs. And inside my toiletry bag was an index card.

I love you, Trigena. Please be safe. K

I smiled, a lump in my throat as I continued to find items she'd included. In addition to almost every piece of thermal underwear I owned, she'd stuck in about ten pairs of wool socks and an equal number of polypropylene sock liners. I laughed out loud as I discovered another card.

You always tell me the most important thing is to keep your feet clean and dry.

Finally, I pulled out a box of cinnamon coffee cakes, the packaged ones with tons of preservatives and fat and all the bad stuff I loved. Karrie didn't like me to eat junk food like that, but she sometimes surprised me with them in my lunch. I hadn't seen any in months. I had no idea where she managed to hide stuff like that.

I walked slowly down the steep stairs with my slippers on—another item I wouldn't have even considered. I held the box of coffee cakes in my hand, and RJ spotted them as I came down.

"Karrie's work?" he asked.

"I thought they would be good with coffee while we try to make a plan."

"Have I ever told you how much I love your wife?" We were stressed and anxious, but our friendship ran deep.

I eyed him. "You better be careful."

"Okay, folks, almost ready. I got one of them K-cup things," Mac called from across the room in the kitchen. "My son got it for me for Christmas last year. At first I hated the crazy contraption, but now I hate waiting for the coffee pot to brew. Damn thing spoiled me." He laughed again.

RJ and I sat at his small round table in the center of the kitchen. "What time is it?" I'd taken off my watch and left it in the loft.

RJ glanced at his wrist. "Almost eleven."

"Damn. I hoped we'd have the crew by now. Okay, Mac. What do you know?"

"Yes, ma'am—Trigena." He grabbed a piece of paper next to the radio that had been chirping quietly in the background.

"That your only comms?"

"Yes, ma'am. Trevor has a cell phone, but we don't get service up here. He just uses it when he goes to town." Mac put on a pair of old wire-rimmed reading glasses and started in. "Trevor took the call at about four this afternoon. Here's what he wrote. It's a little cryptic, but…okay. Looks like we only have Carson, no specific details on what trail or where they may have hiked. Man and woman, Donna and William, mid-thirties with two children, boy and girl. They went for two overnights and were to return by…looks like he wrote noon yesterday. It says here their neighbor called forest service at two p.m. That's all there is. Oh, and here at the bottom it says…ahhh…Ralph somebody is bringing snowmobiles, and there's another name bringing… ahh…I think it just says gear. Here. See if you can read it." He handed me the paper. "Trevor was never good at handwriting."

"He means Ralph Markham. I know him. Does it say when he's coming?" RJ asked.

I hovered over the page, squinting to make out the words. It was all scratches written in a quick hand. "I'm surprised you could read that much. Well, it's not much, but let's get the maps and see if we can find some logical places they would take kids hiking in the middle of the winter." I shook my head. I hated winter camping. I liked fall and early spring. I didn't even mind a dusting of snow, but I just didn't enjoy having to fight to stay warm all the time. The minute I stopped moving, the cold would go all the way to my bones, and I could never get warm again.

RJ and I pulled out our maps, and Mac brought over a few detailed land-navigation charts of the area. We sat down and began to highlight trails and sites that might be worth taking kids to see. I wasn't very familiar with this forest land and was grateful to have Mac's ideas. We ended up with fifteen different areas and were planning some routes in and out when four vehicles drove up at the same time. They were volunteers from all over the state.

About an hour later our new trainee from the fall, Mark Kline, showed up. He was happy to see RJ and me. We all sat down around Mac's fire, and finally an older man who I didn't know came in. He introduced himself as Paul Bond and informed us that he was assigned as incident commander. He assured us all that he had a lot of experience. I was relieved because the weight of this was no longer on me. I hadn't realized how stressed I was until he arrived.

We turned over all the maps to our new incident commander and waited for him to start giving instructions. He asked us to run through what we'd worked out. Mac was at hand to explain some of our ideas. It was almost two in the morning when Trevor opened the front door, and a new gush of cold air followed him.

"I got food supplies in my Jeep. Can I have a hand?" All the volunteers who'd arrived when Paul did were spread across Mac's living-room furniture and floor. They all jumped up at once, and after some quick introductions Mac's son had them running trips back and forth with boxes loaded with food and cold-weather gear. They carried in eight boxes filled with food and left two more with frozen goods outside. Mac herded the group back out of the kitchen, and he and Trevor put things away the best they could, considering the limited space.

I liked Paul immediately and knew he was going to do a great job with the team. I was feeling better about leaving, but going home scared me. I knew I hadn't figured anything out or what to say to convince Karrie I could do this, probably because I still didn't know if I could. Even after nearly nine months, I hadn't solved the problem—I'd ignored it. What was one night in the mountains going to do to solve it?

RJ and I sat with Paul until I was so exhausted I could barely hold my head up. I got RJ's attention and tapped my wrist where a watch should have been.

"It's late," he said.

"We need to get these people to bed, Paul."

He did his own watch check and nodded.

"You should know I'm going to head out first thing tomorrow," I finally told him.

He looked up at me with big eyes. "Trigena, your reputation precedes you." He put his hand on mine to keep me at the table. "I would really like it if you could take a team out first thing in the morning. We're very short on experienced volunteers. I'll bring you in by noon. We should have more people by then." He seemed desperate.

"I can't. I really need to get home. I came to help get things organized in case there were no experienced folks up here. Our ABQ group has dwindled, and we didn't know who would be here. Since you are, you don't need me."

"I do need you. If you stay I can send out three teams. If not, I'm down one, and that's a lot of territory to cover."

I looked at RJ, who said, "Trig, do what's best for you, but you know Karrie can call Aaron, and Mac has great comms with this radio."

Paul chimed in. "And I got a sat phone."

"I'll think about it, but I can only stay till noon." I walked away and started my ascent up the steep stairs, instantly regretting setting up my bag before everyone else. There was only one other woman with the group, and she was next to me. Three other dudes were spread out on the loft floor, and I had to trip over the snoring beards to make my way to the corner.

As I stumbled through the sleeping bags, I heard a deep voice in the dark. "Hey, Trig. Can I team up with you in the morning?" I recognized Mark's baritone.

"It's up to the leader, but I'll suggest it. Did you pick yourself up some good gear?"

"Spent like seven hundred bucks on all the stuff on your list."

I smiled and winked at him before I realized he probably couldn't see me. "Good deal."

I made my way to my bag. As much as I loved Karrie for packing my PJs, it was too much trouble to try to change now, so I climbed in with my clothes on. There was no need to try to break a trail back to the bathroom to change. I'd be back up in about four hours, if I managed to get any sleep at all.

Chapter Twenty-five

As soon as RJ and Trigena drove off, I regretted pushing Trigena to go. Our house wasn't that big, but it felt huge when Trig was gone. Our tile floors and cathedral ceilings always created a bit of an echo, but when I was home alone, it was deafening. Every minute we'd spent talking just made my heart hurt more and more. How could we be happy together as a family if Trigena didn't want kids? And how could I be happy without her?

I sat on the love seat in the front room and stared out the window with a million thoughts running through my head. How could I not have known she felt so strongly about not wanting kids? I'd always thought it was part of her tough-girl image. I don't know what I could've done about it if I'd known, but as I ran my hands against my extended belly, I knew I couldn't do anything now.

I tilted my head and rubbed my round middle. "What are we going to do, little buddy? I know she'll love you when she sees you. We can't make it without her."

After sitting there lost in my thoughts for way too long, I got up and called Natalie to let her know they were on the road, and we arranged to meet for lunch. She suggested a matinee in the afternoon, but I wouldn't be comfortable sitting through a movie in the theater, so we settled on lunch at noon.

Now I just had to wait—and worry. I finally got my computer and sketchpad, took them into the kitchen, and made some tea. I was settling in for a long night of working. I knew I wouldn't be able to sleep anytime soon, and if I could keep my mind busy perhaps I could escape all this even for just a while. I was working on some sketches for a series of paintings I really wanted to start. I wanted to depict the life of a tree with a child playing beneath it in different stages of life, ending as an old man with a huge family of kids and grandkids surrounding him, but I just couldn't imagine standing at my easel for very long with my big belly.

When I finally got everything all set up at the table, my stomach started to rumble. It was almost seven p.m. After sleeping most of the day and fighting most of the afternoon, I'd completely forgotten to eat. I put some leftover grilled chicken in the microwave and pulled out the lettuce and some tomatoes for a salad. I paced from one end of the house to the other until the microwave beeped.

Trigena would be an asset to the search, but now I was thinking she was right. She'd decided that her family was most important, and I'd encouraged her to go. I knew she would be thinking about that lost child until she heard word, so it was probably best that she'd left. Maybe after I ate and started my project, I could stop worrying about her.

Chapter Twenty-six

I woke up to noises below me at four in the morning. Somehow I'd managed to fall asleep for a bit, but my back was killing me now. Sleeping on that hardwood floor was worse than sleeping on the ground. I climbed over everyone with my toiletries, hoping to get in the bathroom before the rush.

"Hey, Trig," RJ whispered. He came out of the spare room at the same time I approached the bathroom.

"Were you headed for the bathroom?" I asked him.

"You first."

"Thanks. I'll be quick."

I took care of all the important parts and got my teeth brushed. I was in and out in less than five minutes.

"You're fast." He winked and we traded places.

As I was about to climb the stairs and get my trail buddy out of his sack, Paul came in through the front door. "You're up."

"Yeah, where have you been? Didn't you sleep?"

"A little, but I woke up a couple hours ago and went out to my truck and started looking at these maps." He held up a bundle of partially folded ones. "This doesn't make sense, Trigena. I think we can eliminate a few areas. Come take a look." He headed to the table. "Good morning, Mac."

"You two want some coffee?" The old man held up two full mugs. "I got that big thing over there going, but it's going to take a while. In the meantime...Keurig." He set the cups down on the table.

"Thanks, Mac." I sat across from Paul.

"Look here." He started pointing to some of the areas RJ and I had highlighted last night. "I don't think if I was taking my kids out, I'd want them so close to this steep canyon. It's just one more danger they'd have to deal with."

"But would you take your kids on a winter backpacking trip? Seriously, what the hell were they thinking?" RJ walked up as we were bent over the map.

"RJ!" I scolded him. "You'll have time to discuss that with them after we get them home safely."

"Sorry. You're right. But I don't think we should exclude those areas."

I spoke up. "I agree with RJ. I know it's too much for us to cover it all, but by midday you'll have more people, and we need to cover every logical trail."

"Hmm." Paul scratched the stubble on his chin. "Well, okay...but we should make them a low priority. Let's send out three teams this morning in these areas." He'd marked three sections on the map.

"That's a lot to cover." RJ shook his head and looked at me.

I shrugged to let RJ know I wasn't in charge. "We better get started then." I drained the rest of the coffee and started up the stairs.

"Trigena," Mac called to me. "Trevor got these breakfast bars. You need to eat." He held out two.

I smiled at our wonderful host. "Thanks, Mac."

Most everyone was getting packed as I crested the top of the stairs. My teammate was still out cold, like only a young person could be with the commotion going on all around him. I threw one of the bars at him. "Hey, Mark. How long before you're ready to walk?"

"I'm ready." He jumped up and started rolling his bag like he had to save it from a fire.

"Fifteen minutes, 'kay?" I headed for my corner and started packing my gear.

"Yes, ma'am."

"Daypack with emergency blankets. We're returning at noon," I instructed him.

"Noon? I only have one pack."

"Yeah. You'll go out with someone else this afternoon. I'm going home." I looked up from my bag. "My wife's having a baby."

"No way." His face lit up. And suddenly I missed Karrie so much I just wanted to run to the truck and drive as fast as I could to her. I shook off the feeling and stuffed the rest of my gear into my bag.

"Yeah. In like two weeks. I'm worried sick about her, so as badly as I want to help find these people, I got to get back to my wife."

"You're right. You do. Family comes first." He sat to pull on his boots, first unwrapping the breakfast bar. It disappeared in two bites.

"That's why we've got guys like you to take over for us."

"Just tell me what to do."

"Well, let's get our gear ready and see what area we're responsible for. Meet me outside where Paul has a table set up with the maps displayed." Even though it was still very dark, Paul had set up a large table at the side of Mac's cabin. He and Trevor had started a generator, with a floodlight blinding everyone who came within ten feet of its glow. As roomy as Mac's cabin was, there wasn't room to spread the whole group out and provide clear instructions.

"Yes, ma'am," Mark said and headed out to his Jeep. He was far too excited about this, but his energy motivated me. I just wanted to get home, and watching him made me realize that for the next five or six hours I needed to focus on looking for a lost family.

Mark was already standing next to Paul and Trevor when I returned with my daypack. I'd pulled out only the gear I needed for a short trip, since I'd be back here before noon. I felt a little bad about leaving Mark with someone else this afternoon, but a fresh crew would be here by then, and he'd learn more by working with different people.

"How's your wife, Trigena?" Trevor asked as I walked up to the table.

"Trevor! Motorcycle guy from Amanda's. I didn't recognize you under that beard. Wow. What a small world." It was the young man who'd ridden out to RJ to give him the message when I left him with the training group in the fall. "She's good, actually. Due in two weeks."

"What the heck you doing up here then?" He walked over to me and gave me a one-armed hug.

"We didn't get good information yesterday. We didn't know Paul was going to be here, and RJ wanted some more experience with him. Since we got Paul, I'm just going out this morning until more folks get up here. Then I'm out." I thumped the team leader on the shoulders and startled him from his intense focus on the maps and his notes. I looked back up at Trevor, "Are you going out with us?"

"No. My old man wants me to monitor the radio. It's going to drive me crazy sittin' here all day. He hates talking on the thing and is afraid he'll mess up a message. He'll be getting chow ready for folks. My dad will cook all the damn day to keep busy and make sure no one goes hungry."

"If there's a call from the ABQ group for me, will you make sure to come out and find me immediately? I told Karrie to have them contact me if she needed anything."

"You got it. I'll be on high alert." He winked, and I felt a little better that someone would be listening for me.

"Paul, Mark and I are ready to go out. You want us to wait? I'd rather get started, so we can cover as much territory as possible before I leave." I leaned over the table to get Paul's attention.

"Hold up for a few more minutes, Trigena. I want everyone to get all the information. I have some descriptions, and I want to pass on some other instructions. Give me just a bit." He flipped through his notebook and scanned the pages. "Trevor, will you go get everyone out of the cabin. Trig's right. We need to get started at first light, and that's only a few minutes away." He turned back to me. "You trust your teammate?"

"Absolutely. I trained him myself." I was aware there was so much he didn't know, but I also knew he respected me and would listen. He was strong and eager to do some good work. I'd take him over a complacent experienced guy any day.

"Okay. I'll get you started as soon as possible. Just be patient a little longer." Sometimes getting a large group like this on its way was the hardest part. Once the teams were organized and on the trail, things usually went pretty smoothly. "I'm going to put you on area three. I think you can cover this top portion here before noon." He folded up the map for area three. He had a map cut and taped for each section so each team would have their own.

I took our section. "Did you sleep at all last night?" He was very organized and knew what he was doing. This rescue effort was in good hands. If we didn't find the family, it wouldn't be because the rescue was poorly coordinated.

"Good, okay." I turned to Mark. "Get the big picture in your head. See this big drop-off here? We're going to walk straight there. Get some coords for me and punch them in." I took the GPS from around my neck. He leaned over and squinted at the map, then ran his fingers across the map, trying to create the straight line he need to get the coordinates.

"That won't be accurate enough for walking in. Here." I handed him a template, and he nodded and went back to work.

"Do you have an extra GPS?" Paul asked.

"Not with me." I cocked my head, concerned with such a question.

"I got one." Mark spoke up quickly and proudly pulled his brand-new GPS out of his pocket. "And I got the supply guy to issue me that Landsat compass you told me I should have."

"Landsat compass?" Paul asked.

"Lensatic." I corrected Mark, and Paul laughed.

"We don't have enough GPSs?" I asked.

"Yeah. One guy doesn't have his own, and another guy told me last night he can't get his to work. I'll have to keep a team in if we don't have an extra."

RJ walked up in the middle of our discussion. "I guess we don't need both of ours, and we both have compasses."

"Trig. Mark hasn't been certified for landnav yet. It's not a good idea. Maybe another team has two."

Paul shook his head.

"Or maybe you should just leave one team back this morning."

"RJ, it's fine. We're only going to be out for a few hours. We won't even be out all that far." I handed Paul my GPS and leaned down to Mark. "Show me when you have those coords in. We need to double-check each other."

"You don't trust me?" He looked up from his work.

"I do trust you, but I'd be a fool if I didn't double-check," I said, and he nodded.

RJ gave me a stern look and pulled me away from the group. "Trig, what are you doing? You gave away your GPS, and you only have a daypack. You know you're required to have gear for twenty-four hours. I know you want to get back to Karrie, and I'm sorry I dragged you out here, but you want to get back to her safely."

"What's with you? You saw the areas he's plotted. I could yell from where we're going, and you could hear me. Stop being an old hen." I was perturbed at him for telling me what I would've told a younger volunteer.

"Fine. Fine. Be safe, and I'll see you when we get back home." He turned to walk away.

"Dude, I'm sorry. You're right. I'll get a sleeping bag. Even if I don't need it, the lost hikers are bound to be suffering from hypothermia." I didn't say the next few words I was thinking.

At this point I was worried that they hadn't made it through the night, but we never suggested someone might not have survived. We were always looking for survivors.

"Thanks, Trig. I didn't mean to be up your ass. I just want you to be okay." He paused and smiled. "It's not like I really care what happens to you. I'm just afraid Karrie would kill me if you didn't make it home safely."

"You're right to be scared of her." I punched him on the arm. He grabbed my fist and pulled me into a hug. RJ and I had been friends for a long time, and I trusted him with my life, but it was odd for him to give me a hug like that. We just weren't the hugging kind.

"Seriously, Trig, please be careful. I…I gotta…ah. Just be careful." He uncharacteristically stammered. "You have enough water, and you got food, right?"

I gave him a smirk. "Yes, Mom. I got water and food, and I'll be in by curfew."

"Okay, okay. I'll see you and your new baby real soon." He rushed away from me.

"You got that GPS set up? We need to be ready to walk as soon as Paul gets us all briefed." Mark handed it over without a word and stood watching while I double-checked the location. "Perfect, good work." I marked our current location with a big red circle and pointed out some major landmarks on the map. I handed him the map and turned to Paul. "You got another one for me?"

"Ahhh…no. You're going to have to share it."

"You can't send teams out with only one map. Everyone needs their own." As organized as Paul was, I was starting to worry about how prepared we were.

"I know. You're the only team without two maps. I thought since you were going to be back by noon, you could go without. There's a group coming up later this morning with more maps and some GPSs and other gear." He sucked in air deeply through his teeth. "I'll understand if you don't want to go out."

Chapter Twenty-seven

It was after eight when I finally woke up on the couch with my sketchpad next to me. The last thing I remember was the stupid *Saturday Night Live* news report with Seth Meyers. I couldn't believe I'd slept all night on the couch. When I got up with a terrible backache, I wished I hadn't. I walked to the front door to see what the weather was like. It was cold but no precipitation.

Natalie was supposed to come by to pick me up at eleven for lunch. I needed to have a little something for breakfast and get ready. I pulled out the eggs and then put them back in the refrigerator. I didn't want to eat a big meal since she'd be here in a couple of hours. I took down a loaf of whole-wheat bread, put two slices in the toaster, and got out some strawberry preserves I'd picked up at the farmers' market last weekend. Then I heated some water for tea and flipped the TV to the news.

The local news announced, "…sent to the Carson National Forest in search of a lost family said to have been backpacking on New Year's Eve." I clicked the volume up. "Kathy is at the forest-service office at the base of the mountain where the family is thought to be. Kathy, the weather is expected to turn in the next few hours. Is there any word on the missing family?"

I stood inches from the TV, ignoring the toaster's pop. "No, Sandy. None. They're still assumed to be missing. Since I arrived here early this morning, about a dozen new volunteers have been going up the mountain. There's a group at a base camp up the mountain already that is said to have started the search. The weather report is predicting three to six inches of snow later this afternoon, and the temperatures are expected to drop another ten degrees as the storm comes through."

"It looks pretty cold there already. Thank you, Kathy." I watched the woman on the split screen shivering even with her expensive down ski jacket, hat, and gloves. Where was my phone? I should find it in case Trig called and needed something. I rushed around the room searching for it. Last night I'd wanted it next to me when I went to lie on the couch in case Trig called. After throwing the blankets, pillows, and cushions on the floor, I finally found it under the front edge of the couch, but there were no missed calls or messages.

I turned down the local news, which was now talking about a series of robberies in the Northeast Heights. I went to get my now-cold toast and finished my tea, then began to get ready for Natalie. Maybe she'd know something. If the conditions got too bad, they'd call off the search and that family wouldn't have a chance. I couldn't help but wonder if Trigena was putting herself at risk for a family that might already be dead from exposure or some crazy accident. I knew I wasn't supposed to think those thoughts; Trig had warned me about negative vibes during a search.

She would be home tonight. If she knew about the weather, she'd clear out even earlier, but what if she was put in charge? She couldn't leave then. I could remember only one other time when Trigena was made to be the commander, but it was because the more experienced staff wasn't available. Being an incident commander required additional training, and Trig had talked about it but decided she preferred to be out in the field instead of running the operation. She was extremely organized and would have been great at the job, but she wanted to get her hands dirty—that's the way she described it. I think she just couldn't stand sitting back at the base camp while others were out risking their lives.

I couldn't imagine that she would've agreed to be a commander on this search since I was so close to having a baby, but I also knew her, and she wouldn't have left a group of volunteers up there without leadership. She would've been so torn and mad, but she'd have stayed and spent as much time trying to get a replacement as she did managing the operation. Or would she be glad she had a reason to avoid dealing with the baby?

I had to stop worrying. She'd said she'd be home tonight. I went to our bedroom to get ready, and as I was undressing, a cramp hit me so hard it nearly brought me to my knees. I grabbed the door frame and held on until it passed. "Woo." I couldn't believe how such an intense cramp came out of nowhere. I stood there several minutes, waiting to see if I'd have another, but everything seemed fine. I finally got in the shower, then took my time getting dressed and putting my hair in a French braid. I pulled on a pair of my maternity slacks and a red blouse Danielle had given me. I didn't feel good in anything right now.

By the time I finished it was nearly time for Natalie to arrive. I cleaned up the kitchen a bit. I'd left my dishes from last night and this morning, and three teacups were sitting around on the countertops. I never left anything out when Trig was here. If I did, she would've been walking around behind me putting things away.

The bell rang as I was finishing, and I grabbed my purse on the way to the door.

"Hi, Karrie." Natalie greeted me when I opened the door. "Are you ready?"

"Yeah. Do you want me to drive?" I asked.

"No. My car's already warm. You're going to want a coat. I think we're getting some temperatures from that pending storm already."

"Oh, yeah. Come on in. I'll be right back." I grabbed a jacket from our closet. Nothing was going to fit around my belly, but at least I'd have something over my shoulders, and I wouldn't be out that much. "Okay. This is the best I can do."

She smiled. "You look so good, Karrie. I remember I was like a horse with Jonathan."

"Oh, you're too kind. I'm pretty sure I'm in the horse category right now."

We walked out to the car and climbed in. I was grateful for its warmth. The car thermometer indicated it was twenty-two degrees outside. "Have you heard from RJ?"

"No, nothing yet."

"The local news had a story and said that storm is going to hit hard up there." I gripped the strap of my purse and twisted it.

"Karrie, now is not the time for you to be worried. They know what they're doing. Those two are the most prepared SAR members on the team. Really. They'll be fine. And Trig's coming home today, right?" She looked over at me, and I nodded. "She'll probably miss the storm."

Chapter Twenty-eight

It was after six by the time Paul finished briefing all the teams and got everyone all set to start in their designated search areas. I was glad we'd waited though, because we acquired some good information about the family. We were looking for thirty-seven-year-old William Madison, who the neighbor described as a big, hairy mountain man. His wife was Donna, also thirty-seven; she was said to be tall and thin. Their two children were Willy and Samantha. Willy was fourteen and an athlete. The girl, Samantha, however, was described as small for her ten years and extremely shy. But everyone in the family was believed to be a fit and healthy outdoor adventurer. I hoped this meant they were well prepared for their winter backpacking excursion.

William owned a concealed-weapons permit and likely had a handgun with him, and that scared me a bit. I worry when I don't know the person behind a loaded gun. It was nice to have descriptions of all four, but that probably wasn't too important at this point, since anyone we found out in these conditions was likely in need of rescuing. Their best hope was to stay in one place and all together.

Mark and I started to head down the trail made by Trevor and his motor-cross bike, when I heard RJ calling me. "Trig, wait."

I turned and stood still with my hands on my hips, waiting for him to make his way to our location at the trailhead. "Dude, you're killing me. Should I just send Mark with you and get in my truck right now? You're never going to let me out on this search."

"Why are you going out before daylight? Just wait another twenty minutes, and it'll be light. Are you trying to put yourself at greater risk?" He placed himself between me and the trail and looked from me to Mark, pleading with the young man to encourage me to wait.

"Are you trying to piss me off? Seriously. Trevor said his trail will be obvious for about five miles toward our destination. There'll be plenty of light by the time we travel five miles. I won't be able to go in farther than another three or so, and that's if we're making good time. That'll take us to the canyon, and hopefully we can get some idea if they've been in the area at all. If we don't start walking now, it'll be a complete waste of time for me to go out at all." I turned and pushed Mark toward the trail.

RJ sighed and let me pass. "Be careful," he called as I brushed past him.

I put Mark in the lead with the map and the compass. I had a pretty good image of the route in my head and wanted him to get some confidence and knowledge, so when he went out this afternoon with a new team member he'd have some useful situational awareness. I was beginning to feel like I was wasting my time, but I was committed now.

A thick forest of pines surrounded us as soon as we entered the trail. The little bit of ambient light we were getting from the stars and moon immediately vanished within the first twenty steps. The calm stillness in the woods was a little eerie, and the blanket of white that layered the trees seemed to intensify the silence. The only sound was the crunching of old snow under our boots.

After about twenty minutes of walking in silence with our headlamps beaming brightly ahead of us, Mark finally spoke. "Almost one mile."

"We need to pick it up. How are you feeling? Can we walk faster?"

"Yeah, sure." He immediately extended his stride and moved us more quickly down the trail. "There's some reason RJ doesn't want you out here today."

"I know. He has a bad feeling, but he can't say that. It's a bad omen to tell someone something negative when they're about to enter a search operation." I was beginning to breathe harder and regretted telling this young, energetic man to step up the pace. I took a deep breath. "We're going to be fine, and we'll be able to come back with information about the canyon." I gasped for air again.

"Should I slow down?" Mark asked, looking back at me and reducing his speed slightly.

"No, not yet. I'll let you know when I can't hang." I smiled back at him and matched him stride for stride.

"You think they're in that canyon, don't you?"

"I don't think anything yet. All I know is we don't know where they are, so we don't know where they're not either." I spoke between panting. "I can't talk and keep up this pace, so just keep pressing until we see Trevor's trail turn west." I was getting warm at this speed and didn't want to start sweating, so I unzipped my Gortex and my fleece liner. We moved quickly down the well-worn trail, with Mark giving me an update as each mile passed. At each new one, I took a big gulp of water and instructed Mark to do the same. After mile three, the dawn was peeking through the sky, and I turned off my lamp.

"Mark, now that we have some light and we're getting closer to the canyon, you're going to have to do some serious multitasking. Watch for signs of anyone on this trail, and keep your eye on that GPS. We don't want to stick to the trail. We veer off, remember? And watch out for low-hanging limbs." I barely got the words out before he faced forward again and a small branch smacked him in the face. We both laughed.

Just before mile four, a light snow started to fall.

"I didn't think that was supposed to start until afternoon." Mark spoke over his shoulder while keeping one eye forward.

"Yeah. That's not good. If they were in this area, all signs of them will be covered soon."

We jogged rhythmically down the trail without a word for the next mile and a half. I was on high alert. I had my own feelings about this search area. I was sure we were going to get some indication that the family had been out here before we returned to base camp.

"Five miles. The trail should turn soon," Mark announced.

I looked at my watch. We'd covered five miles in one hour and ten minutes. We were practically running on the down slopes. Mark had succeeded in moving us quickly down the trail, but I needed a break. I knew we could make it to the canyon and do a thorough search of it over the rim and still make it back before noon. If I could get on the road as soon as we got back, then I could call K at the bottom of the mountain when I was on a main road. I would have cell service then. But at the pace Mark was setting, it might kill me first. I was in pretty good shape, but not good enough to keep up with a twenty-something dude without a break now and then.

"Mark, okay, I give. I need a break just for a minute." I panted as I pulled off my day pack, tiny by comparison to Mark's full-sized backpack. "You want to take your pack off?" I settled myself on a rotted tree that had fallen several seasons ago. Trevor had probably moved it out of the way of his motor-cross trail.

"Nah. I won't want to put it back on if I take it off." He leaned against a tall pine with no limbs for about seven or eight feet from the ground.

"I'm going to call back with an update." I reached for the hip strap on the backpack and pulled off the little radio Paul had given us this morning as part of his bag of gear.

I keyed the mic and realized the stupid little thing wasn't even on, so I switched it on and heard some static. "Base camp, this is Trig and Mark. How copy?"

Mark and I both sat quietly listening for a few seconds before I made the same call again. Still we heard only static. Finally, I faintly heard broken words, "Tri…this is Ma…John…copy?" I knew it was Wayne, and I'd met John last night.

I looked up at Mark and said, "Wow, these little plastic things suck." Then to the radio, "Wayne, you're broken. I'll try base camp again later. Out." I shrugged.

"Is this your first baby?" Mark asked out of nowhere.

"Yeah, first. Stay focused, Mark. We should be thinking of only one thing until we get off this trail, right?" I said it even though I knew I wasn't following my own advice.

"Yeah, you're right. Man, woman, boy, and girl."

"Good. Yeah. You got any feelings?" He looked at me with a cocked head. "You know, like feelings about where they might be."

"Ahh…no. Should I?" He questioned himself. I shrugged and he went on. "I don't think I know enough to have a gut feeling yet. You?"

"Yeah. I think they're in this section."

"What makes you think that?" He leaned forward to stretch his back.

"Don't know. Let's go. We should hit the canyon in about three miles, right? Less than an hour at the rate we've been traveling. You still up for taking lead and setting pace?"

"Yes, ma'am." He pushed himself away from the tree, lifted my pack like it was empty, and held it up for me to wiggle into. Then he took off at his lightning hiking speed, and I kept pace, at least for a while.

Mark called back, "You okay?"

I realized I was losing ground. "Mark, keep this pace as long as I can see you. I won't slow you down, but that canyon is going to pop right out of the forest at about the eight-mile point, so be careful." I think he went even faster after I spoke, and occasionally I forced myself to jog up to catch him, but I must've looked down for a second and he was gone. "Mark," I yelled and then started jogging.

Chapter Twenty-nine

"Jules, it's Karrie. It's not an emergency, but I wanted to let you know I've been having some pain. It feels kind of like menstrual cramps. They aren't too intense and they're sporadic, but I'm a little concerned. Please give me a call when you get this message." I hung up and looked at the clock; it was four thirty, and I still hadn't heard a word from Trig. I didn't really expect her home until late, but I thought sure she would call. As confused and hurt as I was concerning Trig's feelings about our baby, I missed her and wanted her home with me. I had no idea what we were going to do or how we were going to salvage things, but I was scared for her and me.

My cell phone rang as I was pacing around the kitchen island. I grabbed it and answered without looking—confident it was Trigena finally within cell service again. "Hello."

"Hi, Karrie. How are you doing?" Jules's calm voice came through the line.

"Oh, hi. I'm doing okay. I'm a little scared."

"Don't be scared. It's probably Braxton-Hicks. Tell me what you're experiencing and how you feel."

"Well, I felt an intense cramp at about ten thirty or so, but it was just one, and when it passed without any after it, I convinced myself it was nothing. I went to lunch with a friend, and when I came back I lay down for a nap, and another bad one woke me up. I'm not sure if it was really that bad or if it was just the shock of it waking me. I got up and started doing some things around the house, and over the past couple hours I've had maybe as many as four, kind of randomly."

"Okay, and have you had one since we've been on the phone?"

"No. The last one was right before I called you about ten minutes ago." I looked down at my watch. I thought I was keeping better track of when they were coming, but I wasn't sure when it was.

"Okay. Sounds good. He might be getting anxious, but it's probably not the real thing just yet. Braxton Hicks are pretty commonly experienced in the third trimester, especially for first-time moms. The muscles in your uterus can tighten for as long as thirty to sixty seconds. It's just your uterus preparing for the real thing. This could be early labor, but I don't think we're going to be having a baby tonight. Drink a big glass of water. Sometimes being dehydrated can cause your uterus to get a little grouchy. And try to relax and get some rest. If this is the beginning of labor, you'll want to be rested and ready for the work later. First-time mommas usually have a long road to travel. Maybe Trigena could run you a nice bath—"

I totally lost it when she said Trig's name, and I started crying. "Trig's not here." I grabbed a Kleenex and wiped my nose.

"Where's Trigena? Are you okay? What happened?" Jules was firing questions at me, probably thinking the worst.

"She was called to a search-and-rescue up north. She didn't want to go, but I pushed her to help. She's so good. She has an instinct for finding people." I was practically bawling at this point. I'm surprised Jules could even understand what I was saying. "There's a child lost, and I wanted her to be there. Now she's not back, and I can't have our baby without her. And I'm scared she's hurt or—"

"Slow down, slow down. Is there someone you can call to stay with you?"

I sniffed hard and blew my nose. "I could call Dani and Justine. You met them."

"Yes. Good idea. Have them come over. I'm sure Trigena is fine, and she'll be back as soon as she can. But you need to get some rest and take care of you right now and not worry. That baby needs a safe, comfortable place to be welcomed into. Take some deep breaths, make some nice chamomile tea, and call your friends. Try to just lay low and get some rest. I can come over if you need me to, but until the contractions are closer and harder, he's not going to be coming tonight."

"Okay. I'll call Dani and Justine. Thanks, Jules. I'm sorry I'm such a wreck."

"It's going to be fine, and you're okay. You're not the first pregnant woman to call me crying, and if you're the last, then I've done something wrong. If Dani and Justine aren't home, you call me back, and I'll come over, okay? I'm sure Trigena will be home very soon. Try not to worry. Now make some tea, get your girls over to take care of you, and relax so you can have a baby," Jules said in her sing-song voice, assuring me that I had only one thing to worry about right now.

"I can't have him before she gets home. I can't do it without her." I started crying again. I hated losing control like this, but I was scared. I knew something was wrong. She wanted to get back to us. Or maybe she didn't want to come back. Something had happened, and I could only think the worst.

"It's going to be okay. I really don't think he'll arrive before she does, and if she's not back when the baby decides he's coming, then you'll make her proud by having him all wrapped up and ready for her to hold when she walks in." Jules had a way of calming me.

"Okay." I took a deep breath and thought through my plan for the night.

"Karrie, listen to me. Start writing down the times of your contractions and give them a ranking of one through ten, with ten being the most painful. If you have five or more that rank seven or higher on the pain scale, are less than ten minutes apart and a minute long, or your water breaks, call me back no matter what. Okay?"

"Okay."

"Now get some rest. I'll wait to hear from you."

I couldn't decide if I felt better after talking to her or not, but at least I had a plan and wouldn't have to make more trips around our kitchen island. I put the kettle on and punched Dani's contact and let the phone ring.

"Hey, girl," she answered.

I swallowed down my tears. "Can you and Justine come over?"

"Sure. Are you okay?"

"I'm sorry to keep doing this to you, but Trig is with RJ on a search-and-rescue mission. I'm having some contractions. I sure would appreciate it if you could come stay with me until she gets home."

"Of course. We'll be right there."

Just as I sat down with my tea, the bell rang. Dani and Justine came in with hugs. I took them into the living room and told them about the call Trigena had received.

"She'll be home soon. I'm sure of it. Let Dani and me get that tub thing set up."

We pulled out all the stuff in the plastic storage container that Jules had brought over three weeks earlier, and among the three of us, we had the tub set up in no time. I hadn't had a contraction since they arrived, so I was convinced the pain was gone for the night. And maybe Jules was right. Maybe it was just practice contractions.

By nine they encouraged me to go to bed, but I couldn't fall asleep, because every time I started to, my uterus would tighten. Besides that, all I could think about was Trigena. I knew something was wrong now. When I called Natalie she hadn't heard from RJ, but she reminded me how once they got started on something, their focus often caused them to forget about others who might be worrying about them. I must've dozed off, because at midnight I woke when I heard our phone ring.

Chapter Thirty

I woke up to wet snowflakes falling on my face and a throbbing headache. When I tried to push myself up, my left arm crumpled under my weight, and I screamed as the pain shot up from my forearm to my shoulder. It was so intense I felt it deep in my chest, and my whole body went weak. For just a few minutes, I was sure I was going to pass out. I lay completely still, panting through the pain. I finally slowed my breathing and deeply inhaled the cold, crisp air. The intake of oxygen cleared my head a bit, and I looked around, taking in the red-and-yellow rock and sandstone cliffs that surrounded me. It was coming back, but where was Mark? I sat there struggling to remember what had happened.

Mark must've stayed on the trail, and when I ran after him, I found the canyon, or it found me. I used my right arm and pushed myself up to a sitting position and leaned against the rock wall. The movement brought back the intense pain, and I started taking in quick, short breaths again to get through it. The pain subsided a bit, and I tried to focus. I looked up the steep canyon wall. I could barely see the top; it looked like maybe eighteen or twenty feet up. Even if I wasn't injured, I couldn't scale that wall without ropes.

My arm kept throbbing mercilessly; I was sure it was broken. I couldn't think of what to do. I just sat there, probably in shock, watching the snow come down in huge flakes. The weather seemed to have turned in a second, but when I finally got my arm into a position to see my watch, I was aware enough to realize three hours had gone by since the last time I made a radio call—a useless one. The radio—I could try to make a call; maybe someone would hear me. The rescue team must be going crazy at the base camp, especially since I'd hoped to be returning to camp by now. I remained still for a few more minutes, slowly getting my bearings back and remembering my years of survival training.

Finally, I was thinking clearly. I assessed my condition, and, besides a sore hip, a few scrapes on my face, and a banged-up shoulder, it appeared the gash on the side of my head and my arm were the only serious injuries. My head was matted with blood, but the cold air had stopped the scalp wound from bleeding. It probably looked worse than it was. The impact had knocked me out and the bump was egg-sized, but my headache was dull by comparison to the sharp pain in my arm. When I looked back up the cliff I'd fallen down, I realized how truly lucky I was. If I'd broken a leg or seriously injured my head, I could be in an extremely dangerous position. As many times as I'd taught techniques for those conditions, I'd never actually been in such a situation and never wanted to be. Even having all the best training and skills didn't guarantee you'd survive difficult injuries in harsh weather and challenging terrain.

I lowered my arm into my lap and reached for the radio on the hip strap of my daypack. The little plastic radio, purchased because of its small size and light weight with significant donations from generous community members, was smashed. The screen was busted, and the back of the case that held the lithium battery was missing, as was the battery. I looked around for the battery, but even if I had found it, I doubted the radio would work. It was destroyed. That explained the pain in my hip. I'd obviously landed on my left side. A wave of doubt consumed me, and for a few minutes, I continued to sit motionless, watching the snow begin to cover my legs.

I slowly got to my feet, using only my legs to lift myself upright and staggering like a drunk woman as I rose. I held my left arm tight to my body with my right arm; keeping it still didn't alleviate the pain, but it helped a little. I didn't want that nauseous feeling flooding through me again because I'd go back to the ground if it did. I needed to get my pack off and see what I had in it for first aid, but the thought of moving my arm to get it off stopped me where I stood. I contemplated my options for what seemed like hours and finally lowered my left arm along the side of my body, with the help of my right hand, to prepare to release the weight from my back, but the agony dropped me to my knees.

"Damn it!" I yelled at the top of my lungs, and my eyes began to water. I heard my voice echo through the canyon. I didn't want to cry. It was too cold, and I had to get out of this hole in the ground. And home. For the first time since I woke up I thought of Karrie. I just kept thinking how stupid I was for coming out here. She needed me, and instead of being by her side I was stuck out in a canyon with a broken arm. As much as I was emotionally punishing myself, thoughts of Karrie motivated me to make it through this and get back to her. I knew I had to take it slowly or I'd pass out, and if I went out again, I might not survive the cold. Slowly and methodically, over the course of nearly an hour I managed to get my pack off and immobilize my arm under my parka next to my body with long strips of duct tape wrapped around my chest. I even found some ibuprofen and took four pills, forcing myself to drink as much water as I could tolerate.

I got everything back together and stood up to look for a way out of the canyon. I still felt weak and was a little afraid of moving, but I had to do something since darkness was only a couple of hours away. I'd lost so much time. I looked down at my pack, staring at it like it was a foreign object. I didn't want to leave it. I knew better than to abandon my supplies, but I also knew I couldn't carry it on my back. I walked twenty or thirty feet in both directions, looking for a quick solution. Everything hurt with each step, but at least I wasn't going to pass out now.

I wasn't that far from base camp. If I could just get out of this hole, I could get back before dark. But all I saw in both directions were more steep canyon walls and no easy way to climb out. I tied my rope around my pack and my waist and slowly dragged the thirty-pound weight behind me. I stumbled down the canyon floor in the direction I thought would take me closer to base camp, pulling the pack over obstacles along the way. It wasn't a good solution, but I couldn't think of anything else. As I walked I felt the moisture running down my brow. Thinking I was sweating, I ran a dirty-gloved hand through my hair, pushing my hat off, and pulled my hand away to find it coated with coagulating blood. All the activity must have started my head wound bleeding again. I picked up my blood-soaked stocking hat and pulled it down tight on my head, hoping it would stop the blood flow.

I'm sure shock was having an effect on me, but I had no sense of time. I didn't even notice it was getting dark until it began to be difficult to see. I walked back to the pack I was still dragging to get my headlamp, but it wasn't there. I must have lost it when I fell. I didn't remember putting it away when we'd turned them off this morning, so it was likely still on my head until the fall. I hadn't noticed it in my loopy state, and while I was sure I hadn't gone too far, I wasn't about to go back. My progress was too slow to lose any gains I'd made. I was going to have to settle in for the night because it was becoming dangerous to keep moving in the poor visibility. The terrain of the canyon floor was pretty flat but there were some large boulders, and in my current state, I didn't want to risk further injury.

I had very few options for shelter, so I settled for a small overhang that would keep some of the snow off me if it started coming down again. I didn't know when, but sometime during my slow walk, the snow had stopped. I collected as much brush and as many small sticks as I could find and pulled over a large branch that had fallen into the canyon. I wasn't sure if I could keep a fire going all night, but if I could warm my military MRE a bit and get some warm food and water in my body, I could probably stay warm enough in my bag through the night. I had no idea what I was going to do in the morning. The options to get out of the canyon weren't looking good. The small portion of map I had with me cut off with only a corner of the canyon. I was even considering walking back the other way, but right now I only wanted to make it through the night.

Flashes of Karrie worrying about me kept running through my head. How was I ever going to make it as a mom if I would leave my pregnant wife two weeks from her due date? I had to focus on getting warm and getting some food in my system, or I wouldn't have a choice about how to make things right. I was only slightly aware that I hadn't eaten since I left base camp nearly ten hours ago. Having one arm strapped to me made gathering wood and preparing a shelter difficult, but I managed to get a pretty good bundle of sticks together. I was hopeful that I could make it last several hours if I kept the fire small.

I felt a little better after I ate some warmed-up spaghetti, which was actually one of the better MRE food choices. I'd ended up with it by chance, since I'd just grabbed two without looking. I was usually a little choosier, but when I left early this morning, I didn't think I would be eating any of the military's gourmet meals. I was sure grateful for it now; thankfully I'd listened to RJ when he insisted I take some.

I cleaned up all the packaging, which was by far the biggest disadvantage of these GI meals—there was more packaging than food. I put some more fuel on the fire and then went to relieve myself. As I walked back to the fire, I stopped short and stared at the silhouette across the blaze.

Chapter Thirty-One

I heard the landline ring, which was unusual. I didn't know anyone even knew that number anymore. The only reason we kept the stupid thing was for the fax capability, and we rarely even used that anymore. Once in a while someone would want Trig to fax an estimate—old school. I got up to answer it just in case the number had been on some leftover roster of the search-and-rescue group and glanced at the digital clock next to our bed. It was after two in the morning. I'd fallen asleep, and Trig still wasn't here. Panic rushed through me, and I staggered when my knees started to give, but when the phone rang again I forced myself forward.

I ran to the front room, where it sat on a small desk Trigena sometimes used, but mostly it just collected papers that she stacked in neat little piles. Dani was talking on the phone. I had forgotten Justine and Dani were here. "What is it?" I yelled.

She held up her hand and continued to nod and mumble, "Mmm-hmm, okay." I walked back and forth in front of her, waiting. Finally, she hung up.

"What is it? Is Trig okay? Where are they? Why isn't she home?" I was in her face, firing questions in a bit of hysterics.

Dani stood up and put both hands on my shoulders. "Calm down, K. Just listen." By then Justine was standing next to me. She was waiting too, but much more patiently.

"Dani, tell me what's going on," I demanded and jerked out of her grip. I was scared, and not knowing anything was making me crazy. I was also mad at myself for falling asleep when my wife was still not home. How could I have rested?

"Natalie's on her way over. She's heard from RJ and wants to give you all the—"

I grabbed her shoulders and screamed at her. "Where is Trigena? Tell me what's going on. Dani!" Before I could do any real harm, Justine wrapped her arms around me.

"Karrie, Trigena is missing. RJ has had the crew up most of the night. He said to tell you he *would* find her." She paused, and I crumpled to the floor in Justine's arms. Dani sat down with us and said, "Natalie wrote down everything he said with all the information. She'll be right over to tell you everything they know, but she said RJ told her to remind you of how good Trigena is in the woods, and that she had the right gear with her."

"Why was she alone?" I was barely audible through my sobs. The fire was gone; terror had taken over. And every time I started to get angry my belly would tighten and I'd have to pause, but the sensation was more annoying than painful now.

"Dani, call Jules and let her know," Justine said while still sitting behind me on the floor with her arms wrapped tightly around my shoulders. I fell over into her lap and just curled up.

"Yeah, okay." Dani went for my cell phone, which still lay on my nightstand.

After what seemed like hours the doorbell rang, and Dani ran to the door. I rose for the first time since I'd collapsed in Justine's lap. Dani had run around the house getting blankets and pillows, creating a little nest for Justine and me.

As soon as Natalie closed the door, I started talking to her. I didn't even greet her. "Why did I tell her to go?"

"Oh, Karrie. I know, I know." Natalie lowered herself onto the floor with us.

"Where are your kids?" I asked. I don't know why I asked her that, but I was immediately distracted by the thought of her two young children.

"My mom is with them. They're fine." She sat there waiting for me to come back to the real issue.

"Natalie, tell me what happened." I sat shaking in a ball on the floor with three women trying to comfort me.

Chapter Thirty-two

It was a small girl with curly blond hair—my dream. Was I dreaming?

Her long curls hung down below the edges of her sock hat, which had a few little twigs poking out of it. Her big, puffy jacket made her look tiny. I couldn't tell if her little face was dirty like the girl in my dream, but her features were the ones I saw four months ago, right down to the Sorel boots on her feet. They were clearly too big for her. She stood a few feet from the fire like a little statue. I took one step forward, and she looked up.

"Samantha? I'm Trigena. I was sent with a team to find you."

She crumpled to the ground, and I ran to her. Her tired little body had evidently given up the fight. I sat on the ground next to her tiny frame and pulled her on to my lap. With my right arm wrapped around her, I scooted on the ground toward the fire. I wrapped her in my sleeping bag and set her on my lap in front of the fire. I got out the remains of the MRE and warmed the applesauce packet and heated some more water with Gatorade mix in it. I held her tight to me. This poor sixty-pound girl had survived alone and had wandered all day long. It was a miracle she was here.

"Samantha, wake up, honey." I held her face against mine and spoke her name over and over softly. Finally, her eyes opened a little bit.

"Here, baby. Take small sips. We're going to be okay. They're looking for us—my friends. They'll find us."

All I got from her while she was eating the warm applesauce was a few grunts and a mumbled thank you. When she finished, I pulled out some crackers and the peanut butter pack, but she shook her head. I nodded back but encouraged her to drink all the sports drink. I was sure she was dehydrated.

"Okay, now we need to bundle up in this sleeping bag so we can keep warm through the night." I pulled off her dirty, pink down jacket and tucked her in the bag as quickly as I could. Maternal instincts I never knew I had flooded through me as I rushed to keep her warm.

"Are you an angel?" These were the first real words she had spoken to me.

"No, baby. I'm just an ordinary woman." I smiled at her, and she pulled me down to her and hugged my neck.

"You're a mommy?"

"Not yet," I said, and a vision of my beautiful wife pacing around the house came to mind. I had to get out of here and go home. I snuggled into the bag next to her, doing my best to wrap myself around her while keeping pressure off my injured arm. It was hurting again, but it was more of an ache than the initial searing pain I'd felt.

I woke up to a slight change to the light around me. It wasn't light out, but it was a different color. I could see only a few inches in front of my face, but all I really spotted was white. I was amazed that I'd slept at all, but sheer exhaustion and shock had probably put me right to sleep. I felt the warm body next to me and knew Samantha had fallen asleep too. I didn't want to move because I feared waking her, but I was sure I hadn't changed from the position I fell asleep in, and I was aching all over. I squirmed around a little, but the small person beside me didn't move an inch.

After wiggling for several minutes, I was finally out of the bag and could better take in my surroundings. A dusting of snow covered the top of most of the sleeping bag, which I had pushed deep under our poorly built shelter. The fresh blanket of snow was beautiful, but now that the storm had passed, it was actually colder. After being snuggled in that warm bag, I was thanking God, and especially thanking RJ, for making me bring it. I wasn't sure how Samantha had survived the previous night, but the only way we would've survived last night without it was if I'd kept a fire going constantly, and I'm not sure I could've stayed awake.

Thinking of the fire got me in gear. I didn't want to wander too far with Samantha still snuggled in the bag, so I started pulling pieces off the brush I'd used for the shelter. Being restricted to one arm was really getting annoying, and all the movement was bringing back the pain, but it was also making me warmer, so the pros might have slightly outweighed the cons. With a little more work and the sacrifice of part of my first-aid handbook, I got the fire going.

By the time I finally looked at my watch the dial showed eight fifteen, and the sun was starting to peek over the canyon wall. I knew I shouldn't waste a single minute of daylight since the days were so short, and I really didn't want to risk another night in these extreme conditions. I warmed some water for more Gatorade—I sure would have loved a cup of coffee but was grateful for anything to put in the water. I still had one more MRE; I remembered being reluctant to put in a second one. They're so heavy and bulky. I opened it and pulled out the jelly pack—grape, my favorite, and the large crackers. There were two crackers in each pack, and they were as dense as quarter-inch particleboard. They tasted a little like it too, but they would provide enough energy for Samantha and me to get started. I put the jelly on a rock a few inches from the fire and scooted over to the bag where the little dirty-faced girl slept peacefully. I hated to wake her. I hadn't made her talk last night. I was in no condition to initiate a search on my own, and it seemed best to just get her warm and keep her safe, but eventually I was going to need to find out if she knew where the rest of her family was.

I looked around at my surroundings for a few seconds and realized we were stuck. I remembered some shorter canyon walls along my walk yesterday—short enough, in some cases, I might've been able to hoist Samantha up to the ledge. But even if I could push her over it, I wouldn't be able to climb out on a rope she could secure for me. I tried not to worry because I knew RJ wouldn't stop until he found me, even if it was because he was afraid Karrie would kill him. I couldn't quite decide what to do. Perhaps leaving the spot where I'd fallen in might've been a mistake, but at the time I'd been sure I'd find a way out. Also I wouldn't have found Samantha, but now that I had her, maybe I should go back there. Eventually the team would figure out where Mark and I got separated and begin the search there.

I put those thoughts aside for a minute and lightly touched Samantha's little cheek—the tiny bit of pink surrounded by dirt. "Samantha, wake up, honey. We need to get rescued today. Samantha." I spoke her name softly.

Her crystal-blue eyes looked up at me, and she smiled for just a second. Then the worry and fear from all she'd experienced appeared. She crinkled her little eyebrows, and tears began to form in her eyes.

"It's okay, baby. We're going to be okay."

She sniffed and wiped her eyes with her sleeve.

"Come on out, honey. Let's get your coat and shoes on." I'd put her jacket and her little boots next to the fire as soon as I got it going, and they were nice and warm inside. She didn't complain or even speak; she just crawled out of the warm space, and I wrapped her in her jacket. She pulled on her boots and looked at me as if to say, "What's next?"

I held out the little tin mug from my mess kit, and she took it in her mittened hands and started to put it to her month. "Careful, sweetheart. It's very hot." She'd already pulled it back when it touched her lips. "Blow on it."

I squeezed out a blob of purple jelly on one of the crackers and handed it to her, and did the same with the other cracker for me. I ate quickly and started packing. I was beginning to wonder if she'd clammed up on me or if she was still sleepy, but finally she spoke.

"Where are we going?" She'd already realized the obvious. We weren't getting out of this canyon soon.

"Well...remember how I told you there was a team looking for your family?" She nodded and I went on. "I think it would be best if we went back to the place where I fell, because I think they'll start looking for me there."

Samantha took a bite of the cracker and sat on a rock next to the fire. She looked up at the red canyon wall next to where we slept. The other wall was about thirty feet away on the opposite side, and the dry riverbed next to us was covered in snow. Besides the crack of the dry wood in our fire, the wind coming through the canyon was the only sound.

"Samantha, can you tell me how you got separated from your family?"

"I got lost," she mumbled.

"Can you tell me about it?" I started packing up our gear. I'd managed to get my little camp stove set up with one hand, but I was having trouble getting it packed back into its carrying case. Samantha held out her hand for me to give her the mess I was making. I did, and she deftly folded up the equipment.

"It's just like my dad's," she said. Then after a long pause she spoke again. "Mom asked me to go get water. We were camping a long way from the stream, and I didn't want to go by myself, but my brother wanted to go with Dad. We spotted some elk when we hiked in, and they wanted to go take some pictures. I wanted to go too, but Dad said no." She blinked back tears and continued to pack items neatly in my pack.

I just sat there watching her. "He never tells me no, so I was mad. I ran down the hill toward where I knew the stream was, but I must've gotten turned around. It wasn't there. The next thing I remember is the canyon walls." She pointed at the wall next to us.

"Did you fall into the canyon or walk in?" I asked. If she'd walked in, then we could walk out, but she'd been moving for at least a day and could've been going in circles. I wasn't confident that we could find her entry point.

"I didn't fall." She paused, evidently thinking about it for a minute. "I'd remember that, wouldn't I?"

"I think so."

"So your mom...she was at the campsite?"

"Yeah. I was supposed to be bringing water to help her clean up the cooking gear so we could walk out." Tears began to stream down her face. "Are Mom and Dad and Willy okay? It's my fault. If I hadn't been so mad I would've been able to find the stream. I'm a good backpacker. I've been in the woods since before I could walk." Samantha sniffed hard and held her head up and then held my perfectly packed bag up for me to admire.

"Yes. I can see you're a very good backpacker. Can you help me with the sleeping bag?"

"Yeah. That's easy." She rushed over and started stuffing it in the carrying sack. I only helped when the last few inches wouldn't go in. With both of us shoving it, we finally got it tied up. I started to attach the rope on my bag to drag it again, but she lifted the bag and threw the pack on her back. It was light by normal backpacking standards, but it probably weighed close to twenty-five pounds. She looked so tiny under the pack, but the weight didn't seem to faze her.

"You're very strong."

She smiled up at me. "Does your arm hurt?"

I hadn't thought about it for a while, so I'd either gotten used to the pain or it was feeling a little better. Perhaps it wasn't broken after all. "It's not too bad right now. Why don't you carry that for a little while, and I can give you a break and put it on my good shoulder in a bit."

"I can carry this for hours." She started walking.

"Where you going?" She was heading in the opposite direction than I'd planned to walk.

"This is the way out."

"How can you be sure?" I started to open the map. Though it didn't have this part of the canyon on it, I thought I knew where we were, and if we continued in the direction I'd been going all day yesterday, I was sure we were getting farther and farther from the base camp. I also felt our best hope was to get pulled out by the team instead of trying to find a path out of the canyon.

"I just know." She walked over to a broken tree limb about ten yards from our campsite. I simply stood and watched her.

"I broke limbs every fifty steps. This is the last one I broke before I saw you." She held up the broken limb.

I stood there staring at her. This amazing child had survived on her own, knew how to mark a trail, and was as strong as a person twice her size. I looked at my watch—almost nine thirty. It had taken longer to get ready than I thought. I couldn't decide what to do: follow this child's instincts or my own. Mine seemed a little off right now, but I also knew if we kept going down the canyon we'd be going farther from the area my map covered, and I'd be completely lost instead of the sort-of lost I felt right now.

I looked in the direction Samantha was walking, then back in the direction I thought I'd come from. She wanted to take us south. That was the direction of the base camp, but I didn't know how far off course I was. I wasn't even sure I could find the location where I fell. I hesitated too long. Samantha finally turned back and glared at me. With both hands on her hips, leaning slightly forward from the weight of the pack, she reminded me of Karrie being disgusted with me always trying to be in control. She told me I should trust sometimes.

"Are you coming?" Samantha asked.

"Yeah, okay, lead the way."

Samantha's short legs set a consistent but slow pace. At first, I had trouble adjusting myself to her speed, but after only about an hour I was grateful to be going so slowly. My arm ached from the tips of my fingers deep into my shoulder, but my head hurt even more. I'd practically forgotten about my head wound. I hadn't taken off my hat or dared to unwrap my arm. I had no idea what my head looked like, but I was beginning to be sure my arm was broken. It was feeling so bad now that I just wanted to lie down in the snow and cry. If I slipped or made a misstep, the agony shot up through me like a scalding-hot metal rod. And my vision was distorted from the pain in my head.

I walked on methodically. I was trusting, for sure. I couldn't do anything but put one foot in front of the other. Somehow I'd gotten behind again. When I finally looked up from the small prints in the snow I could barely see Samantha. I realized as sweat poured down the side of my face in this fourteen-degree weather that I was in bad shape. I lowered myself in the snow and called out, "Samantha." My voice was dry, and I barely made a sound, but she heard me. I must've blacked out, because the next minute she was kneeling beside me pulling the sleeping bag out of the sack.

"You have a bad fever." Her eyes were wide and she bit her lower lip. "This is bad."

"Motrin," I croaked. "In the pack."

"Okay, good." She panted and struggled to pull the bag up and cover me.

The next thing I remember she was holding the tube of my Camelbak to my lips and two little orange pills in her hand.

I tried to get my right arm out from under the bag to take them, but she pushed it back down. "Open," she commanded, and I obeyed. The water on my throat helped. I had no idea I'd gotten in such bad shape. I was lucky we'd made it through the night. "Give me a few minutes for the Motrin to kick in, and I'll be ready to go again."

"I don't know." I heard her voice quiver. This young girl had been so strong for so long. Finally, she'd reached her limits, and tears ran down her face. "I don't know what to do. I can bandage...and—"

"Samantha, we're going to be okay. I can get up. We'll keep going." I started to stand, and she watched as I stumbled and nearly passed out.

"Trigena, you can't go." She looked around us and jumped to her feet. "I'll make a big fire."

Chapter Thirty-three

It wouldn't have taken Natalie so long to tell me everything if I could've just listened to her, but I interrupted every sentence with a question she was either about to answer or didn't know how to respond to. I paused, oddly calm by the time she finished.

Natalie finally spoke again. "RJ will find her. He won't stop until he does."

I leaned back against the leg of the solid-oak futon Trig had built. As with every room in our house, Trigena had made all the furniture in this one.

"We had a huge fight before she left," I said without looking up.

"Oh, honey," Justine said and took my hand.

"She never wanted kids." I laughed and rubbed my giant abdomen. "Why would she agree to this if she didn't want kids?" I was still laughing a little too loud. They all three just stared at me. I'm sure they thought I'd lost my mind. I suppose you could call it that, with all the stress, the fight, the cramping, and now my wife missing.

Dani scooted over closer and took my other hand. "Because she loves you, Karrie."

"If she'd told me how strongly she felt about not wanting kids…"

"Then you would've been okay with that?" Dani said. "You changed her. She was lost and struggling to know how to be happy, and you changed all that. You never saw the Trig we knew." She nodded toward Justine.

Justine continued with the story. "When she met you...actually I'd have to say the day she first saw you painting in that little room, she changed."

Dani went on. "We were scared for her 'cause she hadn't even talked to you, yet she was convinced you were the one for her. It was weird how she knew you'd be great together." She stopped and pulled the tissue box off the coffee table that matched the craftsman-style futon. Tears were streaming down my face; I had no idea why I was crying. I remembered falling in love with her. It was the best time of my life.

"After the two of you started dating she told me you wanted kids, and I was sure that was the end of the relationship. I thought she'd run like she did in every other relationship I ever saw her in. But she loved you, and I don't think she ever loved anyone else. She told me once that maybe you would change your mind. When I warned her how dangerous it was to count on that, she just winked at me and then said, 'Well, then maybe I'll change mine.'"

"She tried," I said. "I know she tried, and I know she would be a great mom. I guess it's just not who she is." I looked at my round middle again, pulled my hands away from the girls, and cradled my belly. "What am I going to do? I can't raise him by myself, and I can't live without her."

Natalie chimed in. "She's going to be fine. You have to trust her skills and RJ's."

"Oh, God. I was thinking of me. She could be injured or—"

"No. No, K. She's going to be home with you before the baby comes, and you guys will work this out. She'll love that baby as much as she loves you as soon as she sees that she can do it. She's just scared. She's out there now trying to get back to you. I know Trigena, and I know how much she loves you." Justine spoke quickly.

Chapter Thirty-four

I have foggy memories of the rest of the morning. It was like I was in a dream where I was running but couldn't get anywhere. I struggled and struggled to go faster, but the harder I worked at it the slower I went. I just kept talking to Samantha so she wouldn't take off on her own. I had no idea what the solution was, but I knew it would be worse if we were separated again. We weren't more than five to seven miles away from the base camp. There should be a big search team there now, and sooner or later, and I really hoped for sooner, someone would find us. I was more worried about Samantha. I was no longer an asset but instead a huge liability for her. She was smart and resourceful, and if I could've kept going I'm sure she would've led us out of the canyon, and then maybe I could've navigated back to base camp. Now I was keeping us in one spot.

"I'll get you all wrapped up in the sleeping bag, and I can walk back out."

"No. Stay with me. Let me get warm again, and we'll start together." I went back and forth from miserably hot to freezing. I was freezing now, and she had me wrapped up tight. I must've blacked out for a few minutes because when I looked around she was gone.

"Samantha!" I tried to yell, but her name barely came out in my dry, weak voice.

"I'm here. I got some wood. Some of it's dry enough for me to use to build a fire with, and I dug up some pine needles from an overhang just over there." She pointed.

"You scared me." I tried to get my right arm out to touch her, but I was wrapped too tight, and I didn't have the strength to struggle.

"I'll try to get this started." She looked at the pile of sticks and needles she had. "I'm not very good at making fires. My brother teases me."

I rose a bit so I could see what she was doing. "You'll find matches and a lighter in the front pocket of the pack."

Samantha dug them out and held them up, clearly waiting for more instruction.

"You should clear the snow." I panted, trying to hold myself up to watch her. She moved the snow away quickly with her boot and then brushed it down to the ground with her hands.

"Okay. Now the little stuff, right?"

She began making a pile.

"Yeah. Just a little though. No. That's too much." I cautioned her as she picked up a handful of pine needles. "They're probably a little damp, and if you just have a few you can get them dry enough to start."

It was a tedious process that took about an hour before she had a real fire going, but her patience and persistence helped her get the mostly wet materials going one tiny branch at a time. By the time it was going well I was barely conscious, but I kept hanging on.

"Okay. I'm going now," Samantha said quietly.

I was so nearly asleep I almost missed her words, but when they finally sank in, I jerked to a sitting position and then screamed as I jammed my arm. I must've scared her badly. She jumped away and stood staring down at me. Then she looked up the canyon wall.

"I heard someone talking." She backed away so she could see over the ledge and yelled, "We're down here. Help."

Chapter Thirty-five

We were all sitting in the kitchen when Natalie's phone rang. They were trying to get me to eat while they drank their third or fourth cup of coffee. It was nearly noon, and none of us had slept since Natalie arrived in the middle of the night. It seemed like hours since anyone had spoken. We all jumped and stared at her cell phone ringing and buzzing like a large square jumping bean on the kitchen island.

Natalie grabbed it. "Hello."

"Put it on speaker," I yelled. She didn't, but the smile on her face eased my concern.

"You tell her."

"Is it Trig?" I asked, taking the phone she extended toward me.

She shook her head no and wrapped her arms around me as I took the phone.

"Hello."

On the other end of a crackling line, I heard a young man's voice. "Is this Karrie?"

"Yes. This is Karrie. Is Trigena okay?"

"Yes." He sighed before he went on. "They found her this morning, and they're bringing her back to base camp now."

"Oh...I, oh. Thank you."

"Yes, ma'am. I'm glad I'm making *this* call," he said.

"When can I talk to her?"

"They should be back here in a couple of hours, and the doctor's here."

"The doctor?" I screeched. "Is she hurt?"

"Ah..."

"What happened to her? Is she okay? What—"

"He's here just to make sure she's okay—to check her over. I'm sure she's fine, but I was only asked to call you and tell you they found her. I'm sure she's okay." He was stammering and talking fast. "She should be back here in a couple hours. I'll have her call you when she gets in. Please don't worry."

"Don't worry! That's all I've been doing since she drove off."

Justine and Danielle were both hovering over me, with Natalie now, trying to calm me down.

"I'm sorry. I'll call with more news as soon as I get some." He was sure trying to get off the phone with me.

"Yes. Yes, call as soon as you know something." I realized I was yelling at the messenger.

"Yes, ma'am. Good-bye." The line went dead.

"They found her," I said to no one and everyone.

"Oh my gosh. That's great." Dani wrapped her arms around me.

"Yes, it is. That means she'll be home before dark," Justine said.

I sat still for a minute, partly relieved, but I also knew I wouldn't be able to completely relax until I had her in my arms. "I think she's hurt. There's a doctor waiting at the base camp for her."

"It's probably basic exposure. She's smart. She knows how to take care of herself out there," Natalie said.

"I wonder if they found the missing child." I don't know why I thought of the lost kid with all the other things on my mind, but I did.

"Karrie, you should lie down now. Maybe you can rest a little now." Justine tried to encourage me toward my bedroom.

"I don't want to. I don't think I could sleep,"

"Will you just go lie down for a few minutes?" Danielle asked.

I didn't have the energy left to argue anymore. So I got up and headed to the bedroom, leaving my three amazing friends standing in my kitchen.

Chapter Thirty-six

The next thing I remembered was being put on a stretcher. I saw RJ running around in a panic. "RJ," I called, my voice so soft and scratchy I could barely hear it, so I was sure no one else heard me. I tried again. "RJ." It was loud enough that one of the volunteers strapping me in heard me.

"She's conscious."

RJ hovered over me in a second. "Trig, we're getting you out of here."

"Karrie—call K," I squeaked out.

"Already done. I radioed back and Trevor called her on the sat phone," RJ assured me.

"Is she okay?"

"I'm sure she's fine. We'll get you back there as soon as we can."

I was moving now, and RJ was keeping pace with the two volunteers carrying the stretcher. I recognized Mark above my head. He was working like an ox, sweat dripping down the side of his face.

"Samantha? Where's she?"

"She's on her way back to the base camp with her family. They're all safe. The doctor's checking everyone out. They're probably a little dehydrated and suffering from exposure, but everyone will be fine."

"Oh." I panted a bit. I felt so tired. Probably the fever had taken all my strength. "That's good."

"She didn't want to leave you. That little girl may have saved your life." RJ had his hand on my good shoulder.

I could see tears in Mark's eyes. "Mark, I'm okay."

"It's my fault." He was visibly struggling to hold back the tears.

"Here, kid. Switch places with me," RJ said and tried to take the end of the stretcher from him.

"No. I got it." He sniffed hard and looked straight ahead.

"It wasn't your fault." I tried to say more but I just couldn't.

RJ bent down closer and spoke softly to me. "He hasn't slept. He backtracked the path all night long. He finally found the spot where you fell this morning when it got light. That's how we found you."

"Thank you, Mark," I said. He didn't even look down at me; he just kept moving at a pace that was probably pushing the lead man.

"Try to rest. There's a doctor at the cabin, and he knows we're on the way."

For the first time in hours I wasn't cold. They had every sleeping bag and blanket available wrapped around me. I tried to stay awake, but I must've been out immediately, because the next thing I knew I was lying on the sofa in Mac's cabin.

"Yeah, that arm's broken, and this head wound may be infected. It's probably what's causing the fever. Also she's seriously dehydrated. I'll get an IV started, and we can get her to Santa Fe to the hospital," a short, fat man with a gray beard said authoritatively.

"I have to go home." I must've shocked the doctor because he actually jumped.

"Hey there, Trigena. I'm Dr. Klein. We better get that arm set and some good antibiotics into your system."

"RJ, take me to Karrie."

"Doc, her wife's pregnant and due in a few days. I can drive her down to Albuquerque and take her to the hospital there, if you think she can travel okay," RJ explained to the doctor.

"Are you allergic to anything?" The doctor looked back at me while inserting the IV.

"No. Nothing." I spoke quickly, encouraged that he might let RJ take me home.

"Okay." The doctor sighed and searched through his bag. "I'm going to leave your arm the way it is. I'll secure it a little better. I'll also give you some pain medication and start you on some antibiotics." He continued to work as he talked. "Someone write this down."

Trevor walked over and stood next to him, holding a notepad and pen. "Tell me what to write." The doctor called out numbers and medications, and I saw Trevor scribbling down what he said.

I laughed and then stopped when it hurt so bad.

"What are you laughing at?" RJ asked.

"Only a doctor will be able to read Trevor's writing." I smiled at the young man.

"I wrote very neatly." He smiled back. "I'm so glad to see you back here."

"Thanks, Trevor. I'm glad to be here."

"Now all you guys get out of the cabin for a minute while I work on getting her arm stabilized for the drive down." Dr. Klein scolded the group of men who were hovering over me like curious children.

When we were alone he started helping me out of all my gear. I'd wrapped tape around my thermal undershirt, and taking it off and rewrapping it was going to be excruciating.

"Wow. I'm surprised you were able to get it wrapped up so well with only the use of one arm. I'm going to leave it as it is. They'll put you under to take it off and set it."

I vaguely remembered doing it. I'd really been out of it when I wrapped it up. The doctor helped me get my shirt back on and opened the door. The first thing through the door was a dirty-faced blond girl in a pink jacket. She rushed over and then stopped in front of me as if she was scared.

"Where'd you come from?" I held out my good arm for her. "You keep sneaking up on me out of nowhere."

She carefully climbed up on my lap. "They made me leave you out there. I wanted to wait and come with you."

"I know, sweetie, but they wanted to make sure you were okay."

She held on tight, her face buried in my shirt. I was still amazed that she'd survived alone and more amazed that she had saved me. We just sat there holding each other. Everyone seemed to be working on getting the base camp cleaned up so they left us alone.

I couldn't help but think this should never have happened. I hadn't met her parents yet, but I couldn't believe they'd sent her for water alone. I'd never send a child of mine out alone in the woods, no matter how skilled they were. I squeezed her a little tighter and smiled at the thought. I sounded like a mom.

"Can I stay with you?" Samantha's small voice was muffled in my shirt.

My heart melted, and all I could think about was my wife and the baby she was going to have soon. I wanted to get home.

"You know, Samantha, we're each other's guardian angel now, and you know what that means? That means we'll always be there for each other. You can call me anytime, and I can call you. We can visit each other and even go camping." She smiled up at me. "And you'll get to meet a brand-new baby, my son, who'll hear all about how brave you were and how you helped me." She squeezed tighter and it hurt like hell, but I just held on.

"Hello, Trigena. I'm William and this is my wife Donna. You saved our little girl's life. Thank you." He held out his hand, and Donna just stood shyly behind him.

"You're welcome. She's precious. Please watch out for her." I wanted to say so much more, but RJ came back in.

"You ready, Trig? I got your gear packed, and Mark's driving your truck down."

"Okay, sweetie," I said as Samantha held on. "Trevor." I called out, trying to see if he was in the cabin.

"Yeah. Whatcha need?" I heard from behind me.

"Got any more of that paper?"

He put the pad and pen in my hand. "Ahh, could you write down my number and address for Samantha." I couldn't write with one arm strapped to me and the other wrapped around Samantha.

"You got it. Fire away."

Finally, I got Samantha to let go, and with tears in her eyes she waved to me as RJ pulled out of the drive.

Chapter Thirty-seven

As soon as I got in the bed, I began to start calculating in my head how long it would take before I'd see Trigena again. I missed her. I had no idea what the future held for us, but I had to see her.

It normally took only about three hours to get to the Colorado border. I didn't know where they were exactly. I didn't have a map; I only had coordinates, and if I got up and started punching them in the computer to find out where she was, my three exhausted friends, who needed sleep as much as I did, would yell at me. I had to be happy with just estimating. So if it normally took three hours, the snow would likely double their time in the mountains, so I'd add about ninety minutes—that was four and a half plus the time it would take them to get Trig to the cabin and for the doctor to check her out.

As I was thinking through it all, I realized she must be hurt. I couldn't just lie in the bed. I got up and walked the length of our bedroom three or four times, and as I was thinking about what could've happened to Trig, I felt that familiar tightening in my abdomen.

"No, no, buddy. Not yet," I whispered to our son.

If walking around was causing the pain, I'd have to lie still. Maybe doing some more calculations about Trig's possible arrival time would ease my anxiety about her injury and allow me to rest. I also looked at the clock. It was 4:37 in the afternoon. How did it get so late? Considering all the math I'd done I was hoping to see Trig by midnight, and that was probably wishful thinking.

"Ahhh." I felt another twinge, more intense than the first, and when I looked at the clock it was 4:45. I was trying to remember what Jules had said. Was it five or more contractions that ranked seven on the pain scale, less than ten minutes apart? Or was it seven contractions? I definitely ranked that one above a seven. In the midst of all this processing, the pain shot like fire again.

"Fuck." Okay, that one was an eight, and the digital-clock numbers read 4:49. This had to be the real thing.

"Okay, son. Listen. We have to wait till your other mommy gets here. I can't do this without her." I tried to remain perfectly still, taking deep breaths while I slowly rubbed my belly. I almost dozed off, but another hard contraction brought me back to full consciousness. I was sure several minutes had passed so I could start all over with the count, but the clock showed 4:54. I had to start writing this down. When I began to get up, I nearly went to my knees from the agony of another contraction.

"Dani, Justine. Are you guys awake?" Hearing nothing, I walked to the living room to see my two friends sound asleep on the sofa bed. I knew how uncomfortable that thing was, so I felt badly for them. Natalie must have gone back home.

I reached for the pad of paper sitting by the phone and quickly wrote the times I could remember.

"Oh my God." Another one hit me, and I sat down on the bar stool at the kitchen island. "You aren't kidding around, are you?" I looked at the clock on the stove and realized if this didn't stop, I was probably going to have our baby before Trig got home.

"K, are you okay?" Justine raised up and looked across the big open room into the kitchen.

I realized then that I had no control and started to cry. "I think I'm having real contractions. I've had five very intense ones less than ten minutes apart. I can't have him until Trigena gets here. I can't do this without her. She doesn't want kids. What am I going to do?"

Justine was beside me with her arms wrapped around my shoulders before I could say anything else. "It's going to be okay. You can do this. She's trying to get back to you now." Justine's warm soft embrace must've calmed my baby boy for a bit, because I got a reprieve from the pain.

Dani was sitting up in the bed watching. "Let's call Jules."

I looked at the clock, slightly relieved. "It's been more than ten minutes. Maybe they've stopped for now. Maybe they were just Braxton-Hicks again. I had those before. She told me first-time moms have lots of false starts. Let's wait. I don't want to bother her." Just as I finished the sentence my strong little boy made himself known again. "Ooooh." I inhaled deeply and blew out a breath.

Dani was up and searching for my phone before I had a chance to try to convince her I was okay. I must have believed if Jules weren't here I wouldn't have a baby.

Chapter Thirty-eight

By the time we started down the snow-packed forest road it was after nine p.m. I was pretty out of it from the pain meds the doctor gave me, and I slept off and on through the initial treacherous drive. I heard RJ calling back on the little radio, checking on Mark behind us, but I wasn't sure what they were saying.

After we'd driven about an hour, I woke up with the realization that I hadn't called K on the sat phone when I was at the cabin. "Stop!" I yelled. I must have scared the shit out of RJ, because he tried to do just what I'd said and slammed on the brakes—the worst thing a person can do driving down a snow-packed mountain road.

"Trig, what the fuck?" He pulled his foot off the brake immediately and tried to gain control, but it was too late. The damage was done. I looked back to see Mark approaching us quickly and time seemed to slow; the experience was dream-like. RJ's truck seemed to be moving on its own as RJ spun the steering wheel first one way and then another. I saw the grille of my Toyota coming closer and closer.

"I'm sorry, RJ. Steer right…no, straighten up. Oh, shit. Watch the ditch."

"Shut up," he yelled and pulled the wheel back and forth as we fishtailed down the hill like a bobsled out of control.

"You got it." I exhaled. Then I saw a turn approaching and looked back to see Mark still trying to gain control. We still had too much momentum, and when RJ turned the wheel to make the turn, the truck did its own thing.

Mark managed to keep from hitting us, but only because RJ went into the ditch. Mark brought my truck safely to a stop about two hundred yards from where RJ and I sat. RJ was trying to drive out by switching back and forth from drive, then reverse, but he was only making it worse by spinning the tires and causing them to dig deeper into the snow.

He stopped and threw the truck into Park. "What the fuck were you thinking, Trig?" He looked over at me when we realized how stuck we were.

I couldn't help but laugh, probably in relief that we weren't wrapped around a tree or off the canyon on the other side of the road. "I'm sorry, dude. I…I wasn't…it's the drugs." I looked at him and he laughed too. "I forgot to call Karrie from the sat phone. She must be worried sick."

"Well, shit."

Chapter Thirty-nine

Jules arrived about twenty minutes after Dani had called her. While they were on the phone, Jules had told Dani to fill the birth pool up with water and have me do some weird squatting exercises, but I refused. I was lying in the bed as still as I could when she walked through the door. She helped me to relax and encouraged me to build a "cave" of safety and security so the baby would come.

"Hey there. You ready to have a baby?" Her cheery face did me in.

"No. I can't have him until Trig gets here. We have to work out our problems before I have a baby. I need her," I gasped through sobs.

"Oh, sweetie. I'm sure everything's going to be okay." She turned to Justine and Dani and spoke softly, but I could still hear her. "When was the last contraction?"

Justine looked at the pad of paper. "At 5:43, just a few minutes before you walked in."

"I'm here, you know," I said, no longer crying.

"Yes. Let's listen to his heartbeat."

"Jules, you're not listening to me. Is there anything we can do to stop the contractions? He can't come now."

"No, honey. I hear you and I'm listening to you. I know you're sad and scared. Trig will be here soon and so will your baby boy. Right now, I want you to focus on relaxing. Dig deep inside you to find the strength that I know you have, and find peace so you can safely welcome your baby boy when he makes his appearance. Is there anything we can do to help you get to that space? Do you need to have a good cry? Maybe you'd like to get into the pool with some candlelight and soft music?" Jules looked over at Dani and Justine, and they both jumped up to help. Jules opened her bags and pulled out the little monitor. "Karrie, it's going to be okay. Let's just see what this little guy's doing. Okay?"

"Okay." I sniffed back my tears and tried to relax. I was hoping she wouldn't hear anything that concerned her. Then I could just wait until Trig got home.

The room was silent while Jules rubbed the cool, blue jelly on my skin and put the Doppler against my belly. I immediately heard the familiar sound of the baby's heart, which sounded like pressurized air escaping rapidly from a tiny valve in quick spurts. Normally it was a calming sound that I could have listened to all day long, like the waves hitting a rock repetitively, but today I could tell it was faster and more irregular than any time before. I was sure that was a bad sign. My fear was confirmed when Jules looked up at me. Her brow was furrowed, and she shook her head slightly.

"He sounds really good. You just have a little more work to do."

Just as she finished, he made that fact known to me again. The contraction was so intense it took my breath away and seemed to last forever.

Chapter Forty

It seemed to take days to get the truck out, especially since I was basically useless. Mark and RJ put chains on the tires of my truck and spent about an hour digging the snow out from around RJ's truck, after the first couple of attempts at pulling it out almost put my truck in the ditch as well.

As they dug in the heavy snow, several other members of the rescue crew started making their way down the mountain as well. At one point, I think six of them were digging and pushing. All I could do was sit in the truck and watch. I did provide obvious observations about the failed attempts every time they tried something that didn't work. "Hey, I think the right front tire is still packed in. Try digging it out some more," I yelled and quickly rolled the window back up.

"Thanks, Trig. I think we got it out here." RJ was clearly exhausted, having spent the entire night before looking for me and now spending this night trying to get me back to Karrie.

"Let's just get in my truck and come back to get yours in a few days." I tried again to get RJ to give up on getting his truck out.

"Trig. Please! Just sit there and chill. One more try, okay?" He was tired of hearing from me, and I was tired of waiting. I just wanted to get home to let Karrie know I wanted so much to have a family with her. Having a baby in our life didn't mean I'd have to share her love. I knew now that it meant we'd have even more love in our lives.

RJ climbed back in. I shivered as he rolled down the window and yelled instructions to Mark. "Easy does it, Mark. Accelerate slowly. Good." RJ gave his truck just a little gas, and the other guys pushed from behind. I felt RJ's truck lurch as my Toyota dug in.

"Yes. Easy. Take it easy. You got it." I cheered as RJ steered his pickup back onto the road.

RJ gave a big sigh. "Okay, Mark. That's good," he yelled out the window before he rolled it back up and looked over at me. "I told you."

"You did. Now can you please just take me home so I can go wrap myself around my beautiful wife?"

"Yes, if you can manage to keep your mouth shut until we get on a clear, dry road."

"Deal."

I'd been so absorbed in watching the whole crew work at getting the truck out, I'd totally lost track of time. When I looked down at my watch I could see it was almost eleven, and we still had at least three hours ahead of us.

Chapter Forty-one

"Karrie, one more good push and you're going to have your baby. I can feel his head."

As kind as she was, I was sick of hearing Jules's calm voice. I was so exhausted I could barely speak anymore. I felt like I'd run a marathon in the rain. I'd been in and out of the birth pool about a dozen times, and still he wouldn't come out. As much as I wanted Trigena to be here, more than anything, I just wanted our baby to get here so I could get this over with.

"I can't keep on going." I panted between contractions.

"You can do it! K, you can do this. Dig deep." Dani supported my back in the pool while Justine let me squeeze the hell out of her hand.

"Let me get out. I want out of this pool." I tried to get up, but the next contraction hit me like a punch to the gut. "Fuck."

"That's it, K. Get angry and push this baby out."

I made it through another contraction, and nothing happened. "I can't do this anymore."

"Yes, you can."

I exhaled deeply and shook my head at Jules, and when I looked up, I saw Trigena standing in the doorway of our bedroom.

"Trig. Oh, my God. Your head…arm." I started crying and reached out for her.

"I'm fine, babe. It looks like you need to focus on our baby." Trigena walked over to hug me. "It's okay." She pulled my head to her chest and held me tight.

"What…happened…you?" I tried to ask through the pain. Tears were still streaming down my face, and I attempted again to stand up, but another contraction hit. Trigena quietly slid in where Dani had been. I could hear her soothing voice quietly in my ear. "I love you so much. You can do this. I can't wait to be a mom with you. Push, K."

"That's it, K. Just a little more." Jules looked up at me as I panted through the pain, and I pushed with all I had left.

"Oh my God, K. He's here." Trig raised up as Jules lifted our son up out of the water and onto my chest.

"Is he okay?"

"He's perfect," Jules said as she rubbed his gooey back, causing him to make a little squawk.

"You were supposed to catch him." I looked up at Trig, who was leaning over the tub to see our son.

"I'm not sure I could've done it with one hand. He's amazing."

I held my sweet baby to me, and tears started streaming down my face. "What are we going to do? I need you so much, but I can't make you be a mom if you don't want to."

"Karrie, I want to be a mom with you. I found out I can do it. She was there, K, and we took care of each other."

"Who?"

"The girl from my dream, Samantha. We found each other. She's very special, and she told me I'd be a great mommy. I'm going to be the best one I can be for our boy. I want you to meet her, K. I want her to be part of our lives. I want to make sure she's taken care of."

"I'd like that." I smiled.

Epilogue

I stood in the doorway of K's studio holding six-month-old Mylo as he slept on my shoulder. I listened in as Samantha told Karrie how good she was at sitting still. At the same time, I watched her wiggle all over the chair.

"Yes, you're very good at posing for a portrait." Karrie looked up from her painting and smiled at me.

"Mylo would move around too much," Samantha said.

"Hey, pretty ladies. Lunch is ready. I'm going to put Mylo in the crib. Come eat. Your mom will be here in just a little bit, Samantha," I said.

"Can I stay the night with you and Karrie?"

I looked over at Karrie and she nodded. "Sure. If it's okay with your mom."

"Yah," Samantha squealed. "Karrie's going to teach me to paint."

I looked down at our baby boy, sure he would be awake, but he was still sound asleep. "Let's go call your mom."

About the Author

Jan Gayle was raised in a small farming community in central Illinois. Upon graduating from college with a B.S. in social studies education, Jan joined the U.S. Air Force. She later accepted a commission and served for twenty years as an Air Force officer. As a new lieutenant, she deployed to Desert Storm. She returned to the Middle East for another deployment to Operation Iraqi Freedom fourteen years later. While on active duty, Jan visited over forty countries and was assigned to locations all over the United States. She continues to work for the Air Force as a civil servant, but her true passion is her small woodworking business where she builds custom wood furniture.

Jan lives with her wife Jules and their two boys. She started writing on a dare and was immediately hooked. *Live and Love Again* is Jan's debut novel.

Jan can be contacted at: jggourley@gmail.com

Books Available from Bold Strokes Books

Forsaken Trust by Meredith Doench. When four women are murdered, Agent Luce Hansen must regain trust in her most valuable investigative tool—herself—to catch the killer. (978-1-62639-737-8)

Her Best Friend's Sister by Meghan O'Brien. For fifteen years, Claire Barker has nursed a massive crush on her best friend's older sister. What happens when all her wildest fantasies come true? (978-1-62639-861-0)

Letter of the Law by Carsen Taite. Will federal prosecutor Bianca Cruz take a chance at love with horse breeder Jade Vargas, whose dark family ties threaten everything Bianca has worked to protect—including her child? (978-1-62639-750-7)

New Life by Jan Gayle. Trigena and Karrie are having a baby, but the stress of becoming a mother and the impact on their relationship might be too much for Trigena. (978-1-62639-878-8)

Royal Rebel by Jenny Frame. Charity director Lennox King sees through the party girl image Princess Roza has cultivated, but will Lennox's past indiscretions and Roza's responsibilities make their love impossible? (978-1-62639-893-1)

Unbroken by Donna K. Ford. When Kayla and Jackie, two women with every reason to reject Happy Ever After, fall in love, will they have the courage to overcome their pasts and rewrite their stories? (978-1-62639-921-1)

Where the Light Glows by Dena Blake. Mel Thomas doesn't realize just how unhappy she is in her marriage until she meets

Izzy Calabrese. Will she have the courage to overcome her insecurities and follow her heart? (978-1-62639-958-7)

Escape in Time by Robyn Nyx. Working in the past is hell on your future. (978-1-62639-855-9)

Forget-Me-Not by Kris Bryant. Is love worth walking away from the only life you've ever dreamed of? (978-1-62639-865-8)

Highland Fling by Anna Larner. On vacation in the Scottish Highlands, Eve Eddison falls for the enigmatic forestry officer Moira Burns, despite Eve's best friend's campaign to convince her that Moira will break her heart. (978-1-62639-853-5)

Phoenix Rising by Rebecca Harwell. As Storm's Quarry faces invasion from a powerful neighbor, a mysterious newcomer with powers equal to Nadya's challenges everything she believes about herself and her future. (978-1-62639-913-6)

Soul Survivor by I. Beacham. Sam and Joey have given up on hope, but when fate brings them together it gives them a chance to change each other's life and make dreams come true. (978-1-62639-882-5)

Strawberry Summer by Melissa Brayden. When Margaret Beringer's first love Courtney Carrington returns to their small town, she must grapple with their troubled past and fight the temptation for a very delicious future. (978-1-62639-867-2)

The Girl on the Edge of Summer by J.M. Redmann. Micky Knight accepts two cases, but neither is the easy investigation it appears. The past is never past—and young girls lead complicated, even dangerous lives. (978-1-62639-687-6)

Unknown Horizons by CJ Birch. The moment Lieutenant Alison Ash steps aboard the Persephone, she knows her life will never be the same. (978-1-62639-938-9)

Divided Nation, United Hearts by Yolanda Wallace. In a nation torn in two by a most uncivil war, can love conquer the divide? (978-1-62639-847-4)

Fury's Bridge by Brey Willows. What if your life depended on someone who didn't believe in your existence? (978-1-62639-841-2)

Lightning Strikes by Cass Sellars. When Parker Duncan and Sydney Hyatt's one-night stand turns to more, both women must fight demons past and present to cling to the relationship neither of them thought she wanted. (978-1-62639-956-3)

Love in Disaster by Charlotte Greene. A professor and a celebrity chef are drawn together by chance, but can their attraction survive a natural disaster? (978-1-62639-885-6)

Secret Hearts by Radclyffe. Can two women from different worlds find common ground while fighting their secret desires? (978-1-62639-932-7)

Sins of Our Fathers by A. Rose Mathieu. Solving gruesome murder cases is only one of Elizabeth Campbell's challenges; another is her growing attraction to the female detective who is hell-bent on keeping her client in prison. (978-1-62639-873-3)

The Sniper's Kiss by Justine Saracen. The power of a kiss: it can swell your heart with splendor, declare abject submission, and sometimes blow your brains out. (978-1-62639-839-9)

Troop 18 by Jessica L. Webb. Charged with uncovering the destructive secret that a troop of RCMP cadets has been hiding, Andy must put aside her worries about Kate and uncover the conspiracy before it's too late. (978-1-62639-934-1)

Worthy of Trust and Confidence by Kara A. McLeod. Special Agent Ryan O'Connor is about to discover the hard way that when you can only handle one type of answer to a question, it really is better not to ask. (978-1-62639-889-4)

Amounting to Nothing by Karis Walsh. When mounted police officer Billie Mitchell steps in to save beautiful murder witness Merissa Karr, worlds collide on the rough city streets of Tacoma, Washington. (978-1-62639-728-6)

Becoming You by Michelle Grubb. Airlie Porter has a secret. A deep, dark, destructive secret that threatens to engulf her if she can't find the courage to face who she really is and who she really wants to be with. (978-1-62639-811-5)

Birthright by Missouri Vaun. When spies bring news that a swordswoman imprisoned in a neighboring kingdom bears the Royal mark, Princess Kathryn sets out to rescue Aiden, true heir to the Belstaff throne. (978-1-62639-485-8)

Crescent City Confidential by Aurora Rey. When romance and danger are in the air, writer Sam Torres learns the Big Easy is anything but. (978-1-62639-764-4)

Love Down Under by MJ Williamz. Wylie loves Amarina, but if Amarina isn't out, can their relationship last? (978-1-62639-726-2)

Privacy Glass by Missouri Vaun. Things heat up when Nash Wiley commandeers a limo and her best friend for a late drive out to the beach: Champagne on ice, seat belts optional, and privacy glass a must. (978-1-62639-705-7)

The Impasse by Franci McMahon. A horse packing excursion into the Montana Wilderness becomes an adventure of terrifying proportions for Miles and ten women on an outfitter led trip. (978-1-62639-781-1)

The Right Kind of Wrong by PJ Trebelhorn. Bartender Quinn Burke is happy with her life as a playgirl until she realizes she can't fight her feelings any longer for her best friend, bookstore owner Grace Everett. (978-1-62639-771-2)

Wishing on a Dream by Julie Cannon. Can two women change everything for the chance at love? (978-1-62639-762-0)